TALES OF MAGIC, TIMES GONE BY. . . .

"Draco, Draco" by Tanith Lee—Dragon or dragonslayer, which should they fear the most?

"The Harvest Child" by Steve Rasnic Tem—She came to them in a swirl of dust and mystery to change their fortunes—but for good or ill?

"Stoneskin" by John Morressy—For a warrior, magical invulnerability can be his most valuable weapon—or his greatest weakness!

"The Foxwife" by Jane Yolen—She enchanted him with gentle loveliness . . . but was she beauty—or the beast?

These are just a few of the spellbinding tales brewed up in this latest collection of—

THE YEAR'S BEST FANTASY STORIES: 11

Look for these other exciting DAW Anthologies:

THE YEAR'S BEST FANTASY STORIES: 11

Edited by
Arthur W. Saha

DAW BOOKS, INC.
DONALD A. WOLLHEIM, PUBLISHER

1633 Broadway, New York, NY 10019

DEDICATION

*For Don and Elsie
With respect and admiration*

First Printing, November 1985

1 2 3 4 5 6 7 8 9

PRINTED IN U.S.A.

Acknowledgments

Draco, Draco by Tanith Lee first appeared in *Beyond Lands of Never.* Copyright © 1984 by George Allen & Unwin (Publishers) Ltd. Reprinted by permission of the author.

The Harvest Child by Steve Rasnic Tem first appeared in *Elsewhere,* Vol. III. Copyright © 1984 by Steve Rasnic Tem. Reprinted by permission of the author.

Love Among the Xoids by John Sladek first appeared as *Drumm Booklet No. 15.* Copyright © 1984 by John Sladek. Reprinted by permission of the author.

Stoneskin by John Morressy first appeared in *The Magazine of Fantasy & Science Fiction,* June 1984. Copyright © 1984 by Mercury Press. Reprinted by permission of the author.

Unmistakably the Finest by Scott Bradfield first appeared in *Interzone* Summer 1984. Copyright © 1984 by *Interzone.* Reprinted by permission of the author.

The Foxwife by Jane Yolen—The *World Fantasy Convention* 1984 Program Book. Copyright © 1984 by Jane Yolen. Reprinted by permission of Curtis Brown, Ltd.

Golden Apples of the Sun by Gardner Dozois, Jack Dann and Michael Swanwick first appeared in a slightly shorter version as "Virgin Territory" in *Penthouse,* March 1984. Copyright © 1984 by Penthouse International, Ltd. Reprinted by permission of the authors' agent, Virginia Kidd.

My Rose and My Glove by Harvey Jacobs first appeared in *Omni,* May 1984. Copyright © 1984 by Omni Publications International Ltd. Reprinted by permission of the author.

Strange Shadows by Clark Ashton Smith first appeared in *Crypt of Cthulhu* No. 25. Copyright © 1984 by Richard E. Kuhn. Reprinted by permission of the author's estate and Brown University Library.

A Little Two-Chair Barber Shop on Phillips Street by Donald R. Burleson first appeared in *Rod Serling's The Twilight Zone Magazine,* April 1984. Copyright © 1984 by TZ Publications. Reprinted by permission of the author.

Taking Heart by Stephen L. Burns first appeared in *Sword and Sorceress.* Copyright © 1984 by Stephen L. Burns. Reprinted by permission of the author.

The Storm by David Morrell first appeared in *Shadows 7.* Copyright © 1984 by David Morrell. Reprinted by permission of the author.

A Cabin on the Coast by Gene Wolfe first appeared in *The Magazine of Fantasy & Science Fiction,* Feb. 1984. Copyright © 1983 by Mercury Press, Inc. Reprinted by permission of the author's agent, Virginia Kidd.

Contents

INTRODUCTION

Over the last several years I have been speaking about science fiction and fantasy at various schools to classes ranging from sixth grade to high school seniors. I have found an ever increasing interest in and enthusiasm for the fiction of the fantastic not only on the part of those who have already discovered the vast amount of reading material available to them but also on the part of those whose acquaintance with the genre has up to now been limited to movies and television shows.

It really should not come as a surprise that imaginative fiction is popular with the young (and those who are still young in spirit). We are after all living in an age when space flight is no longer fiction, when computers are revolutionizing the world, when industrial robots are becoming commonplace, an era when new discoveries are changing our perception of the world, nay, the universe, almost every day.

It is also, of course, a world beset by a multitude of problems: air and water pollution, acid rain, hunger in many parts of the world, wars and revolutions which seem to be constantly with us, and finally the possibility of a nuclear holocaust.

It's no wonder then that today's readers are more ready to accept the many futures postulated by science fiction writers. In a changing world it's easy to accept the possibilities of even further change. And insofar as the dangers our world faces, it's certainly preferable to read about a nuclear winter than to actually experience one.

I suspect that such possibilities are at least part of the reason that fantasy fiction has remained and even become more popular in recent years. It provides us all with an escape into worlds that are very different from our real world. These are worlds that we know really don't exist, but they do take us away for at least a little while from our familiar surroundings and everyday lives and allow us to dream an occasional dream about how different our lives might be. The young and young at heart will always want to escape for a while into another world, and fantasy fiction will continue to provide one doorway through which to make that escape.

This year's volume in our continuing series presents many different types and varieties of fantasy stories, some taking place in mythical pasts, some in today's world albeit not exactly the world with which we're acquainted.

Now without further ado I invite you to step through that doorway into the realm of fantasy.

ARTHUR W. SAHA

In the world of myth and legend great reputations were acquired by men who gained for themselves the appellation "dragonslayer." They were both honored and respected. Whether such reputations were actually deserved is questionable, as evidenced by this tale about a swordsman, a maiden and a dragon—and a very pragmatic narrator.

DRACO, DRACO

Tanith Lee

You'll have heard stories, sometimes, of men who have fought and slain dragons. These are all lies. There's no swordsman living ever killed a dragon, though a few swordsmen dead that tried.

On the other hand, I once traveled in company with a fellow who got the name of 'dragon-slayer'.

A riddle? No. I'll tell you.

I was coming from the North back into the South, to civilization as you may say, when I saw him sitting by the roadside. My first feeling was envy, I admit. He was smart and very clean for someone in the wilds, and he had the South all over him, towns and baths and money. He was crazy, too, because there was gold on his wrists and in one ear. But he had a

11

sharp gray sword, an army sword, so maybe he could defend himself. He was also younger than me, and a great deal prettier, but the last isn't too difficult. I wondered what he'd do when he looked up from his daydream and saw me, tough, dark and sour as a twist of old rope, clopping down on him on my swarthy little horse, ugly as sin, that I love like a daughter.

Then he did look up and I discovered.

'Greetings, stranger. Nice day, isn't it?'

He stayed relaxed as he said it, and somehow you knew from that he really could look after himself. It wasn't he thought I was harmless, just that he thought he could handle me if I tried something. Then again, I had my box of stuff alongside. Most people can tell my trade from that, and the aroma of drugs and herbs. My father was with the Romans, in fact he was probably the last Roman of all, one foot on the ship to go home, the rest of him with my mother up against the barnyard wall. She said he was a camp physician and maybe that was so. Some idea of doctoring grew up with me, though nothing great or grand. An itinerant apothecary is welcome almost anywhere, and can even turn bandits civil. It's not a wonderful life, but it's the only one I know.

I gave the young soldier-dandy that it was a nice day. I added he'd possibly like it better if he hadn't lost his horse.

"Yes, a pity about that. You could always sell me yours."

"Not your style."

He looked at her. I could see he agreed. There was also a momentary idea that he might kill me and take her, so I said, "And she's well known as mine. It would get you a bad name. I've friends round about."

He grinned, good-naturedly. His teeth were good, too. What with that, and the hair like barley, and the rest of it—well, he was the kind usually gets what he wants. I was curious as to which army he had hung about with to gain the sword. But since the Eagles flew, there are kingdoms every-where, chiefs, war-leaders, Roman knights, and every tide brings an invasion up some beach. Under it all, too, you can feel the earth, the actual ground, which had been measured, and ruled with fine roads, the land which had been subdued but never tamed, beginning to quicken. Like the shadows that come with the blowing out of a lamp. Ancient things, which are in my blood somewhere, so I recognize them.

But he was like a new coin that hadn't got dirty yet, nor learned much, though you could see your face in its shine, and cut yourself on its edge.

His name was Caiy. Presently we came to an arrangement and he mounted up behind me on Negra. They spoke a smatter of Latin where I was born, and I called her that before I knew her, for her darkness. I couldn't call her for her hideousness, which is her only other visible attribute.

The fact is, I wasn't primed to the country round that way at all. I'd had word, a day or two prior, that there were Saxons in the area I'd been heading for. And so I switched paths and was soon lost. When I came on Caiy, I'd been pleased with the road, which was Roman, hoping it would go somewhere useful. But, about ten miles after Caiy joined me, the road petered out in a forest. My passenger was lost, too. He was going South, no surprise there, but last night his horse had broken loose and bolted, leaving him stranded. It sounded unlikely, but I wasn't inclined to debate on it. It seemed to me someone might have stolen the horse, and Caiy didn't care to confess.

There was no way round the forest, so we went in and the road died. As it was summer, the wolves would be scarce and the bears off in the hills. Nevertheless, the trees had a feel I didn't take to, somber and still, with the sound of little streams running through like metal chains, and birds that didn't sing but made purrings and clinkings. Negra never balked nor complained—if I'd waited to call her, I could have done it for her courage and warm-heartedness—but she couldn't come to terms with the forest, either.

"It smells," said Caiy, who'd been kind enough not to comment on mine, "as if it's rotting. Or fermenting."

I grunted. Of course it did, it was, the fool. But the smell told you other things. The centuries, for one. Here were the shadows that had come back when Rome blew out her lamp and sailed away, and left us in the dark.

Then Caiy, the idiot, began to sing to show up the birds who wouldn't. A nice voice, clear and bright. I didn't tell him to leave off. The shadows already knew we were there.

When night came down, the black forest closed like a cellar door.

We made a fire and shared my supper. He'd lost his rations with his mare.

'Shouldn't you tether that—your horse,' suggested Caiy, trying not to insult her since he could see we were partial to each other. 'My mare was tied, but something scared her and she broke the tether and ran. I wonder what it was,' he mused, staring in the fire.

About three hours later, we found out.

I was asleep, and dreaming of one of my wives up in the far North, and she was nagging at me, trying to start a brawl, which she always did for she was taller than me, and liked me to hit her once in a while so she could feel fragile, feminine and mastered. Just as she emptied the beer jar over my head, I heard a sound up in the sky like a storm that was not a storm. And I knew I wasn't dreaming anymore.

The sound went over, three or four great claps, and the tops of the forest reeling, and left shuddering. There was a sort of quiver in the air, as if sediment were stirred up in it. There was even an extra smell, dank, yet tingling. When the noise was only a memory, and the bristling hairs began to subside along my body, I opened my eyes.

Negra was flattened to the ground, her own eyes rolling, but she was silent. Caiy was on his feet, gawping up at the tree tops and the strands of starless sky. Then he glared at me.

"What in the name of the Bull was that?"

I noted vaguely that the oath showed he had Mithraic allegiances, which generally meant Roman. Then I sat up, rubbed my arms and neck to get human, and went to console Negra. Unlike his silly cavalry mare she hadn't bolted.

"It can't," he said, "have been a bird. Though I'd have sworn something flew over."

"No, it wasn't a bird."

"But it had wings. Or—no, it couldn't have had wings the size of that."

"Yes it could. They don't carry it far, is all."

"Apothecary, stop being so damned provoking. If you know, out with it! Though I don't see how you can know. And don't tell me it's some bloody woods demon I won't believe in."

"Nothing like that," I said. "It's real enough. Natural, in its own way. Not," I amended, "that I ever came across one before, but I've met some who did."

Caiy was going mad, like a child working up to a tantrum. *"Well?"*

I suppose he had charmed and irritated me enough I wanted to retaliate, because I just quoted some bastard nonsensical jabber-Latin chant at him:

Bis terribilis—
Bis appellare—
Draco! Draco!

At least, it made him sit down.

"What?" he eventually said.

At my age I should be over such smugness. I said, "It was a dragon."

Caiy laughed. But he had glimpsed it, and knew better than I did that I was right.

Nothing else happened that night. In the morning we started off again and there was a rough track, and then the forest began to thin out. After a while we emerged on the crown of a moor. The land dropped down to a valley, and on the other side there were sunny smoky hills and a long streamered sky. There was something else, too.

Naturally, Caiy said it first, as if everything new always surprised him, as if we hadn't each of us, in some way, been waiting for it, or something like it.

"This place stinks."

"Hn."

"Don't just grunt at me, you blasted quack doctor. It does, doesn't it? Why?"

"Why do you think?"

He brooded, pale gold and citified, behind me. Negra tried to paw the ground, and then made herself desist.

Neither of us brave humans had said any more about what had interrupted sleep in the forest, but when I'd told him no dragon could fly far on its wings, for from all I'd ever heard they were too large and only some freakish lightness in their bones enabled them to get airborne at all, I suppose we had both taken it to heart. Now here were the valley and the hills, and here was this reek lying over everything, strange, foul, alien, comparable to nothing, really. Dragon smell.

I considered. No doubt, the dragon went on an aerial patrol most nights, circling as wide as it could, to see what might be there for it. There were other things I'd learned. These beasts hunt nocturnally, like cats. At the same time, a dragon is more like a crow in its habits. It will attack and kill, but normally it eats carrion, dead things, or dying and immobilized. It's light, as I said—it has to be to take the skies—but the lack of weight is compensated by the armour, the teeth and talons. Then again, I'd heard of dragons that breathed fire. I've never been quite convinced there. It seems more likely to me such monsters only live in volcanic caves, the mountain itself belching flame and the dragon taking credit for it. Maybe not. But certainly, this dragon was no fire-breather. The ground would have been scorched for miles; I've listened to stories where that happened. There were no marks of fire. Just the insidious pervasive stench that I knew, by the time we'd gone down into the valley, would be so familiar, so soaked into us, we would hardly notice it any-more, or the scent of anything else.

I awarded all this information to my passenger. There followed a long verbal delay. I thought he might just be flabbergasted at getting so much chat from me, but then he said, very hushed, "You truly believe all this, don't you?"

I didn't bother with the obvious, just clucked to Negra, trying to make her turn back the way we'd come. But she was unsure and for once uncooperative, and suddenly his strong hand, the nails groomed even now, came down on my arm.

"Wait, Apothecary. If it *is* true—"

"Yes, yes," I said. I sighed. "You want to go and challenge it, and become a hero." He held himself like marble, as if I were speaking of some girl he thought he loved. I didn't see why I should waste experience and wisdom on him, but then I said, "No man ever killed a dragon. They're plated, all over, even the underbelly. Arrows and spears just bounce off—even a pilum. Swords clang and snap in half. Yes, yes," I reiterated, "you've heard of men who slashed the tongue, or stabbed into an eye. Let me tell you, if they managed to reach that high and actually did it, then they just made the brute angry. Think of the size and shape of a dragon's head, the way the pictures show it. It's one hell of a push from the eye into the brain. And you know, there's one theory the eyelid is armored, too, and can come down faster than *that*."

"Apothecary," he said. He sounded dangerous. I just knew what he must look like. Handsome, noble and insane.

"Then I won't keep you," I said. "Get down and go on and the best of luck."

I don't know why I bothered. I should have tipped him off and ridden for it, though I wasn't sure Negra could manage to react sufficiently fast, she was that edgy. Anyway, I didn't, and sure enough next moment his sword was at the side of my throat, so sharp it had drawn blood.

"You're the clever one," he said, "the know-all. And you do seem to know more than I do, about this. So you're my guide, and your scruff-bag of a horse, if it even deserves the name, is my transport. Giddy-up, the pair of you."

That was that. I never argue with a drawn sword. The dragon would be lying up by day, digesting and dozing, and by night I could hole up someplace myself. Tomorrow Caiy would be dead and I could leave. And I would, of course, have seen a dragon for myself.

After an hour and a half's steady riding—better once I'd persuaded him to switch from the sword to poking a dagger against my ribs, less tiring for us both—we came around a stand of woods, and there was a village. It was the savage Northern kind, thatch and wattle and turf banks, but big for all that, a good mile of it, not all walled. There were walls this end, however, and men on the gate, peering at us.

Caiy was aggrieved because he was going to have to ride up to them pillion, but he knew better now than to try managing Negra alone. He maybe didn't want to pretend she was his horse in any case.

As we pottered up the pebbled track to the gate, he sprang

off and strode forward, arriving before me, and began to speak.

When I got closer I heard him announcing, in his dramatic, beautiful voice,

"—And if it's a fact, I swear by the Victory of the Light that I will meet the thing and kill it."

They were muttering. The dragon smell, even though we were used to it, sodden with it, seemed more acid here. Poor Negra had been voiding herself from sheer terror all up the path. With fortune on our side, there would be somewhere below ground, some cave or dug out place, where they'd be putting their animals out of the dragon's way, and she could shelter with the others.

Obviously, the dragon hadn't always been active in this region. They'd scarcely have built their village if it had. No, it would have been like the tales. Dragons live for centuries. They can sleep for centuries, too. Unsuspecting, man moves in, begins to till and build and wax prosperous. Then the dormant dragon wakes under the hill. They're like the volcanoes I spoke of, in that. Which is perhaps, more than habitat, why so many of the legends say they breathe fire when they wake.

The interesting thing was, even clouded by the dragon stink, initially, the village didn't seem keen to admit to anything.

Caiy, having made up his mind to accept the dragon—and afraid of being wrong—started to rant. The men at the gate were frightened and turning nasty. Leading Negra now, I approached, tapped my chest of potions and said:

"Or, if you don't want your dragon slain, I can cure some of your other troubles. I've got medicines for almost everything. Boils, warts. Ear pains. Tooth pains. Sick eyes. Women's afflictions. I have here—"

"Shut up, you toad-turd," said Caiy.

One of the guards suddenly laughed. The tension sagged.

Ten minutes after, we had been let in the gate and were trudging through the cow-dung and wild flowers—neither of which were to be smelled through the other smell—to the headman's hall.

It was around two hours after that when we found out why the appearance of a rescuing champion-knight had given them the jitters.

It seemed they had gone back to the ancient way, propitiation, the scapegoat. For three years, they had been making an offering to the dragon, in spring, and at midsummer, when it was likely to be most frisky.

Anyone who knew dragons from a book would tell them this wasn't the way. But they knew their dragon from myth. Every time they made sacrifice, they imagined the thing could understand and appreciate what they'd done for it, and would therefore be more amenable.

In reality, of course, the dragon had never attacked the village. It had thieved cattle off the pasture by night, elderly or sick cows at that, and lambs that were too little and weak to run. It would have taken people, too, but only those who were disabled and alone. I said, a dragon is lazy and prefers carrion, or what's defenseless. Despite being big, they aren't so big they'd go after a whole tribe of men. And though even forty men together undoubtedly couldn't wound a dragon, they could exhaust it, if they kept up a rough-house. Eventually it would keel over and they could brain it. You seldom hear of forty men going off in a band to take a dragon, however. Dragons are still raveled up with night fears and spiritual mysteries, and latterly with an Eastern superstition of a mighty demon who can assume the form of a dragon which is invincible and—naturally—breathes sheer flame. So, this village, like many another, would put out its sacrifice, one girl tied to a post, and leave her there, and the dragon would have her. Why not? She was helpless, fainting with horror—and young and tender into the bargain. Perfect. You never could convince them that, instead of appeasing the monster, the sacrifice encourages it to stay. Look at it from the dragon's point of view. Not only are there dead sheep and stray cripples to devour, but once in a while a nice juicy damsel on a stick. Dragons don't think like a man, but they do have memories.

When Caiy realized what they were about to do, tonight, as it turned out, he went red then white, exactly as they do in a bardic lay. Not anger, mind you. He didn't comprehend anymore than they did. It was merely the awfulness of it.

He stood up and chose a stance, quite unconsciously impressive, and assured us he'd save her. He swore to it in front of us all, the chieftain, his men, me. And he swore it by the Sun, so I knew he meant business.

They were scared, but now also childishly hopeful. It was part of their mythology again. All mythology seems to take this tack somewhere, the dark against the light, the Final Battle. It's rot, but there.

Following a bit of drinking to seal the oath, they cheered up and the chief ordered a feast. Then they took Caiy to see the chosen sacrifice.

Her name was Niemeh, or something along those lines.

She was sitting in a little lamplit cell off the hall. She wasn't fettered, but a warrior stood guard beyond the screen, and there was no window. She had nothing to do except weave flowers together, and she was doing that, making garlands for her death procession in the evening.

When Caiy saw her, his color drained away again.

He stood and stared at her, while somebody explained he was her champion.

Though he got on my nerves, I didn't blame him so much this time. She was about the most beautiful thing I ever hope to see. Young, obviously, and slim, but with a woman's shape, if you have my meaning, and long hair more fair even than Caiy's, and green eyes like sea pools and a face like one of the white flowers in her hands, and a sweet mouth.

I looked at her as she listened gravely to all they said. I remembered how in the legends it's always the loveliest and the most gentle gets picked for the dragon's dinner. You perceive the sense in the gentle part. A girl with a temper might start a ruckus.

When Caiy had been introduced and once more sworn by the Sun to slay the dragon and so on, she thanked him. If things had been different, she would have blushed and trembled, excited by Caiy's attention. But she was past all that. You could see, if you looked, she didn't believe anyone could save her. But though she must have been half dead already of despair and fright, she still made space to be courteous.

Then she glanced over Caiy's head straight at me, and she smiled so I wouldn't feel left out.

"And who is this man?" she asked.

They all looked startled, having forgotten me. Then someone who had warts recalled I'd said I could fix him something for warts, and told her I was the apothecary.

A funny little shiver went through her then.

She was so young and so pretty. If I'd been Caiy I'd have stopped spouting rubbish about the dragon. I'd have found some way to lay out the whole village, and grabbed her, and gone. But that would have been a stupid thing to do, too. I've enough of the old blood to know about such matters. She was the sacrifice and she was resigned to it; more, she didn't dream she could be anything else. I've come across rumors, here and there, of girls, men too, chosen to die, who escaped. But the fate stays on them. Hide them securely miles off, across water, beyond tall hills, still they feel the geas weigh like lead upon their souls. They kill themselves in the end, or go mad. And this girl, this Niemeh, you could see it in her. No, I would never have abducted her. It would have been no use. She was convinced she must die, as if she'd seen it written in light on a stone, and maybe she had.

She returned to her garlands, and Caiy, tense as a bowstring, led us back to the hall.

Meat was roasting and more drink came out and more talk came out. You can kill anything as often as you like, that way.

It wasn't a bad feast, as such up-country things go. But all through the shouts and toasts and guzzlings, I kept thinking of her in her cell behind the screen, hearing the clamor and aware of this evening's sunset, and how it would be to die . . . as she would have to. I didn't begin to grasp how she could bear it.

By late afternoon they were mostly sleeping it off, only Caiy had had the sense to go and sweat the drink out with soldiers' exercises in the yard, before a group of sozzled admirers of all sexes.

When someone touched my shoulder, I thought it was Warty after his cure, but no. It was the guard from the girl's cell, who said very low, "She says she wants to speak to you. Will you come, now?"

I got up and went with him. I had a spinning minute, wondering if perhaps she didn't believe she must die after all, and would appeal to me to save her. But in my heart of hearts I guessed it wasn't that.

There was another man blocking the entrance, but they let me go in alone, and there Niemeh sat, making garlands yet, under her lamp.

But she looked up at me, and her hands fell like two more white flowers on the flowers in her lap. "I need some medicine, you see," she said. "But I can't pay you. I don't have anything. Although my uncle—"

"No charge," I said hurriedly.

She smiled. "It's for tonight."

"Oh," I said.

"I'm not brave," she said, "but it's worse than just being afraid. I know I shall die. That it's needful. But part of me wants to live so much—my reason tells me one thing but my body won't listen. I'm frightened I shall panic, struggle and scream and weep—I don't want that. It isn't right. I have to consent, or the sacrifice isn't any use. Do you know about that?"

"Oh, yes," I said.

"I thought so. I thought you did. Then . . . can you give me something, a medicine or herb—so I shan't feel anything? I don't mean the pain. That doesn't matter. The gods can't blame me if I cry out then, they wouldn't expect me to be beyond pain. But only to make me not care, not want to live so very much."

"An easy death."

"Yes." She smiled again. She seemed serene and beautiful. "Oh, yes."

I looked at the floor.

"The soldier. Maybe he'll kill it," I said.

She didn't say anything.

When I glanced up, her face wasn't serene anymore. It was brimful of terror. Caiy would have been properly insulted.

"Is it you can't give me anything? Don't you have anything? I was sure you did. That you were sent here to me to—to help, so I shouldn't have to go through it all alone—"

"There," I said, "it's all right. I do have something. Just the thing. I keep it for women in labor when the child's slow and hurting them. It works a treat. They go sort of misty and far off, as if they were nearly asleep. It'll dull pain, too. Even—any kind of pain."

"Yes," she whispered, "I should like that." And then she caught my hand and kissed it. "I knew you would," she said, as if I'd promised her the best and loveliest thing in all the earth. Another man, it would have broken him in front of her. But I'm harder than most.

When she let me, I retrieved my hand, nodded reassuringly, and went out. The chieftain was awake and genial enough, so I had a word with him. I told him what the girl had asked. "In the East," I said, "it's the usual thing, give them something to help them through. They call it Nektar, the drink of the gods. She's consented," I said, "but she's very young and scared, delicately bred too. You can't grudge her this." He acquiesced immediately, as glad as she was, as I'd hoped. It's a grim affair, I should imagine, when the girl shrieks for pity all the way up to the hills. I hadn't thought there'd be any problem. On the other hand, I hadn't wanted to be caught slipping her potions behind anyone's back.

I mixed the drug in the cell where she could watch. She was interested in everything I did, the way the condemned are nearly always interested in every last detail, even how a cobweb hangs.

I made her promise to drink it all, but none of it until they came to bring her out. "It may not last otherwise. You don't want it to wear off before—too early."

"No," she said. "I'll do exactly what you say."

When I was going out again, she said, "If I can ask them for anything for you, the gods, when I meet them. . . ."

It was in my mind to say: Ask them to go stick—but I didn't. She was trying to keep intact her trust in recompense, immortality. I said, "Just ask them to look after you."

She had such a sweet, sweet mouth. She was made to love and be loved, to have children and sing songs and die when she was old, peacefully, in her sleep.

And there would be others like her. The dragon would be given those, too. Eventually, it wouldn't just be maidens, either. The taboo states it has to be a virgin so as to safeguard any unborn life. Since a virgin can't be with child—there's one religion says different, I forget which—they stipulate virgins. But in the end any youthful woman, who can reasonably be reckoned as not with child, will do. And then they go on to the boys. Which is the most ancient sacrifice there is.

I passed a very young girl in the hall, trotting round with the beer-dipper. She was comely and innocent, and I recollected I'd seen her earlier and asked myself, Are you the next? And who'll be next after you?

Niemeh was the fifth. But, I said, dragons live a long while. And the sacrifices always get to be more frequent. Now it was twice a year. In the first year it had been once. In a couple more years it would happen at every season, with maybe three victims in the summer when the creature was most active.

And in ten more years it would be every month, and they'd have learned to raid other villages to get girls and young men to give it, and there would be a lot of bones about, besides, fellows like Caiy, dragon-slayers dragon slain.

I went after the girl with the beer-dipper and drained it. But drink never did comfort me much.

And presently, it would be time to form the procession and start for the hills.

It was the last gleaming golden hour of day when we set off.

The valley was fertile and sheltered. The westering light caught and flashed in the trees and out of the streams. Already there was a sort of path stamped smooth and kept clear of undergrowth. It would have been a pleasant journey, if they'd been going anywhere else.

There was sunlight warm on the sides of the hills, too. The sky was almost cloudless, transparent. If it hadn't been for the tainted air, you would never have thought anything was wrong. But the track wound up the first slope and around, and up again, and there, about a hundred yards off, was the flank of a bigger hill that went down into shadow at its bottom, and never took the sun. That underside was bare of grass, and eaten out in caves, one cave larger than the rest and very black, with a strange black stillness, as if light and weather and time itself stopped just inside. Looking at that, you'd know at once, even with sun on your face and the whole lucid sky above.

They'd brought her all this way in a Roman litter which somehow had become the property of the village. It had lost its roof and its curtains, just a kind of cradle on poles, but Niemeh had sat in it on their shoulders, motionless, and dumb. I had only stolen one look at her, to be sure, but her face had turned mercifully blank and her eyes were opaque. What I'd given her started its work swiftly. She was beyond us all now. I was only anxious everything else would occur before her condition changed.

Her bearers set the litter down and lifted her out. They'd have to support her, but they would know about that, girls with legs gone to water, even passed out altogether. And I suppose the ones who fought and screamed would be forced to sup strong ale, or else concussed with a blow.

Everyone walked a little more, until we reached a natural palisade of rock. This spot provided concealment, while overlooking the cave and the ground immediately below it. There was a stagnant dark pond caught in the gravel there, but on our side, facing the cave, a patch of clean turf with a post sticking up, about the height of a tall man.

The two warriors supporting Niemeh went on with her towards the post. The rest of us stayed behind the rocks, except for Caiy.

We were all garlanded with flowers. Even I had had to be, and I hadn't made a fuss. What odds? But Caiy wasn't garlanded. He was the one part of the ritual which, though arcanely acceptable, was still profane. And that was why, even though they would let him attack the dragon, they had nevertheless brought the girl to appease it.

There was some kind of shackle at the post. It wouldn't be iron, because anything fey has an allergy to sable metals, even so midnight a thing as a dragon. Bronze, probably. They locked one part around her waist and another round her throat. Only the teeth and claws could get her out of her bonds now, piece by piece.

She sagged forward in the toils. She seemed unconscious at last, and I wanted her to be.

The two men hurried back, up the slope and into the rock cover with the rest of us. Sometimes the tales have the people rush away when they've put out their sacrifice, but usually the people stay, to witness. It's quite safe. The dragon won't go after them with something tasty chained up right under its nose.

Caiy didn't remain beside the post. He moved down toward the edge of the polluted pond. His sword was drawn. He was quite ready. Though the sun couldn't get into the hollow to fire his hair or the metal blade, he cut a grand figure, heroically braced there between the maiden and Death.

At the end, the day spilled swiftly. Suddenly all the shoulders of the hills grew dim, and the sky became the color of lavender, and then a sort of mauve amber, and the stars broke through.

There was no warning.

I was looking at the pond, where the dragon would come to drink, judging the amount of muck there seemed to be in it. And suddenly there was a reflection in the pond, from above. It wasn't definite, and it was upside down, but even so my heart plummeted through my guts.

There was a feeling behind the rock, the type you get, they tell me, in the battle lines, when the enemy appears. And mixed with this, something of another feeling, more maybe like the inside of some god's house when they call on him, and he seems to come.

I forced myself to look then, at the cave mouth. This, after all, was the evening I would see a real dragon, something to relate to others, as others had related such things to me.

It crept out of the cave, inch by inch, nearly down on its belly, catlike.

The sky wasn't dark yet, a Northern dusk seems often endless. I could see well, and better and better as the shadow of the cave fell away and the dragon advanced into the paler shadow by the pond.

At first, it seemed unaware of anything but itself and the twilight. It flexed and stretched itself. There was something uncanny, even in such simple movements, something evil. And timeless.

The Romans know an animal they call Elephantus, and I mind an ancient clerk in one of the towns describing this beast to me, fairly accurately, for he'd seen one once. The dragon wasn't as large as elephantus, I should say. Actually not that much higher than a fair-sized cavalry gelding, if rather longer. But it was sinuous, more sinuous than any snake. The way it crept and stretched and flexed, and curled and slewed its head, its skeleton seemed fluid.

There are plenty of mosaics, paintings. It was like that, the way men have shown them from the beginning. Slender, tapering to the elongated head, which is like a horse's, too, and not like, and to the tail, though it didn't have that spade-shaped sting they put on them sometimes, like a scorpion's. There were spines, along the tail and the back-ridge, and the neck and head. The ears were set back, like a dog's. Its legs were short, but that didn't make it seem ungainly. The ghastly fluidity was always there, not grace, but something so like grace it was nearly unbearable.

It looked almost the color the sky was now, slatey, bluish-gray, like metal but dull; the great overlapping plates of its scales had no burnish. Its eyes were black and you didn't see them, and then they took some light from somewhere, and they flared like two flat coins, cat's eyes, with nothing—no brain, no soul—behind them.

It had been going to drink, but had scented something more interesting than dirty water, which was the girl.

The dragon stood there, static as a rock, staring at her over the pond. Then gradually its two wings, that had been folded back like fans along its sides, opened and spread.

They were huge, those wings, much bigger than the rest of it. You could see how it might be able to fly with them. Unlike the body, there were no scales, only skin, membrane, with ribs of external bone. Bat's wings, near enough. It seemed feasible a sword could go through them, damage them, but that would only maim, and all too likely they were tougher than they seemed.

Then I left off considering. With its wings spread like that, unused—like a crow—it began to sidle around the water, the blind coins of eyes searing on the post and the sacrifice.

Somebody shouted. My innards sprang over. Then I realised it was Caiy. The dragon had nearly missed him, so intent it was on the feast, so he had had to call it.

Bis terribilis—Bis appellare—Draco! Draco!

I'd never quite understood that antic chant, and the Latin was execrable. But I think it really means to know a dragon exists is bad enough, to call its name and summon it—call twice, twice terrible—is the notion of a maniac.

The dragon wheeled. It—*flowed*. Its elongated horse's-head-which-wasn't was before him, and Caiy's sharp sword slashed up and down and bit against the jaw. It happened, what they say—sparks shot glittering in the air. Then the head split, not from any wound, just the chasm of the mouth.

It made a sound at him, not a hissing, a sort of *hroosh*. Its breath would be poisonous, almost as bad as fire. I saw Caiy stagger at it, and then one of the long feet on the short legs went out through the gathering dark. The blow looked slow and harmless. It threw Caiy thirty feet, right across the pond. He fell at the entrance to the cave, and lay quiet. The sword was still in his hand. His grip must have clamped down on it involuntarily. He'd likely bitten his tongue as well, in the same way.

The dragon looked after him, you could see it pondering whether to go across again and dine. But it was more attracted by the other morsel it had smelled first. It knew from its scent this was the softer more digestible flesh. And so it ignored Caiy, leaving him for later, and eddied on toward the post, lowering its head as it came, the light leaving its eyes.

I looked. The night was truly blooming now, but I could see, and the darkness didn't shut my ears; there were sounds, too. You weren't there, and I'm not about to try to make you see and hear what I did. Niemeh didn't cry out. She was senseless by then, I'm sure of it. She didn't feel or know any of what it did to her. Afterward, when I went down with the others, there wasn't much left. It even carried some of her bones into the cave with it, to chew. Her garland was lying on the ground since the dragon had no interest in garnish. The pale flowers were no longer pale.

She had consented, and she hadn't had to endure it. I've seen things as bad that had been done by men, and for men there's no excuse. And yet, I never hated a man as I hated the dragon, a loathing, deadly, sickening hate.

The moon was rising when it finished. It went again to the pond, and drank deeply. Then it moved up the gravel back towards the cave. It paused beside Caiy, sniffed him, but there was no hurry. Having fed so well, it was sluggish. It stepped into the pitch-black hole of the cave, and drew itself from sight, inch by inch, as it had come out, and was gone.

Presently Caiy pulled himself off the ground, first to his hands and knees, then on to his feet.

We, the watchers, were amazed. We'd thought him dead, his back broken, but he had only been stunned, as he told us afterwards. Not even stunned enough not to have come to, dazed and unable to rise, before the dragon quite finished its feeding. He was closer than any of us. He said it maddened him—as if he hadn't been mad already—and so, winded and part stupefied as he was, he got up and dragged himself into the dragon's cave after it. And this time he meant to kill it for sure, no matter what it did to him.

Nobody had spoken a word, up on our rocky place, and no one spoke now. We were in a kind of communion, a trance. We leaned forward and gazed at the black gape in the hill where they had both gone.

Maybe a minute later, the noises began. They were quite extraordinary, as if the inside of the hill itself were gurning and sharling. But it was the dragon, of course. Like the stink of it, those sounds it made were untranslatable. I could say it looked this way comparable to an elephantus, or that way to a cat, a horse, a bat. But the cries and roars—no. They were like nothing else I've heard in the world, or been told of. There were, however, other noises, as of some great heap of things disturbed. And stones rattling, rolling.

The villagers began to get excited or hysterical. Nothing like this had happened before. Sacrifice is usually predictable.

They stood, and started to shout, or groan and invoke supernatural protection. And then a silence came from inside the hill, and silence returned to the villagers.

I don't remember how long it went on. It seemed like months.

Then suddenly something moved in the cave mouth.

There were yells of fear. Some of them took to their heels, but came back shortly when they realized the others were rooted to the spot, pointing and exclaiming, not in anguish but awe. That was because it was Caiy, and not the dragon, that had emerged from the hill.

He walked like a man who has been too long without food and water, head bowed, shoulders drooping, legs barely able to hold him up. He floundered through the edges of the pond and the sword trailed from his hand in the water. Then he tottered over the slope and was right before us. He somehow raised his head then, and got out the sentence no one had ever truly reckoned to hear.

"It's — dead," said Caiy, and slumped unconscious in the moonlight.

They used the litter to get him to the village, as Niemeh didn't need it any more.

We hung around the village for nearly ten days. Caiy was his merry self by the third, and since there had been no sign of the dragon, by day or night, a party of them went up to the hills and, kindling torches at noon, slunk into the cave to be sure.

It was dead all right. The stench alone would have verified that, a different perfume than before, and all congealed there, around the cave. In the valley, even on the second morning, the live dragon smell was almost gone. You could make out goats and hay and mead and unwashed flesh and twenty varieties of flowers.

I myself didn't go in the cave. I went only as far as the post. I understood it was safe, but I just wanted to be there once more, where the few bones that were Niemeh had fallen through the shackles to the earth. And I can't say why, for you can explain nothing to bones.

There was rejoicing and feasting. The whole valley was

full of it. Men came from isolated holdings, cots and huts, and a rough-looking lot they were. They wanted to glimpse Caiy the dragon-slayer, to touch him for luck and lick the finger. He laughed. He hadn't been badly hurt, and but for bruises was as right as rain, up in the hayloft half the time with willing girls, who would afterwards boast their brats were sons of the hero. Or else he was blind drunk in the chieftain's hall.

In the end, I collected Negra, fed her apples and told her she was the best horse in the land, which she knows is a lie and not what I say the rest of the time. I had sound directions now, and was planning to ride off quietly and let Caiy go on as he desired, but I was only a quarter of a mile from the village when I heard the splayed tocking of horse's hooves. Up he galloped beside me on a decent enough horse, the queen of the chief's stable, no doubt, and grinning, with two beer skins.

I accepted one, and we continued, side by side.

"I take it you're sweet on the delights of my company," I said at last, an hour after, when the forest was in view over the moor.

"What else, Apothecary? Even my insatiable lust to steal your gorgeous horse has been removed. I now have one of my very own, if not a third as beautiful." Negra cast him a sidelong look as if she would like to bite him. But he paid no attention. We trotted on for another mile or so before he added, "And there's something I want to ask you, too."

I was wary, and waited to find out what came next.

Finally, he said, "You must know a thing or two in your trade about how bodies fit together. That dragon, now. You seemed to know all about dragons."

I grunted. Caiy didn't cavil at the grunt. He began idly to describe how he'd gone into the cave, a tale he had flaunted a mere three hundred times in the chieftain's hall. But I didn't cavil either, I listened carefully.

The cave entry-way was low and vile, and soon it opened into a cavern. There was elf-light, more than enough to see by, and water running here and there along the walls and over the stony floor.

There in the cavern's center, glowing now like filthy silver, lay the dragon, on a pile of junk such as dragons always accumulate. They're like crows and magpies in that shiny things intrigue them and they take them to their lairs to paw possessively and to lie on. The rumors of hoards must come from this, but usually the collection is worthless, snapped knives, impure glass that had sparkled under the moon, rusting armlets from some victim, and all of it soiled by the devil's droppings, and muddled up with split bones.

When he saw it like this, I'd bet the hero's reckless heart failed him. But he would have done his best, to stab the dragon in the eye, the root of the tongue, the vent under the tail, as it clawed him in bits.

"But you see," Caiy now said to me, "I didn't have to."

This, of course, he hadn't said in the hall. No. He had told the village the normal things, the lucky lunge and the brain pierced, and the death throes, which we'd all heard plainly enough. If anyone noticed his sword had no blood on it, well, it had trailed in the pond, had it not?

"You see," Caiy went on, "it was lying there comatose one minute, and then it began to writhe about, and to go into a kind of spasm. Something got dislodged off the hoard-pile—a piece of cracked-up armor, I think, gilded—and knocked me silly again. And when I came round, the dragon was all sprawled about, and dead as yesterday's roast mutton."

"Hn," I said. "*Hn*n."

"The point being," said Caiy, watching the forest and not me, "I must have done something to it with the first blow, outside. Dislocated some bone or other. You told me their bones have no marrow. So to do that might be conceivable. A fortunate stroke. But it took a while for the damage to kill it.''

"Hn*n*."

"Because," said Caiy, softly, "you do believe I killed it, don't you?"

"In the legends," I said, "they always do."

"But you said before that, in reality, a man can't kill a dragon."

"One did," I said.

"Something I managed outside then. Brittle bones. That first blow to its skull."

"Very likely."

Another silence. Then he said: "Do you have any gods, Apothecary?"

"Maybe."

"Will you swear me an oath by them, and then call me 'dragon-slayer'? Put it another way. You've been a help. I don't like to turn on my friends. Unless I have to."

His hand was nowhere near that honed sword of his, but the sword was in his eyes and his quiet, oh-so-easy voice. He had his reputation to consider, did Caiy. But I've no reputation at all. So I swore my oath and I called him dragon-slayer, and when our roads parted my hide was intact. He went off to glory somewhere I'd never want to go.

Well, I've seen a dragon, and I do have gods. But I told them, when I swore that oath, I'd almost certainly break it, and my gods are accustomed to me. They don't expect honor and chivalry. And there you are.

Caiy never killed the dragon. It was Niemeh, poor lovely loving gentle Niemeh who killed it. In my line of work, you learn about your simples. Which cure, which bring sleep, which bring the long sleep without awakening. There are some miseries in this blessed world can only end in death, and the quicker death the better. I told you I was a hard man. I couldn't save her, I gave you reasons why. But there were all those others who would have followed her. Other Niemeh's. Other Caiy's, for that matter. I gave her enough in the cup to put out the life of fifty strong men. It didn't pain her, and she didn't show she was dead before she had to be. The dragon devoured her, and with her the drug I'd dosed her with. And so Caiy earned the name of dragon-slayer.

And it wasn't a riddle.

And no, I haven't considered making a profession of it. Once is enough with any twice-terrible thing. Heroes and knights need their impossible challenges. I'm not meant for any bard's romantic song, a look will tell you that. You won't ever find me in the Northern hills calling "Draco! Draco!"

Folk tales have long been a source of material for fantasy writers. This tale about a young girl who appears at the door of a sorely beset dust-bowl-stricken Kansas farm family would seem to be based on some old folk legend. It is not, however. It is in toto Steve Rasnic Tem's creation.

HARVEST CHILD

Steve Rasnic Tem

Two months ago I was doing volunteer work at a refugee camp in Somalia. I've done quite a bit of that—going where lives were so bleak, so devastated, no one but a handful could stand to witness it—since I retired from the army. Lieutenant-colonel. World War II, Korea, Vietnam. I suppose if I'd paid more attention to soldiering and less to sight-seeing disaster areas I'd have done much better than lieutenant-colonel. But I stumbled across a harvest child in each of those places. The last one in Somalia.

I had just gotten off the phone with the United Nations people again. Trying to get food, seeds, anything we needed. We were getting practically nothing; the U.N. had really dropped the ball on that one. None of the refugees had received food rations in two days, and we had no idea when the next truck would arrive. The starving were lying in huts made of thornbush branches, animal skins, and rotten pieces of cloth. No blankets, and only two small hand-dug wells to provide water for 76,000 people. We soon discovered that the two wells were contaminated.

The mothers' breasts were no longer giving milk. The children's bellies were swollen, their eyes more vacant than the worst cases of shellshock I witnessed in my military years. So many unable even to cry, the encroaching starvation a slow, silent death.

The Somalis have an age-old tradition of caring for kinspeople; they will take any number of refugees in, despite the devastating cost to themselves. It was frustrating, watching the armies of starving continue to pour into land already virtually depleted of resources. I understood why the Somalis were doing it, perhaps more than most; my own people back in the Midwest would have done much the same. But that made it all the more painful for me.

There wouldn't be a harvest that year; I had thought about that a great deal the past few days. A terrible drought, almost no rain in nearly five years. Overgrazing, indiscriminate cutting of trees, intertribal war, wind and water erosion: it all aided the desert as it slowly took over more and more of the crop and grazing land. I had seen it happen before; the burning dust brought with it an indescribable chill.

I was walking toward a new group of arrivals, mostly old men and women, when she stepped out of the crowd: dark liquid eyes, glistening hair, mouth and cheeks that added up to the look which promised so much: green crops in the ground, flowing streams, corn, barley, wheat. A harvest child. She brought me back to the Kansas of my childhood— 1934; I was nine years old. And just for a moment she brought back the dust storms that seemed a mile high, that swallowed the horizon and turned the sun rust-colored at noon, that made you afraid you'd be buried in your sleep. So you woke up every few hours from nightmares of suffocation, bothering your mother too many times with it. But one night when you awakened it had grown still outside, the wind gone off somewhere. Everyone else asleep. That was the night she came.

We'd spent most of the day indoors. In my daddy's house, the house my daddy and grandpa built with their own hands, when grandpa was still alive. Straightening nails and wiring up the rafters with bailing wire. A real roughshod affair, I can still remember the lopsided corners and the way the boards met off-angle in places, as if the wind had thrown them there and by some natural process they'd just grown together. I loved that house, even back then. It showed where my daddy's hands had been. My daddy who couldn't touch me, hold me, any of us really, or say more than an occasional kind word.

You couldn't even see to the edge of the front yard for the blinding dust. One of my uncles was due to come in that day but we really didn't expect him; we'd heard they were having to plow several feet of dust drift off the roads to clear them. We'd had to wear goggles over our eyes and handkerchiefs over our mouths and noses the past few days to walk outside at all. Even then the mucus in your nose dried out so bad it formed a rock-hard crust that burned your skin. When you could smell the dust it smelled burnt. "Hell," my daddy would say, and we all knew he meant that was where we were. It didn't seem much like we were in Kansas anymore.

That day had been especially bad, I remember. The wind howled like some big thing lost out there in the dust. Cornstalks hit the side of the house like bones. I'll never forget the way the corn had died: brown spreading from the tips down a dead vein in the center of each leaf, spreading 'til it bronzed the plant completely, the dry stalks leaning in the direction of the

wind. When the winds started picking up topsoil they took
the corn with it.

The dust seemed more persistent in getting into the house
this time. Mama was frantic. Usually you could keep most of
it out by stuffing sheets and rags against the door frame and
the windowsill. Even then a little bit of it would slip in and
gradually build up in the air, so that a fine layer covered all
the furniture and you were always having to brush it off your
clothes. Mama had to keep a cloth over the food. But this
night the wind blew the rags out of the cracks and chinks and
the dust just poured through. Mama ran around crying, trying
to stuff the rags back in. Daddy made us put our handkerchiefs up over our faces, said it wasn't healthy to breathe that
air.

Things calmed down some after supper. And Grandma told
us another one of her stories before bed. Mama didn't approve of her tales, because Grandma believed things a good
Christian woman just did not believe. She'd listen to anybody's tales and repeat half of 'em, Mama always said to my
daddy. But Grandma was my daddy's mama, so Mama never
could say too much. When Grandma was telling her stories
my mama would just sit in her rocker and knit. And frown.

"Won't be a harvest this year, I'm afeared," Grandma was
saying. "Guess it'll be a good time for the good Lord to give
somebody a harvest child."

"What's a harvest child?" I asked my grandma. I didn't
say too much back then, usually. I guess that's why Grandma
looked up at me a little surprised.

"Why that's a gift, youngun, usually a girl. She'd be a
sister for you boys." My brother Jack made a face and she
laughed. "The Lord—or whatever does sech things—" She
looked at my mama quickly. Mama just frowned some more
and kept rocking. "He gives it to you, to make up for the lost

harvest, and just maybe to help bring the harvest back to you someday, all things willing."

"Some gift!" my daddy said. "Just givin' you 'nother mouth to feed."

After we went to bed I thought about that a long time. I'd always wanted a sister, and I knew Jack did, too, although we were both too embarrassed to admit it. There had always seemed something missing in the house, something out of whack. I always figured that somehow a sister would put things right again. Not somebody to take care of, really, but a special friend. Somebody to talk to in a way you couldn't talk to your daddy or your brother or other male kin, even your mother, I guess. I just knew things would be better with a sister around.

When I woke up I stared all around the little house. I couldn't figure what had disturbed me. Everybody else was asleep. And so still—I suddenly realized the wind had stopped blowing. No more whistling, or shaking. And the way the windows glowed, all silver, I could tell that the moon had come out from behind the giant dust clouds.

But then there was a tapping, and I nearly jumped out of bed. I listened hard. Maybe it had just been a tumbleweed blowing against the door. But there it was again, and I knew this time it had to be a knock.

I got up out of bed and padded to the front door, trying not to wake up anybody else. I turned the knob and pulled, just a little bit.

Her face and shoulders were dark, shadowed, as if they were covered with the brown dust. But her hair . . . golden, like it was glowing on its own, moving on its own like the way the wheat heads seemed to sometimes even when there wasn't any wind. The color was like wheat heads, too, I realized, so gold and full and ripe, just before harvest time.

My grandma was suddenly there beside me, pulling the

little girl in. That's what she was, I could see as she passed me so quietly. About eleven years old, same age as Jack.

Soon the whole household was up and surrounding her, wondering who she was and where she'd come from. But she couldn't seem to remember any of that. My mama took to her, and held her, but it was hard to tell if that was helping any. "Poor baby," my mama kept crooning. "Lost out in the storm."

My grandma stood back and looked at her. "Harvest child . . ." she whispered.

Mama looked up at her sharply and no one else said a word. Then we all gathered around the newcomer again, just looking at her. Daddy scratched his head, it seemed like the whole time.

After a while I caught sight of my grandma standing by the window, looking out. I went over to her. She was rubbing her hands, making them look raw.

"What's the matter, Grandma?" I said.

She looked down at me a little funny. Then she tried to smile, but not doing it too well. "A harvest child means many things, child. Most of 'em good." She gripped my shoulder. "But sometimes that means there's a lot more bad got to come first."

She didn't know her name, so we called her Amanda. That was Daddy's youngest sister who died of the croup when he was just a boy. Mama looked at him funny when he came up with the name; that was an unusual thing for him to do, taking that kind of interest. I guess it surprised us all.

There was a time at first, the first month I guess, when Amanda kept pretty much to herself, staying close to Mama and keeping out of the way of the rest of us. Not that she was afraid; more like she was shy. Except with my grandma. I do think she was a little afraid of my grandma. I'm not sure why, but she was even quieter than usual when Grandma was around, keeping behind Mama's skirts and staring at the old woman like a cautious little animal. Of course, that made things even worse between Mama and Grandma. Mama seemed sure that Grandma meant our new sister harm, although even she didn't know why. I never thought that about Grandma. It seemed to me she was just a little nervous about Amanda, as if she didn't know what was going to happen because of Amanda, and that scared her.

That changed a little. Amanda started bringing Grandma fresh-picked flowers, putting them in a vase by her bed, and making such a smile as I've never seen. Even Grandma, for all her nervousness around the child, had to laugh when she saw that smile. Funny thing was, none of us had seen blooming flowers under that dust for some time. We couldn't figure out where she was finding them.

After a while, though, Amanda started acting just like any other little girl her age, laughing and playing with dolls and chasing the hens and chattering away the whole time about all kinds of nonsense. It was hard to believe she hadn't always been with us. She even had fights with my brother Jack like most sisters and brothers do. Catcalling and crying and both of them running to Mama, who just shooed them out the door again.

I couldn't tell any difference at first between her and any other girl. Except that she was my friend.

First time I knew that was when she took the blame for something I'd done. Daddy used to take the things his boys did pretty seriously, with very little humor. He really expected us to be men. With times so hard he seemed to think that was necessary; there just wasn't enough easy time to indulge a childhood. He expected us to grow up fast. "Only way you boys are gonna survive is to be men jes' quick as you can," is the way he used to say it, but not looking at us.

That's how we knew something was bothering him; he'd always looked at us.

I'd been playing around the root cellar. I knew I wasn't supposed to be there, but I liked it so much down there—it was so dark, and cooler than anywhere else around. You could pretend it was a cave, or an Egyptian tomb. I daydreamed a lot down in that old cellar. It was harder to daydream out in the open air; everything was so flat, it used to seem that your daydreams and fancies had nothing to hold on to. The wind just picked them up and blew them away, left them crumpled on the ground, covered with a fine layer of dust.

I'd found a sack with a few potatoes in it. Dried out a little, but not too bad. The eyes were already long as little garden snakes; I figured Mama had just forgotten about them. Or maybe that was just wishful thinking. I picked up one and stared at it. And thought I recognized a face. From some storybook or dream, maybe. Without thinking I pulled Grandpa's old pocketknife out of my pants and started carving into the potato, trying to uncover the face that was hiding there. Sharp, crooked nose and high cheekbones and slash of a mouth framed by long mouthlines. After a while the potato looked like some sort of witch or evil goddess, the eyes making long snakes for hair, wriggling in a disgusting way as I put in the finishing touches: cleft chin and wrinkled neck.

I stared at her. I vaguely remembered a woman like her in one of the school books, turning people to stone with just a look. Only with her gritty feel, the way the leftover peel made streaks in her face and hair, I figured she probably turned people into dust. Like the itinerant preacher who passed through occasionally used to say, "Dust unto dust." That was her. She could turn you, your brothers and your sisters, your whole world into dust with just one look. You had to be careful. Had to watch out. Or she'd turn on you.

That night my mama came into the house carrying the sack of potatoes. I wanted to run out; I didn't know what to do. She started to cry, pulling out the ruined potato. Daddy went over and grabbed it out of her hand, then turned and looked at me.

At the time I wasn't sure why everybody looked so upset over one potato. I guessed it was because we had so little left, even one potato meant more hardship. And then realizing they were upset over just one little potato made them even more upset. Because it told them just how bad off we were.

Amanda stepped up to Daddy and said, "I did it." She didn't even have to look at me. She knew. I listened to Daddy whipping her out past the barn that night with a feeling I'd never had before. Like I was almost devastated with guilt, but that there was something happy about the feeling, too. I never knew if she cried when he whipped her; I couldn't hear her and I couldn't ask Daddy. I was too embarrassed to ask her.

The next day Amanda came home from playing out in the dust with her arms full of potatoes. She wouldn't say where she got them, just that she'd found them in the dust. Daddy and Mama didn't know what to believe. They knew it couldn't have happened the way she told it, but they couldn't come up with a better explanation either. No one lived close enough to us for her to have stolen them. So they finally just took them, and Mama cooked them a little bit at a time, although I think it always bothered her the way we got them.

The next few years things were hard. Us kids knew, although Mama and Daddy would never say we didn't have any money, or that we didn't have enough food. We just didn't talk about it. So I guess in a way we were a little protected from it, and for the most part played and went to school the same as we always had.

Except some of our friends had to go away. We were

lucky; we owned the land and house. A lot of the other families were tenant farmers, and the big land companies decided tenant farming didn't pay in a drought and started kicking people off the land they'd farmed for years, that they had kin buried in.

The land companies sent giant earth movers and tractors to knock the old houses down and plow up everything including the front yards. They planted cotton: green and dry. Daddy said it would ruin the land; the big land companies were just trying to get the most out of it before they sold it to somebody else.

So a lot of our friends had to leave, going to California and other places. That next school year there was just a handful of us left.

Amanda did well in school, although she was still pretty quiet. She still brought vegetables and other things home from playing, and one time a new shawl for Mama. Daddy and Mama had given up asking her about it a long time ago. And always bringing Grandma fresh-picked flowers, even when they weren't in season, even when there weren't any flowers to be had anywhere, the dust having killed them all. Amanda still brought them, giving them to Grandma with a smile.

Grandma asked where she got them, sometimes, shaking her head when Amanda said she couldn't remember.

Of course, Daddy didn't care to ask much of anything by that time. That's when he'd first started drinking. Sometimes he even dragged Jack along to a neighbor's place to drink. To have somebody to help carry him home, I guess. No matter what, he insisted on passing out and sleeping in his own bed, not at a saloon or somebody's place miles away. Mama and Grandma kept saying that was bad for Jack, that the boy would get to be just like him, but he didn't seem to listen.

I wasn't growing up to be like Daddy, or Jack. I realized

that that year. I was different. I used to be like Jack, I know; used to like all the same things: hunting and fishing and scaring the livestock every chance we had. We spent most of our time together. That changed pretty quickly. I started spending a lot of time with Amanda: talking to her, listening to her. Soon I spent all my time with her. Jack stayed with Daddy.

"You gotta be careful," she said to me one day. We'd been about a mile from the house, on a little rise, one of the few places around there that hadn't changed much the past few years; it was still green as ever.

"Careful of what?" I said. She talked . . . abstractly, a great deal of the time. Like she was telling a riddle. I didn't like it all the time.

"Of your anger. . . ." She brushed grass and seeds off her dress.

"Anger? I ain't angry!" I felt anxious. "You know I 'most never lose my temper!"

"We all have anger," she said in a quiet voice. "Even me. You've seen lots of folk angry around here, haven't you?"

I nodded. There were a lot of bitter people. First they got pushed off their land, then for them to get to California and other places they had to sell most of what they owned. And there were always people around to take advantage, offering them far less than what their belongings were worth, just because the people were desperate. I saw one man shoot his horse rather than sell it for far less than what it was worth. The two men had just been standing there with the horse in front of the house, arguing, when the poor farmer went into the house, came back with a shotgun, and stopping on the porch took aim and shot his own horse. I'd never seen anybody as mad as that other fellow, standing there looking down at the fine piece of horseflesh he'd intended to buy.

Mirrors and pictures and good pieces of furniture passed

down from grandparents to parents to children, valuable pieces brought over from the old country, cherished items once owned by dead relatives—I saw them stacked up in people's yards and burned, burned in anger because they couldn't bear to sell them for such shamefully low amounts. Kids' toys and mama's best linen, daddy's tools and grandpa's cedar chest. Anger striking the match. Smoldering. That was the scariest thing about it all: They were all so angry, but quiet about it. Lots of them never said a word. Just lit the match and stepped back, staring blank-eyed and pale.

They left their old houses to the wind and stray animals—birds and mice and skinny dogs and cats. Jack used to go out and break windows, tear down boards, wreck anything he could get his hands on. A lot of our schoolfriends did the same. Jack more than anybody else, though. He'd just spend hours tearing up a place. It worried Mama and Grandma; I don't know how Daddy felt.

I felt strange about it. For some reason I thought Amanda understood what Jack was up to.

I did have the anger, deep down, but I knew Amanda was changing that. With her there, there just seemed to be less reason to be angry.

One night a year later Jack came home from town by himself. Pale and angry and trying not to cry. "Daddy's hole up down the saloon! They can't get him to leave!"

We all went down, even Grandma. All the men were standing in the street, quiet. No one said a word. They all stared at the saloon. A few young boys ran around the street bumping into people, but nobody really paid them any attention. I listened carefully. I could hear Daddy inside the saloon, screaming, busting things up. I looked at Amanda. She had sat down on an old log, her hands folded. She seemed to be waiting.

Nobody would go in. When Grandma tried, it took three men to stop her.

Suddenly, we all saw Amanda walking up the sidewalk toward the saloon. Mama began to scream. A couple of the men tried to catch her, but before they could reach the door she had walked in.

It was quiet for just a minute. Then I could hear my daddy yelling again. "Get away from me! Who asked you to come anyway?" Then I could hear things breaking up in there again. What if he hurt her? I'd never forgive him. . . .

Then we heard him scream. "Get away from me, witch!" And a shot. My mama began to moan to herself.

It seemed like a long time, but then Amanda walked out alone.

No one said anything. Except my grandma. I can still hear her whisper, so low it was almost as if she hadn't intended to say anything and a little breeze just came and picked her thoughts up out of her mouth and turned them into words. "Harvest child. . . ." Those were the words; I do remember.

No one doubted Daddy'd killed himself. Lots of people said they'd seen it coming for a long time. My grandma never replied, except one time to say, "It was time. Time for the harvest," but she was tired, so nobody paid much attention.

Mama never would talk about it, so I don't know what she thought.

Things changed after that. Jack settled down some, enough that we stopped thinking he'd turn out like Daddy. He started doing better in school. And he fell in love with Amanda.

He had the right, I know; she wasn't really our sister. And I'd never thought about her romantically myself; she was my friend. Although I never saw her encourage him, she didn't seem to want to stop him, either. I couldn't blame him—she'd grown into a beautiful young woman, her hair even more golden than when she'd first come to us.

But I still felt it wasn't right. No good would come of it. And I knew Grandma felt the same way. When she looked at the two of them, it was with sadness.

There's something else, too, I realized at the time, although I couldn't quite think it out. My mind seemed to clamp shut when the idea was only halfway in focus. Jack was better without Daddy. Mama and me were, too. We all were. I still hate to think that, but it's true.

Things were getting better all over the Midwest by that time. It was 1940. The government had started a grass-seeding program back in '35 that was showing good results; a good deal of erosion cover had been replaced. Farmers had started using a three-year rotation of wheat and sorghum and a fallow year. There was increased contour plowing, terracing, and strip-cropping. You could see shelter belts of trees on the horizon now, planted to break the high winds. A lot of politicians were saying that the dust bowl years would never happen again.

And old neighbors were returning from California. They were coming home.

I'd noticed that Amanda had grown restless the last few months before school that year. She was seventeen; it'd be her last. But it wasn't the same kind of hurry-up-to-be-grownup I saw in Jack. It was as if she were waiting, and not too happy about what she was waiting for. And each time a storm came up she seemed anxious, sharp with the rest of the family for the first time I could remember. She'd spend long hours out on that little rise where she'd warned me about anger, just staring off into the distance. She looked sad, as if something were ending. I couldn't sleep most nights thinking about her, the way she was acting, and when I'd get up at night to use the bathroom I'd see her sitting out on the porch, looking toward the moon, watching, waiting.

Grandma seemed to be waiting, too. "Things are lookin'

better," she'd say, talking about the way the land was now, and the old neighbors coming back, and all the things the government was doing for us. Then she'd stare off into the distance, just like Amanda, waiting.

Tornado season begins around March in Kansas. The old-timers say you can usually tell a few hours before one hits; the livestock seem restless, people's tempers flare, and the whole countryside seems to hold its breath.

That year the waiting seemed to drag on forever. I thought Jack and I were going to kill each other before school was out, always snapping at each other and quarreling over every little thing. Grandma had to separate us several times when we got into it at home. She was looking more and more worried herself; she and Mama weren't even speaking that spring.

Amanda wasn't paying too much attention to Jack anymore, or me either for that matter. We'd both try to talk to her, but she usually wouldn't reply, just sit there, staring at the dark fingers of cloud reaching down, raking the earth. Fake tornadoes, I used to call them. Those clouds looked a little like tornadoes to a youngster I suppose; they just didn't spin. I used to imagine they did that for protective camouflage, so that airplanes wouldn't fly into them and tear them apart. Self-preservation—back then I figured everything must value that.

Amanda had changed Jack all right. Despite our quarrels, I could tell he really cared about things. He had grown. He was sprouting new things just about all the time. Maybe that's why she didn't pay as much attention to him anymore, or to the rest of us; her work was done.

It was almost time for school to let out that day when the first twister hit. What strikes me the most now that I look back on it is how pretty it had seemed at that first sighting, like a giant gray feather off in the distance, one of those plumes The Three Musketeers might have worn in the book I'd read in school the year before. I said that to Jack and he frowned, poked me, and said it looked just like a big old tree in a heavy rain. One of the girls said it was like spigot water when dust got in the pipe, kind of muddy gray.

We all stood at the windows watching it jump over Thompson's barn and climb over the little rise separating the Thompson place from the school. We watched it coming closer and closer. Some of the kids were getting nervous. The teacher was from back east—our old teacher had stayed out in California with the rest of her family—and I don't think she had ever seen a tornado before. She stood there staring like the rest of us. Some of us recognized the danger, I guess, but we'd been seeing twisters all our lives; they were like old, friendly landmarks. You never really thought about one attacking you. That always happened to other folks.

Then I noticed Amanda.

I have never seen, before or since, such a look. She seemed to be straining upwards on her feet. A tenseness in her back; for a second I was afraid it was going to snap. But the odd thing about it, despite her painful appearance, I was convinced that she was almost thrilled with the approach of the tornado.

"There's another one!" Bobby Collins shouted, and I remember, clearly, the shrill panic in his voice.

Kids scrambled away from the windows and started for the stairs that led to the shelter beneath the school. The teacher shouted, urging them to safety, but they didn't have to be told. I think I may have been the only one who heard her.

"Another one! Three!" Jack yelled, and I thought my brother was going to cry.

Jack and I started down the stairs behind the others. Two of the tornadoes were almost at the schoolhouse. Then I remembered Amanda. "Jack!" I shouted, almost sobbing, and twisted back around, away from his hand.

Amanda had opened the door, and was walking slowly outside.

Jack must have turned around right after me, because he was shouldering past, then running toward the open door.

I'm not sure I'll ever know why I did it, if I was afraid Jack was too late and he'd just get himself killed going out there, or if I sensed Amanda was finally going home, her work completed, and we had no right to stop her. Sometimes I wonder, God forbid, if maybe I just wasn't a little scared of Amanda, and the way she had changed things in our lives, all of our lives. I do know it broke my heart, what I did. I leaped after Jack and grabbed him, held him away from the door, held him away from Amanda, then I knocked us both under the large oak table as the twister thundered past.

My brother finally forgave me. I think maybe after a few years he realized what Amanda was, and understood why I'd done what I'd done. He sent me a painting of a young girl harvesting wheat one year, right about the same time Amanda had disappeared. Her hair golden, a distant look in her eyes.

Everybody said she'd been killed, but no one ever found a body.

I searched all over the Somali refugee camp for the beautiful young black girl, that harvest child. But like my Amanda, I never saw her again. I figured there would be other chances, though. Besides, I now knew the bad times would eventually pass for these people, as they had for my own. It made the work a bit easier, the suffering a little more bearable to watch.

My grandma died in that storm. They found her in bed, looking out the window. They figured her old heart couldn't handle all the excitement.

But she was smiling. And there were newly picked flowers in a vase on her bedtable.

I think about Grandma a lot these days, now that I'm getting older. I wonder about what she saw. I wonder if it was anything like what I saw while I was pulling Jack away from the schoolhouse door. Out in the swirling dust, a young golden-haired girl lifting up her arms.

And three tornadoes bending down, surprisingly gently, to lift her.

When I'm older, Amanda, just a bit older. Bring me fresh-picked flowers. Come smile at me.

There are, of course, people in our society who are seldom noticed or, if noticed, are quickly forgotten. They just seem to fade into the background and are easily overlooked. Suppose, however, that an entire subculture of people whose presence was completely unknown to the rest of us actually existed. Here is a story about just such a group and about their unusual and precarious lifestyle.

LOVE AMONG THE XOIDS

John Sladek

Syd and Mercy got off the bus in the middle of a little flock of old people. They knew exactly how to blend in and totter down the steps with the old people, so no one saw them. The old people didn't notice any young strangers among them, either. They were concentrating on their own tottering, and their eyes would be running, because of the cold wind, you see. Syd and Mercy could always calculate things like that, a cold October wind.

They knew just when to slide into the doorway of a book-store nobody ever visits, how long to wait there, and how to vanish around a corner just when the wind was flinging dead leaves in everybody's face. No one saw them move along to a house that suited them. They walked right in and went straight down to the laundry room in the basement—always a safe bet.

"Here goes," said Mercy. She opened the door of the dryer, ran her hand around inside and came up with something. A sock.

"Blue," said Syd in disgust. "I don't need blue. Why can't they ever leave a pair? I've had one of every kind of sock they've ever dreamed of." At the moment, he showed her, he was wearing a brown dream on his left foot and a yellow-and-green argyle nightmare on his right. "It's not fair."

"Fair?" She laughed. His face tried laughing back, but it was too thin. You could see knots of muscle and cords tying it all up so laughter was impossible. All a thin face like that could do was complain about unfairness.

"Let's go get some breakfast," Mercy said. Silently they flowed up the stairs to the kitchen. There was no one there but a black-and-white cat that immediately sat down and waited to be fed. Yet, even while it licked its chops and cast significant looks at the cupboard door, the cat couldn't help noticing how *different* these humans were. The way they moved, sliding along walls and peering around corners, was not entirely human. They reminded the cat of cats.

There was stale bread in the breadbox, being saved for stuffing, a trace of butter on a butter-paper being saved for baking, and the coffee filter was full of good, reusable grounds. Mercy and Syd insinuated themselves into chairs and started breakfast.

Mercy hated to watch him eat. Two years she'd been with him now, and never had been able to get used to the sight of his jaws working, the anatomy lesson of cords snapping and muscles knotting in his face. Why did he have to be so thin?

Of course thinness helped him be inconspicuous, just as it helped her or any of their friends except Rollo. Nothing like thinness if you're spending lots of time flattened against walls or hiding behind lampposts, staying out of sight.

That's how they all lived, perpetually out of sight. They owned nothing, not houses or cars or even clothes. All they had were castoffs from ordinary society, from "real people." Realpeople were unaware of these invisible guests, who lived unseen all over the city—all over the world, she'd heard.

Thinness was fine, but Syd was too thin. He hated his meals and took them grudgingly, scowling at the plate. To him, the word "food" was an epithet. He would never speak of having breakfast or lunch, only "Let's *grab* some *food*."

Syd liked to watch Mercy eat. She was nearly as skinny as he but she was beautiful. Syd was all too aware of his own ugliness, the nose like a big axeblade, the Adam's apple genuflecting every time he swallowed. Chop, gulp, chop, gulp, God he hated eating. But he had to put on some weight. He had to become somehow more solid and substantial. Otherwise, he knew, Mercy was going to leave him.

If only they were able to have a kid, that would fix everything. She wanted one, but there was something wrong. She never had to borrow any tampons anywhere, that meant something was wrong. The want was there all the same, and it was growing, turning everything sour. *If you were a realwoman, he wanted to say to her, you'd have six kids. We'd all sit at the breakfast table, my wife, my kids, my table. I'd have a big car and maybe an airplane* . . .

"Be winter soon," he said.

"You want to stay here a few days?"

"If you do."

She scratched the cat under the chin. "I don't know. We don't know what they're like here. Might be hard to keep out of their way."

They looked at the floor, as though trying to deduce from it what kind of people lived here. There was little to be deduced from the tile pattern in brown, gold and white. Looked at one way, the brown snakes vanished, replaced by gold, G-shaped plants. Life is like that, they both were thinking. Always something missing.

A face with bulging eyes and bushy hair peered around the doorframe.

"Rollo!" they both exclaimed, though not loud. Never loud.

"Thought I saw you two popping in here. I was at the drugstore, reading magazines." He sat down with them, a slightly plump presence at the table of gauntness. "Nice place you got here. Is that coffee?"

They complimented Rollo on his new suit, a crisp plaid item that had probably been the height of fashion, a few years ago.

"I like to keep my eyes open for stuff," he said, his bulging eyes bulging a little more. "I could pick you up a dress, Mercy. What's your size?"

She looked at Syd, who was frowning at the floor tiles. "Oh, uh, thanks anyway, Rollo. What were you reading?"

None of the people they knew, except Rollo, bothered reading anything. Many were illiterate. They themselves, though they could read street signs and bus names, never had time for any serious reading. Rollo, however, read everything: magazines in stores, old piles of papers left out for the Boy Scouts, the labels on foods at the supermarket. He was a walking encyclopedia of information, and if any of it was a little distorted, shopworn or out of date, no one noticed.

"Fascinating the stuff you can glean, a page here, a page there," he said. "For instance, Syd, I would say that you are suffering from a disease called *anorexia nervosa*, did you know that?"

Syd looked alarmed. "A disease?"

"A nervous disease, it keeps you from eating square meals. Is there some marmalade to go with this bread, by the way?"

"But how would I get cured?"

Rollo helped himself to jam. "I didn't get that part. But I saw another article for you, Mercy. It talked about the problems of women in the upper echelons of the corporate pyramid."

Syd and Mercy, who had never heard of corporate pyramids or echelons, said nothing. Rollo continued: "Oh, by the way, IBM stock holds steady. Thousands die in Iranian earthquake. Local philanthropist honored. Air disaster blamed on faulty maintenance."

Mercy said, "Rollo, you're so well-informed!"

"I try to keep up. The man who knows what's going on in the world is the man who's going to get someplace. After all, world events affect everybody—even us."

"But how?" Mercy put the lid back on the jam, and tried to make it look as though several spoonfuls had not been removed.

"Well for instance, there are these superpowers, and they apparently have a lot of warheads, and they plan to use them to blow up the whole world!"

Syd tried to laugh again. "Come on, now, Rollo. That's a lot of gobbledegook from television. I'm not that ignorant, I've seen a little television myself, you know. Clowns eating hamburgers, cars crashing in flames, *superpowers, warheads*, agreements about salt, I've seen it too."

Mercy said, "Anyway these superheroes or whoever they are wouldn't use their warheads if they had them. It doesn't make sense."

"I'm only telling you what I read," said Rollo. "I'm not saying it's all true." Some of the bulge went out of his eyes, as Rollo seemed to sag a bit. "I guess sometimes I just wish we lived in their world, the realpeople world."

"Who doesn't?" Syd said, looking at his socks.

"I mean, I get so tired sometimes, sneaking around, hiding like some kind of wild animal—I mean, we're as much people as they are. We've got a right to be seen. We could live right out in the open, have houses of our own."

"Work jobs," said Syd.

"Raise children," said Mercy.

"I saw an expression in a magazine the other day that just summed it up. It spoke of coming out of the closet. Well that's what we ought to do, gosh darn it, come out of the closet!" Rollo banged his fist very lightly on the kitchen table.

There was a noise upstairs, of a heavy piece of furniture being moved. Without making a sound, the three cleaned up their crumbs, collected their dishes and ran to the hall closet.

In a moment, a woman came clumping down the stairs, carrying a load of bedlinen. The cat gave up pawing at the closet door and bounded into the kitchen with her, almost tripping her.

"Out of the way, Midnight," she said, using the loud voice realpeople used. "It's not dinnertime."

They could hear her clumping down the basement stairs, clanging the washing machine, singing over the racket of washing. Then back up to the kitchen, where sounds told them she was making coffee, drinking it, listening to the radio, cleaning the stove top, talking on the phone, loud.

"Mother it's okay, I'll *drive* you there . . . I *said* I would, didn't I? . . . Okay, but I have to be back by two, to pick up Donnie from school."

There were the sounds of a coat being slipped on, a nose blown, keys jingled. The back door slammed, and outside a car started. The three, who'd been holding themselves perfectly rigid for an hour, glided out in time to see the woman drive away.

In the silence of the house, Rollo said, "I've got to go myself. See you both at the party tonight?"

The house seemed even quieter with Rollo gone. Mercy walked through the living room, touching things. Realpeople had roomfuls of stuff like this: an onyx cigarette lighter, a dolphin-shaped ashtray, whiskey decanters marked *His* and *Hers*, an electronic organ, a glass cabinet full of tiny glass animals, a shelf of cacti, a painting of a clown on black velvet, a carriage clock, a tank of beautiful fish. On the desk was a pen-and-pencil set in something like gold, and a box of name labels. A plaster shepherd and shepherdess simpered at one another from opposite ends of the mantel, in the middle of which stood a large photo, a family portrait. Mommy, Daddy and Donnie. She began to sniffle.

"Don't start that again," said Syd. He was digging down the back of a sofa for loose change. "You know you can't have a kid, so why keep thinking about it? And even if you could, I'm not so sure we could raise it. We gotta travel light."

"I could raise it," she said hoarsely. "*I* could raise it."

Travel light, that was the rule. The rule was, no children, no pets, vacate the room by ten. It was the eternal rule, graven on tablets at the dawn of time for everyone who had to keep moving and travel light.

Well, she didn't want to travel light. She didn't want to keep moving, keep hiding. She wanted to grow thick and heavy and settle down in one place, while possessions piled up around her. Then one day she could squat down and pop out a nice, rosy baby. A baby girl. She could name it Portia. They would settle down together, with possessions piling up around them. It wasn't having things, that wasn't what was so important. It was having memories to go with them. This carriage clock we bought at that funny place in New Hampshire, remember? And the dolphin ashtray Portia brought back from camp, remember how tan she got? And wasn't that the year . . .

If I was realpeople, Syd thought, I'd just slap her in the mouth when she gets like this. Realpeople do what the hell they want. They talk out loud. They get in their cars and drive like hell, blasting the horn. Out of the way, Midnight. Out of the way, everybody. I'm real, out of my way!

When she'd finished crying, Mercy helped Syd search for coins. Then they slid up to the attic, where they found some old clothes in a trunk, just right for Letty's party. There was a blue chalkstripe suit for Syd, and a red-and-white floral dress for Mercy. They both looked good.

A yellow cab pulled up at a big house on Sumac Street at two a.m. The driver walked up to the front door to pick up his fare—someone leaving a party. While he was away from his empty cab, its back door opened and two shadows slipped out in silence. They moved so quickly that the blue chalkstripes and the red-and-white floral patterns were just blurs. As a realperson came out of the front door of the big house, Mercy and Syd were sliding around to come in the back way.

Letty liked to throw her parties in the wake of realpeople's parties. She would start letting in her guests before all the realpeople guests had left. Then she and her friends would spend some time keeping out of the way of the last, drunken realpeople—who were usually too busy singing, dozing, feeling sick or trying to remember the ending of some story, to notice Letty's friends.

Then when all the reals had been packed off in cars and taxis, or upstairs to bed, the second party would begin. There might be some chipdip and liquor left, or her guests would have visited other parties—drifting through them like cigarette smoke—and from them brought food or bottles. One way or another, there was always some cheer, often a little discreet music—and always, the company of friends.

There was Chauncey, who made the rounds of garage sales to collect anything he knew his friends might need. Though of course he did not pay for the stuff he collected, it was never missed. There was Rollo, the news-gatherer. There was Letty herself, who on Sundays took over an empty dentist's office to work on her friend's teeth. Ethel, a tall woman in pince-nez (one lens missing) likewise acted as a doctor, and was as adept at slipping her patients into empty hospital rooms as Ham was at making funeral arrangements, two bodies to a coffin. Mercy and Syd, like many others, were just providers of supermarket food and abandoned clothing. Finally there was Uncle Darb, now retired and living in a seldom-used darkroom, but still the patriarch and final arbiter on all matters of law.

Uncle Darb was sitting in a corner, telling a small, not very attentive group that their envy of realpeople was sinful.

"We are not meant to be like them," he kept saying. "We are meant to be apart, to live in their shadow, unseen, a secret tribe. We may use only what they won't miss, and only enough for our own survival. I don't say it's sinful to have a little party like this now and then. We do after all need to gather, to see one another and to talk about the rules."

The rules. Mercy took a glass of gin in four big swallows, gagged, and turned to hear what Chauncey was saying.

"These realpeople I'm with keep leaving the television on and going to sleep in front of it. So I drift in and watch all the late-night movies. *Invasion of the Xoids*, one was called. The Xoids looked just like real people, but if you shone a certain ray on them, they'd go pffft like flat tires, and just collapse."

His audience laughed, Mercy hardest of all. But even now, even in drink, she found herself unable to let go and shriek, really shriek the way realpeople did at parties.

"Call this a party?" she said to the nearest man. "I call it a meeting of the ghosts. Of the Xoids."

"Hello, Mercy," he said. "Long time no see. Remember me? Jasper." He was a short, balding man with a thin moustache.

"Jasper, hello. Haven't seen you since—funeral, was it?"

He nodded, emphasizing the baldness. "Aunt Portia's funeral. I, ah, still visit the grave a lot." It sounded like some kind of invitation.

"I keep meaning to visit, myself," she lied. "Only I can never remember the name. On the stone."

"Weiler," he said. "Maxine Weiler. I could, ah, take you out there tomorrow, if you like."

"Poor Aunt Portia," said Mercy. "Since we had to bury her with somebody, the least we could have done would be to put her in with a man. I don't suppose she had so much as a cuddle in her whole life, and now it's too late. I'll never have one."

"*You'll* never have one? I don't understand." His moustache understood, though. It was twitching comically.

She laughed. "I meant *she'll* never have one. A *cuddle*, I meant. Not a baby. O God, I don't feel so well. Jasper, do you think we could get some air?"

As they went out one door, Syd came in the other door with two glasses of wine. He looked for Mercy. Finally he said, "Okay, hell with her. Hell with her." He emptied her glass in one gulp, not minding at all how his Adam's apple genuflected. Hell with everything. He didn't mind anything anymore.

"I don't," he explained to Rollo. "I don't even mind you."

Rollo clapped him on the shoulder. "And I don't mind you, either, Syd old buddy. Let's get drunk. They say the alcohol content of wine—"

"Right," said Syd. Behind him he could hear Chauncey still going on about *Invasion of the Xoids*. "That's us, you know? Xoids. We're the fuckin' Xoids—oh, excuse me," he said to Uncle Darb.

The old man waved a hand. His blind eyes seemed focused on Syd. "Go on, my son. We're Xoids?"

"We're not even alive, we're not even real. We just go around faking everything. Borrowing everything. *Their* houses, *their* food, *their* damned socks. We're nothing, we're nobody!"

"What and whom do you want to be?" asked the patriarch.

"I want to drive a car and honk the horn. I want to be real and solid and important. I want to live in a world where I belong. Maybe in the country, with no realpeople—"

"Realpeople are everywhere," the old man warned. "They are the madness of this world, as it is their asylum. We, thank God, are outside their madness."

"Don't give me all that, I don't buy it anymore. You always end up with the same story, how we've been living like we do since the Dark Ages, how we never take last names because we're not families, we're individuals—I'm sick of all that."

"You want to join the realpeople? Nothing easier, my son. Just stop hiding. Let the realpeople see you. Course they'll probably put you in jail. Or the hospital."

"You're just saying that."

"Nope. There you'll be, a man with no identification cards, no job, no past and no last name. You never had any kind of job, never went to school, never lived at any address. You can't give your parents' full names, you don't know how old you are—"

"Stop! Just stop!" Syd's facial muscles were writhing. He turned and stalked away, out the kitchen door and into the back yard where he almost stumbled over two figures on the ground. He recognized the red-and-white of Mercy's dress, even though it was up around her waist.

Back inside the borrowed house, Syd found a downstairs borrowed bathroom. He went in, turned the borrowed lock, stripped off his borrowed clothes and looked at himself in the borrowed mirror. He borrowed a razor blade and cut both his wrists, then climbed in the borrowed bathtub to keep from messing up the floor. Xoids weren't even allowed to bleed out loud, he thought, as he went to sleep.

Screened by a gang of orderlies going to lunch, Ethel and Mercy slipped along the corridor to Syd's room. He was sitting up in bed, looking cheerful and relaxed—for the first time in years.

"I've made a decision," he said. "I'm joining the real world."

Ethel began changing the dressings on his wrists.

"I hope you'll be all right," said Mercy.

"I will. It doesn't have to be the way Uncle Darb says. I can work into it gradually, traveling and doing odd jobs, meeting just a few realpeople at a time—until I'm real, myself."

To Mercy, though she could not say so, the whole idea of being real included a home and family, pictures on the mantel and a cat in the kitchen. A realperson who traveled and did odd jobs sounded like "the worst of both worlds," as Rollo would say.

"I know what you're thinking," Syd said. "I thought so too."

"Really?"

"It's what everybody thinks, but I can't help it. I'm going."

Ethel nodded. Light danced on her pince-nez, on the single lens. "You can go home today, if you like," she said. "Home or wherever."

"What are you going to do?" he asked Mercy.

"I don't know. I still want a child," she said, looking out of the window. Buses moved along the street, carrying crowds of old people. Snow was making up its mind to fall, or rain. "I don't think I could ever make it as a realperson, though. So unless I can get pregnant—"

"Maybe you and Jasper could have a child," he suggested, already bored with her problems. He wanted to get out of here, get away from ghostly women complaining about their periods. He wanted to hit the street, walk tall, wear a hard hat, be somebody.

"I don't think I want to raise a child, not the way we have to live," she said. "Hiding, hiding, hiding, hiding, hiding." She wiped her eyes. "I'd better go."

Stifling a yawn, Syd said good-bye. Ethel took her arm and steered her along corridors, slipping like smoke past receptionists.

"Is this the way out?"

"No, I wanted to show you something." They glided on to a room with a glass door. Inside, they could see a nurse leaning over a glass crib. She was holding up a string of bright discs. The baby in the crib laughed and reached for them with one arm. The other arm was in a cast. They ducked back as the nurse looked up.

"Do you want that baby?"

Mercy said, "What? That baby? I mean, yes of course, but—but I mean—"

"I've checked her records," said Ethel. "Her name is Rae-Sue Fridley, daughter of Earl and Mae-Rae Fridley. They broke her arm."

Mercy gasped.

"It happens, among realpeople. They go ahead and have children they don't want, and end up hurting them. Now they're putting Rae-Sue into state care. Unless you and I take her first."

No children, no pets. Mercy thought about her own childhood. Folded up in a sofabed every day. Taken along quietly to the playground only late in the afternoon, when all the realkids had gone home to supper. The old rusty bike with rotten tires, on which she'd been allowed to ride around and around the deserted parts of town: weed-grown vacant lots, weed-grown railroad tracks; the grain-elevator part of town where weeds were allowed to show themselves. Folded away in the sofabed during school hours.

"Ethel, I just wouldn't want to make a mistake. I'd want to take good care of her."

"I know you would, that's why I brought you here."

"No but I mean I wouldn't want to make the mistakes my mother—"

"If you know they're mistakes, don't make them," said Ethel. "Anyway, you didn't turn out too badly, for all those mistakes. You know, she named you Mercy after the hospital where she found you."

"What? You mean I was abandoned, too?"

"Most of us are," said Ethel. "For centuries back, very few of our women could ever conceive. It may be our unusual sleep pattern—the fact that we have to be able to jump up and vanish at a second's notice, that we're never very deeply asleep. Whatever the cause, not many of us menstruate. So there's only one way to carry on the tribe."

"Kidnapping." She and Ethel ducked back as the nurse left the room.

"We only take children the realpeople don't want," said Ethel. "The rule still applies. And we only give them names the realpeople don't want." She looked at the clock down the corridor. "You have fifteen minutes to decide."

T, thought Mercy. *Theresa. Thomasina. Terry. Tina. Thea.*

Thora. I can teach her myself. Rollo could give her reading lessons. Letty could teach her painting and sculpture. *Toots.* *Tess.* No folding sofabed for my little—*Tiffany*?

"Titania," she said aloud.

A moment later, they bundled up Titania and slipped out a side door of the hospital. No one saw them sliding along the sidewalk today, because everyone else was running in the other direction, hurrying to see the accident. Ethel and Mercy and Titania sped on their way unnoticed; they were gone like breath vapor on this cold October day.

The man who'd been struck down by a bus was still breathing. Everyone could see the vapor, white as the bandages on his wrists. As the paramedics tried to lift him, he said, "I'm real." the vapor stopped.

"I just never saw him," said the bus driver. "He came at me out of nowhere."

The policeman said, "Don't worry. Your witnesses here all agree the guy jumped in front of you. Like he was daring you to hit him, somebody said."

"That right," said an old man. "And he shouted, I heard him shout. He shouted, 'Get out of my way.' Can I have a transfer?"

Wiping his eyes, the bus driver tore a colored piece of paper from a pad and handed it to the old man. The old man joined a crowd of other old people, tottering from this bus to the next one, waving their transfers like little flags of victory.

After spending the night with a witch, the man who would later be known as Stoneskin was given the gift of invulnerability. While not exactly an Achillean hero, he did learn to use that gift not only to benefit himself but also those who joined him. He also learned in time that the reputation was as potent as the reality.

STONESKIN

John Morressy

He rode through the forest slowly. The hooves of the big warhorse made scarcely a sound on the thick turf. The mist was dense and still, chilling him even through cloak and padded jerkin and heavy breeches. He pulled the cloak close around him, to guard his ring mail from the moisture as best he could, and rode on nodding, half-asleep.

A scream jolted him awake. It came again, from off to the left, and then was cut short. He guided the horse toward the sound, and soon came to the edge of a clearing.

At the far side, dim in the murky light, was a small cottage. A figure burst from it, running, followed by two others. The running figure appeared to be a woman. She fell, and the two men in pursuit stood over her. He heard their laughter.

There were two of them, and he was alone, but he spurred

the horse and rode directly for them, morning star poised to strike. They were ragged louts, on foot, armed with cudgels and no match for a mounted warrior.

They heard him coming, and turned, but they were helpless before his rush. He smashed the skull of the nearest. The other threw down his club and ran. He rode over him and left him whimpering in the mud with a broken back.

He returned to where the woman lay, a huddle of dark rags on the sodden ground. As he dismounted, she stirred, but did not attempt to rise. He looked around warily, then drew his dagger and stepped to her side.

"They're dead," he said in his flat rasping voice. "What were they after? Speak."

She moved again, weakly. A shudder ran through her, and she rose to hands and knees. With his free hand, he reached down and turned her face to him, holding his dagger ready to strike.

Her beauty was so totally unexpected that it shocked him. He drew back; then, recovering his wits, he laughed harshly and sheathed his dagger.

"I see what they wanted. I'll take it for myself."

"No need to take by force what I give you willingly," she said in a voice soft as a caress.

"You're sensible. Or do you go on your back for every man who passes?"

"You saved me. I am yours by right."

"So you are," he said.

He leaned down to clutch at her frayed robes, but she laid her hand on his and said, "Come inside. You need food and rest."

"Time enough for food and rest when I've had my fill of you."

"My house is clean and warm, and my bed is waiting."

He pulled her to her feet. Her beauty, as she stood before

him, was dazzling in its perfection. Under the muddy, dripping rags, her figure was full and inviting.

He cast a suspicious glance at the cottage. "Anyone else in there?" he asked, holding her by the wrist.

"We will be alone. Come," she said.

He motioned for her to lead the way, and followed a few paces behind with drawn sword. The interior of the cottage surprised him. They were alone, as she had said, in a room he had not expected to see in a simple woodland cottage. In the light of a score of candles, it was clean and shining and sweet-smelling as a queen's bower. The floor was of gray flagstones, scrubbed smooth, and the furnishings were of pale oak, carved and joined by a master's hand. A fire burned brightly in the fireplace, warming the splendid bed that stood nearby.

"What would you have of me?" she asked.

He inspected the place quickly. The cottage had no other entrance, and the shutters over the two small windows were barred. He barred the door himself and turned to her.

"I'll have you as a man should have a woman. I've had to satisfy myself with stinking peasants, no better than beasts," he said, looking upon her ravenously.

He threw aside his cloak and pulled off his boots. She began to remove her dark robes, but not quickly enough for him. He tore them from her and forced himself upon her in a frenzy of desire.

When his initial passion was sated, he stripped and lay beside her. He had no notions of love or tenderness, and no trust; but when he awoke in the night and drew her to him, he took her gently.

In the morning, she was not beside him. He raised himself on one elbow, instinctively taking up his sword, and then he saw her, dressed in her ragged robes, seated by the fire, rocking slowly back and forth. She stretched out her hands to the fire, and his mouth went dry at the sight of them: they were chalky pale, and her forearms were as thin as sticks. When she turned to face him, he cried out in horror at the mummified crone before him.

"Where is she? Where's the woman?" he demanded.

"She is here," said the old woman, and he recognized in her cracked voice the one who had whispered to him in the night.

He sprang from the bed, raising the sword for a stroke that would shear the witch in two. Her eyes flashed coldly for an instant. She raised a hand in a languid gesture, and the sword clattered to the flagstones. His arm hung dead and insensate at his side.

"Do not attempt violence on me," she said.

"All right. No violence. But give me back the use of my arm."

"I will give you more than that before you go. Why would you harm me?"

"You deceived me. The beautiful woman was only an illusion."

"Perhaps this is the illusion. Did the woman feel real when she was in your arms? Did you think you were rutting with a shadow?"

"She was real. But why did you do it?"

"It suited me. Do you lust after me as I am now?" she asked, laughing thinly at his stupefied silence. "I thought not. Go, dress yourself. You look like a fool standing there naked, gaping at me."

"Give me back the use of my arm."

"You have it—but leave the sword where it lies."

He dressed quickly. He wanted nothing now but to be away from this place. His work was the work of muscle and steel. Magic was beyond his understanding, and it frightened him.

"Let me take my sword and go," he said as he fastened his cloak. "I will not try to harm you."

"Why are you in such a hurry to leave me? Do I frighten you?"

"I don't like what I don't understand."

With a black grin, she said, "And all you understand is fighting and killing, eh? Raping, burning, looting—you understand them well, eh? Who's your master, soldier?"

"Whoever pays," he said.

"But no one pays now, or you would not be riding in the forest alone, cold and hungry. How long since you've eaten?"

"Yesterday . . . early in the day," he said. As he spoke the words, his empty belly growled and his mouth watered at the smell of roast meat.

"A piece of bread hard as a stone, was it? And a sip of stinking ditch-water? A man like you needs good food. Eat your fill," she said, pointing to a table on which stood steaming platters. He saw roast fowl, crisp and brown; a blood-rare joint of beef; bread of fine wheat, snowy white; heaped fruit whose sweet ripeness glowed in the beaded skin; a pewter flagon and a single pewter goblet. He had not seen any of these things a moment ago, and could not even be certain that they had been there. But the feast smelled real, and when he tore a leg from the fowl and bit into it, it tasted real, and the wine was rich and pungent as only the best wine could be.

He seated himself and settled down to a leisurely meal, the best and most abundant he had ever eaten. When he could cram down no more, he laid his hands on his belly, turned to the old woman, and said, "It was good."

"You're sparing with your gratitude," she said dryly.

"It's seldom I'm called upon to thank anyone," he said. He paused to belch, then added, "but I thank you."

"Good, good," she said. "You've had a night's pleasure

with the most beautiful woman you ever saw, and you've eaten as few kings in this benighted land have ever eaten. Now, I suppose, all you want is a bag of gold to consider yourself well rewarded.''

"I've never refused gold."

"It is there for the taking," she said, and when he looked down, a leather pouch lay beside his goblet. He pulled it open, and spilled the gold onto the table. As he ogled it, she added, "I will give you something better, besides."

"If you have something better than gold, I'll take it."

She turned aside and began to rummage in a chest that stood at her side. "I had a good look at you. You've had four arrows cut out of you, and three sword cuts that took a long time to heal."

"I've recovered. And I've learned a few things."

"Here," she said, turning to face him. She held up a bit of filmy grayish stuff that looked like a scarf. "Put this on. Come, put it on. I'll help you."

He came closer and stood over her. "What is it?"

"A glove. A very special glove, for your sword arm," she said, taking his hand.

She slipped the glove over his fingers and began to work it over his hand and wrist, pressing and smoothing the thin material so as to fit it perfectly to his skin. He watched as the gray faded, and his own skin showed through, dully at first, but soon healthy and fully flesh-colored, as though the gray glove had become transparent, or been somehow absorbed. The tightness he had felt at the first touch was gone from his fingers and hand, but he felt it rising as she worked the glove up his forearm, smoothly fitting it just below his elbow, where a thin black line marked its edge.

"It fits you perfectly," she crowed. "I knew it. I knew you were the one!"

"What do you mean? Have you been waiting for me? That can't be!"

"You know nothing of what can and cannot be. Kembrec accepts you. You are the one, and that is all you need know."

He stared down at his hand and arm. There was no sign of the glove now, only the black line encircling his forearm. He could feel no seam, no trace of a juncture. "Who is Kembrec? What happened to the glove you put on me?" he asked, and there was fear in his voice.

"Kembrec was a man of power, and the glove was once his flesh. His enemies overcame him at last, and as he lay dying they dismembered him. They thought they could destroy him forever by doing so. I took his hand and arm, because I knew the secret. They never suspected," said the old woman, rocking back and forth as she had done when he awoke, looking dreamily into the fire. "I stripped the skin off very carefully, very slowly and carefully, and I preserved it, because I remembered his promise. The others thought . . . ah, who knows what they thought, those frightened men. They wanted him dead, because they feared his power, and they got what they wanted." She looked up, and her eyes were bright. "But I preserved the power."

"What power? What are you saying?"

"I have said enough. You gave me what I sought, and you have your reward. Go now, as you wished. Go!" she commanded.

He took up his sword and left the cottage without another word. His horse was stabled in a small outbuilding. He had been fed and groomed. Harness and trappings were laid out in careful order, but there was no sign of a hostler.

Harnessing his mount, he led it from the building and into the clearing. Looking back, he gasped in sudden fright. The cottage he had left a short time before was now a sagging ruin, as was the stable. With a shudder, he sprang into the saddle and spurred the horse. When he looked back again, there was nothing in the clearing but the morning mist.

He rode without stopping, his mind in turmoil, wanting only to get far away from that witch-haunted spot. He could not understand the things that had befallen him. The beautiful woman had been no illusion; he could still feel her warmth and softness, and picture her beauty. The smell of her hair and the taste of her mouth mingled with the smell of the food and woodsmoke and bedclothes, and the taste of meat and wine; they were as real as the witch who had sat by the fire and talked of incomprehensible things. His arm felt no different, and it looked no different except for the black line below his elbow. There was no trace of the glove she had placed on him so carefully. He wondered what magic had been worked on him.

Late in the day he scented a village in the wind, and turned toward it. He did not like peasants or their ways or their stinking, waddling women, but he did not want to spend this night alone. Even the company of dolts was better than being left to dwell on his troubled imaginings.

The villagers welcomed him, and their welcome seemed genuine. They lived in constant fear of marauding bands, and the presence of a free lance among them gave an unaccustomed sense of security. They fed him on rank meat and gruel and hard bread—poor stuff, but the best fare in the village—and offered him a dry place to sleep. He chose to stay in the loft of the stable, near his horse; the hayloft rats, he judged, would be less bother than the fleas that swarmed in every house.

He awoke in the morning to a great outcry. Quickly donning his mail shirt and taking up his sword, he descended in time to meet three villagers who had come seeking him.

"Raiders, master! They come to plunder!" one cried.

"They will kill us all and burn the village!" said a second, wringing his hands.

"Save us, master! Drive them off!" begged the third.

"Where are they?"

"They are in the village square," the third man said.

Despite the danger of the moment, he could not help but smile at the term. The village was a pile of squalid hovels; the "square" was an open patch of mud, a wider place in the narrow track that ran through it. He shouldered his big two-handed sword and walked outside.

Nine men were in the square, two mounted and the rest on foot. One of the mounted men carried a sword, the other a long-handled battle-ax. There were three pikemen, three swordsmen, and a crossbowman. All were hard-faced men of good size. The village could hope for no mercy from this band.

"Good day to you, swordsman," said one of the men on horseback. "Is this your village?"

"I spent last night here. One night was enough. Nothing here but fleas and rats. And peasant women," he replied, and spat.

"Do you say so? Well, women are women. There's sure to be a bit of food, and the place will make a decent fire to warm our hands when we're done with it."

He did not reply, only stood his ground, the sword still resting on his shoulder. The horseman moved a bit closer.

"That's a fine sword," he said.

"It is."

"And a good mail shirt, too. Give them to me, and I'll let you keep whatever else you have and leave unharmed."

He knew then that he would have to fight, and there was small chance of winning. He was a match for any two of these men—except the crossbowman, who could be deadly—but no man living was a match for nine. Still, it was better to be cut down fighting than to be kept alive, unarmed, to amuse this lot, and he would give them plenty to regret before he fell.

As he shifted his weight, the leader nodded to the crossbowman, who dropped to one knee and released his bolt. He moved so quickly that the swordsman was taken by surprise. Something struck him on the forehead, just above his eye, with an impact no harder than the slap of a child's hand. The bolt spun high in the air, and the swordsman stood blinking in astonishment.

"Pikemen!" the leader cried.

Two pikemen dashed forward. They bore simple lances, made for thrusting, and once he slipped the points and got within striking distance, they were helpless. As the second one went to his knees, clutching at his spilling entrails, the swordsman turned and saw, too late, the third pikeman thrusting for his belly.

The point drove home with all the man's strength behind it, and it felt like nothing more than a pat on a comfortably full stomach. The pikeman cried out and dropped his weapon, and the swordsman made short work of him.

The remaining men were less eager for combat now. He did not understand what had happened, but he saw the fear on their faces and knew that he had a chance to live. The crossbowman was occupied fitting a new bolt; two of the swordsmen fell back, and the third, hesitating only an instant, joined them. They knew that their ordinary blades were like sticks of wood before a two-handed sword that could cleave an armored man in half.

Too late, he heard the horse bear down on him. Before he could dive aside, he was flung down in the mud. He rolled and looked up at the descending hooves of the leader's mount. Twice he evaded those plunging hooves, but the third time they landed full on his knee and thigh. The bones should have been splintered by the impact; but he felt nothing.

Whinnying and shaking its head wildly, the horse drew away from him. He climbed to his feet, uninjured, and as the leader charged, he caught him across the midsection. The leader screamed and toppled from his horse.

At this, the second horseman tried to flee, but the peasants pulled him down. Hearing his cries, the others fell to their knees before the swordsman.

"Spare our lives, master, we beg," one cried.

"Spare us and we'll serve you faithfully," said the cross-bowman, abasing himself.

He stood over them and looked down contemptuously. "Four of you against one, and you surrender. What good is the service of your kind?"

"I've never begged mercy before, master, I swear it," said a third. "But I'll not do battle against a man made of stone. I'll serve that man, but I'll not fight him."

"I saw the bolt bounce off your forehead, and the spear break on your belly!"

He listened, the sword at rest on his shoulder. At last he said, "Get up. Keep your weapons. Take the horses to the stable and wait there." To the ring of peasants that stood around him, he said, "These men are friends, and see that you treat them as such. The ones who would have harmed you are dead. Bring their weapons to the stable."

"As you say, master," one of the peasants replied, and the rest moved to obey.

"Hang the bodies along the road. Let them be a warning to others," the swordsman added.

As the four raiders slogged toward the stable, leading the riderless horses, and the villagers went about their work, he stood alone, thoughtful, in the calm mood that always came over him after violence. He remembered distinctly things that could not have happened. The raiders spoke of them, too, but they could not be. No bolt would have rebounded from his forehead; it would have gone into his skull and killed him on the spot. His chain mail could not stop a pike; his bones could not have withstood the impact of a war-horse's hooves.

He saw a child grope in the mud and bring forth a small object, then turn to gape at him in openmouthed awe. A man, seeing the object, also stared at him.

"What have you got, boy? Bring it to me," he commanded.

The boy came forward fearfully and held out a crossbow bolt. The head was skewed to one side, the tip mushroomed as though it had struck a stone wall full force.

"Bring me the pikes!" he cried.

Two of the pikes were in perfect condition. The head of the third was bent and blunted, and the shaft was split. He let out his breath in a loud puff of sheer wonderment; then he thought of the witch, and her gift. She had made him invulnerable.

He settled in the village while he made his plans. It was an easy, comfortable period, the first rest he had known in a long time. The four raiders proved loyal, and the villagers treated him with a respect that bordered on veneration. They came to call him "Lord Stoneskin."

As the story of his victory spread, new arrivals came to the village, seeking the safety to be found there. He admitted all who wished to join him, and by the end of summer, the village had more than doubled in size.

The price of safety was service. He commanded that all villagers spend part of each day building a hall for him and his men. The hall went up on a rise overlooking the village, with a clear prospect of the approaches. It had a deep well, a cellar for provisions, and formidable defenses. He had no need for protection himself, but deemed it wise to provide it for his followers, and for such goods as he might amass.

He learned more about his gift as the summer drew on. Not

only was he immune to the weapons and the assaults of others, he could not even injure himself voluntarily. His health was better than it had ever been, and his old injuries no longer gave him pain. He could not tell whether this, too, was the witch's doing, or was simply the result of his eating better and resting well. Whatever the answer, it appeared to him that the witch had made him immortal—or close to immortal. He could not fathom her reasons, but in a short time he stopped questioning, and accepted his fortune.

In the autumn, after the harvest, another marauding band came to the village. This band was larger than the first, and better organized. The leader wore a gleaming breastplate and greaves, and rode a fine black stallion. His followers showed soldierly discipline as they took up position in the enlarged village square.

By this time, Stoneskin had added several of the strongest and quickest young men of the village to his little force, arming them with the weapons of the fallen raiders. They took their posts unseen by the newcomers, and waited. He walked into the square alone, bare-chested under an open leather jerkin, his sword resting on his shoulder.

"Is this the village of the one called 'Stoneskin?' " the leader demanded.

"I am Lord Stoneskin, and this is my holding."

"A prosperous village, and well fortified. Surely you do not hold it alone," said the leader. Stoneskin did not respond, or even acknowledge the remark, and he went on, "People have said that you cannot be injured by any weapon of man."

"Have you travelled all this way to find out if they speak the truth?"

"We want food, and a place to lay up for the winter. This village will satisfy us."

"Serve me faithfully, and you're welcome here. Otherwise, there is no place for you."

"Now hear me, Lord Stoneskin," said the leader of the marauders with heavy sarcasm. "There're twelve of us and one of you. I'm sure you have a few loyal supporters hidden here and there, but they'll be no help to you. If our weapons can't bring you down, our numbers will."

There was no point in debating. Stoneskin sprang forward, raising the blade to clear the horse's head and take the rider across the midsection. The leader brought his own blade around and caught Stoneskin at the juncture of neck and collarbone. His blade shattered, and the great two-handed sword sheared through pommel, breastplate, and flesh and tumbled him to the ground in a spray of blood.

Standing over the fallen horseman, Stoneskin said to the others, "You heard my terms. Stay and serve me, or go and don't try to come back."

Six of them charged him, crying out for vengeance; the rest dropped their weapons and stayed back. When four of his attackers went down with four strokes of his blade after he had taken, unharmed, blows with ax and sword that would have killed any man, the last two threw down their weapons and prostrated themselves before him.

"Take your lives and go," he said, when he had regained his breath. "Tell what happened here, and tell it truthfully."

Blubbering their gratitude, they rose. They turned and fled from the village without looking back.

More men came to the village before the snows closed it off, but they did not come to challenge Stoneskin. They came to offer loyal service, and he accepted them. Families came, seeking his protection; camp followers, vendors, and a wandering healer arrived. A tavern opened near the hall, and grew to be a thriving inn.

Three years later, Stoneskin left the village. It was now a prosperous town, protected by a garrison of well-trained fighters and elaborate defensive works, as well as by the power of his name. He had thought his plans through, and was now ready to carry them out.

He traveled to the east, stopping at every village and town to accept tribute and enlist the best fighting men. His name raced before him, and he was everywhere received with deference. There were no challenges.

When winter came, he was master of the province. At the end of the second winter, the two adjoining provinces were his. In five years, he ruled all the land, and proclaimed himself King Stoneskin. No one disputed his claim.

Years of brutal war had left the land devastated and the people demoralized, without trust in their leaders, without faith in anything. Stoneskin offered them hope. To the common people, the issues underlying the struggle had always been obscure. They knew only that since the time of their fathers, life and property had been subject to the whim of armed bands that appeared from nowhere and, for no reason their victims could understand, robbed, raped, killed, and destroyed. Any armed man was the enemy, come to punish them for disloyalty to a leader they did not know and a cause they could not comprehend.

Stoneskin was different. He came to them himself, walked among them unarmed, and offered them a simple choice: serve him and enjoy his protection, or deny him and go on as before. Few wished to risk denying him, and none who had the desire had the courage.

He declared that he was married to his kingdom, and would have no other wife; he took the daughters of the most powerful landholders and warlords as his concubines, and set about building a dynasty.

His children were born mortal. Like the children of ordinary men, most of them did not survive their first days of life. But many lived, and as their number increased, Stoneskin was faced with a problem he had never known before. He was not certain that the witch's gift to him could be passed on; in any case, it could go to only one of his children, and that one might choose to be a tyrant over the rest. Stoneskin realized that he did not want such a thing to happen.

In his entire life, he had never been close to anyone, or cared much for another. He had no memory of parents, or a family, or love. For as long as he could remember, he had been fighting, or preparing to fight, or recovering from battle. Now he had to fight no longer, and he came slowly to care for his children, and his people, and to want to spare them the life he had known.

For a time, the problem was no more than a minor concern; for all he knew, he might outlive generations of descendants. But when he woke one morning with his head burning and his bowels turned to water, and lay for five days alternately shivering and sweating, his mind tossed and wrung by wild imaginings and visions, he knew that the gift of the witch could not protect him from sickness and fever. He might be invulnerable to all weapons of men, but he was mortal still, and must admit that the day would come when he would guide his kingdom no longer.

The new knowledge forced a decision on him. He surrounded himself with wise and farsighted elders, and listened carefully to their words. Slowly he learned to be a ruler. He created structures, and laws, that would enable his descendants to live in domestic peace, and an army to protect them from external aggression.

He ceased eventually to carry weapons or to wear armor. The fact of his invulnerability was known to all by this time, and none came to test him with the sword. Only once was an attempt made on his life, and it was made by subtler means than steel.

He knew that some of the scholarly elders who advised him held him in secret contempt for his lowly origins and sudden rise. Since he did not fear their envy nor seek their admiration, he did nothing to remove them; their wisdom was needed. But when three of them remained behind after a council, and he detected an odd taste to the wine they offered him, he knew that their envy had gone beyond tolerable bounds.

He drained the goblet, wiped his lips, and refilled it. Holding it out to the oldest of the three, he said, "The wine is particularly good this day. Drink it."

Awareness glinted in the old man's eyes, but he did not falter. He took the cup, murmured, "To the king's health," and drank every drop. He turned the goblet upside down and returned it to his master.

The expression of the others was fearful to see as Stoneskin refilled the goblet and, without a word, handed it to the white-haired woman who stood unmoving before him. Her hand shook as she accepted it, and she was pale as mist, but she drank it off in a single draft.

As Stoneskin was refilling the goblet for the third time, the old man groaned and fell to his knees, clutching at his stomach. The third adviser, a middle-aged man of great skill in debate, threw himself to the ground at Stoneskin's feet.

"Be merciful, King Stoneskin!" he wailed. "I was misled. They persuaded me that you would lead the kingdom astray. I did it for your children's sakes, and for your people!"

"Liar!" the old man cried in a broken voice.

The woman pointed an unsteady hand at the groveling figure and said coldly and deliberately, "He turned us to this. Called you a tyrant and usurper. Said . . . only the wise are fit to rule."

Stoneskin sat with the goblet in his hand, brimful, and listened to the agonized cries of the old man and the woman as they died the death they had planned for him. When they were still, the man at his feet looked up and whispered, "Mercy!"

Stoneskin offered the goblet. "Here is my mercy. Take it, or die a worse death."

The man rose to his knees, and with shaking hands, took the goblet from Stoneskin's hand. He raised it to his lips, and under Stoneskin's unblinking gaze, he emptied the contents. When he, too, lay still, contorted by his death agonies, the king summoned his guards to clear the chamber.

No public announcement of the attempt on the king's life was ever made, and Stoneskin never spoke of it to his other advisers. No future attempt was made.

King Stoneskin's territories grew, and his power increased, with each passing year. He received visitors from the neighboring kingdoms, and some from distant lands with unknown names, and he accepted their tribute graciously. It did not surprise him to have emperors and kings seek his friendship; he knew that they were aware of how dangerous an enemy he could be. But when, in all earnestness, they asked his advice on affairs of state, he was astonished. His gift was not statecraft, not wisdom or foresight, it was invulnerability. Wisdom he left to his council.

Since these outlanders sought his advice, he gave it; and when they returned to their own lands and did as he had counseled them to do, they prospered. He came to realize then that in his years of wielding power, he had learned much about its ways and uses. This knowledge changed him. He became more thoughtful, relying less on his gift and more on his judgment.

One day in the sixteenth year of his reign, he received a pair of visitors who came with a strange request. On a cold dawn at the very brink of winter, when no one traveled the roads unforced, a young man came to the court of King

Stoneskin leading a woman whose eyes were covered with a dark band. The woman stepped haltingly before Stoneskin, threw herself on her knees, and begged him to use his power to restore her sight.

"I am no healer, woman," he said gently.

"A healer cannot help me. I ask your magic."

"I am no sorcerer, either. Only a man."

"You are a man with a great gift, a power that lifts you above all others. Use that gift to help me, I beg you," the woman said piteously.

"My gift is not a healing gift. It is a protection that I do not understand, not a magic I can pass on to another."

"You have magic. Magic is all that can help me now," the woman persisted.

He came forward and raised her up. "Tell me how you lost your sight," he said.

"There was a witch. She sought to take my boy from his cradle when he was newborn. I fought her, and drove her away, but she cursed me. That very night my eyes burned with pain. The next day, I saw as through a mist. Soon I could not see at all," the woman said matter-of-factly.

He called for a bench to be set by his throne, and led her to it. "You deserve such help as I can give, madam. I promise you shelter and protection here for the rest of your life, and a place for your son where he can rise as far as his abilities take him. I can do no more."

"Only look at my eyes. Touch them. Will me to see again," she implored.

Her son looked at him in silent appeal. Stoneskin knew he could do nothing to cure this brave woman, but if his touch could comfort her, he was willing to give it. He ordered the room cleared of all but mother, son, and himself.

When the door shut behind the last of his court, the woman unbound the dark cloth covering the upper portion of her face. The eyes were ageless, bright and alive. They flashed as she raised her hand in a swift gesture, and Stoneskin fell back in the throne, numbed in his limbs and powerless to cry out.

"You have prospered," she said, in a voice he well remembered. "The nameless mercenary has become a great king. And all thanks to me."

"I acknowledge that. I'd be dead now, but for your gift."

"My gift, King Stoneskin? No, say rather, 'my loan.' It will now pass on to its proper wearer."

He looked at the young man, who gazed back at him hungrily. "Our son?" he asked.

"So he is. I named him Kembrec, for the one who should have fathered him, and whose flesh he shall wear," she said.

"Talk when it's done, Mother," said Kembrec, drawing his dagger and stepping to Stoneskin's side. He drew back the sleeve covering the limp arm, to reveal the dark line that ringed the forearm. With smooth, surgically exact strokes, he cut around the mark and stripped the outer layer of skin off like a glove.

Stoneskin felt nothing. The arm revealed was as pale and dry as a long-weathered branch, smooth as marble. It bled scarcely at all. But even as he watched, color slowly began to return to it. He tried to flex his fingers, and found that he was now able to move.

Kembrec had slipped the loose gray glove of flesh on his own hand at once. Now he stood with his hand upraised before his face, and his cold laughter rang through the chamber. He pressed the point of his dagger against Stoneskin's chest.

"What will you call yourself now, Father? 'Stoneskin' is no longer appropriate," he said.

"I never chose that name."

"If I kill you, you'll need no name," Kembrec said,

pressing the dagger until it broke the skin. "I could do it easily enough now."

"He's done all he was meant to do. Let him live," said the witch.

"I will let him live," Kembrec said, stepping back. "But not out of gratitude. I want him to learn what it is to live in fear of dying. To live in fear of pain!" he cried, suddenly lashing out and cutting a notch in Stoneskin's ear.

"Why do you hate me so much?" Stoneskin asked mildly as he wiped the blood from his neck.

"Because you wore the skin of Kembrec while I waited. For years, I awoke each day wondering if this would be the day that some wild beast, or a stupid brute with a sword, would take my life before I could claim what was mine by right. I was prey to chance, illness, poison . . . and you were beyond reach of all. And so I hated you."

"I'm beyond their reach no longer," said Stoneskin.

"No, no longer," Kembrec said with relish. "Now you can learn what it's like to be human, and face death."

"That's something I learned before you were born. I've forgotten it these twenty years, but I can learn it again."

"You will learn. I'll teach you fear before I leave this place."

"No, Kembrec. We must leave now," said the witch. "We need time to make our plans."

"*We? We* need nothing. Now *I* will plan, and do as I please."

"You're not ready, Kembrec. Follow my guidance until the proper time. You need my wisdom," she said, reaching out to grasp his arm.

"I need you no more, witch," said Kembrec, plunging his dagger to the hilt in her breast.

She gave a soft little cry and staggered back a step. Turning to Stoneskin, she gaped at him, wide-eyed, and opened her mouth to speak, but no sound came forth. She swayed and fell, and her robes sank around her as she crumbled to dust.

"So much for her," said Kembrec. "She would have tried to use me, just as she used you, and my namesake the sorcerer. I would never have been safe."

"And now there's nothing, and no one can kill you," said Stoneskin.

"Nothing! No one!" Kembrec cried. He slashed at his forearms, with no effect. He drove the dagger against his stomach and, laughing loud, brandished the blunted point.

"What will you do?" Stoneskin asked.

"I'll stay here, as long as it pleases me. This is a tolerable palace, and you'll make me an amusing fool," said Kembrec. He looked around the chamber, and stepped to the center to view it better. "Yes, I'll stay here, I think," he said.

"You surely will," said Stoneskin as he twisted the armrest of the throne and the floor opened under the astonished young man.

He peered cautiously over the edge, but the pit was black. When he kicked the empty heap of rags down, it quickly disappeared into the darkness. He could hear faintly the cries of rage that echoed up the smooth stone shaft, twenty times the height of a man, and wiping his bloody neck, he smiled. When the shaft was filled to the top with stone and mortar—the work would begin within the hour—there would be no more sound.

He pulled up the heavy collar of his robe to conceal the gash in his ear; it was best that no one knew of it. Losing the glove was inconvenient, but need be no worse than that. It was not really necessary to be invulnerable—only to be believed invulnerable. He turned and went to his throne, where he seated himself comfortably and smiled.

He felt almost sorry for Kembrec. The boy really had needed a wise guide. It takes time to learn that invulnerability, in itself, is not the solution to all problems, and that even an invulnerable man will not survive for long unless he learns to use his wits.

Kembrec, he reflected, would have an undisturbed lifetime to learn that lesson.

Sandra Mitchelson was a very unhappy young lady whose life was thoroughly dull and gray. Then she discovered an airwaves evangelist known as Reverend Fanny and started sending money to her with the hope that things would change for her. They really did for at least a while, but then came the inevitable reckoning.

UNMISTAKABLY THE FINEST

Scott Bradfield

Every time Sandra Mitchelson's Daddy came home on the boat he brought her things. French chocolates, a stuffed elephant, a golden heart-shaped locket, a transistor radio, a hand-painted porcelain Japanese doll with a rice-paper parasol. In return Sandra helped him work in the back yard. The front yard was covered with gravel, the back yard with tall yellow weeds. "This will be our family area," Daddy said, knee-deep in the weeds. "We'll have a barbecue, a swingset, a bird bath, a trellis, maybe even someday a swimming pool." They already had a fish pond. The water was dark and smoky, rimmed with algae. Large gold and lead colored fish glimmered dully in the muck, slowly blinking their bulbous eyes like monsters surfacing from some nightmare. Sandra held Daddy's white cloth hat and watched him hit the ground with a shovel. He overturned convexes of damp black earth,

94

severed worms and pulsing white slugs. Sandra liked the pungent, musty odor of the fertilizer, and rode on Daddy's back while he pushed the reseeder. They watered every morning, and soon tiny green shoots appeared. After Daddy disengaged the garden hose he filled his coarse red hands with water from the tap, flung the water into the bright summer sky and told Sandra the sparkling droplets were diamonds. Sandra tried to catch them, but they slipped through her fingers. One day she sat down on the patio and cried. Daddy promptly took her to the store and bought her a tiny "Genuine" brand diamond set in a thin copper band. The next morning he went away on the boat.

The new grass died, the earth turned gray and broken. Mrs. Mitchelson said, "He wants a lawn? Then let him water it his damn self." She toasted her reflection in the twilit picture window. "Here's to your damn lawn. Here's to your damn family area." Bourbon and crushed ice spilled over the rim of her glass. In the afternoons Sandra sat alone on the living room floor and observed through the smudged picture window the gradual destruction of the yard. In the spring, weeds grew—strange enormous weeds as tall as Daddy, bristling with thorns and burrs and furred, twisted leaves. Scorched by the summer sun the weeds cracked and fell and, when the spring returned, the mat of dead weeds prevented new weeds from sprouting. Sandra asked when Daddy would be home. Mrs. Mitchelson said, "Never, if I have anything to do about it," and departed for the pawn shop with the heart-shaped locket, the transistor radio, the tiny "Genuine" diamond ring. "You want to know what all that junk was worth?" Mrs. Mitchelson shouted, looming over Sandra's bed at three a.m. Sandra sat up, blinked at the light, rubbed her eyes. Mrs. Mitchelson's eyes were red and wet and mottled with discount cosmetics. "Twenty bucks. That's how much he loves you. Your wonderful father. Your father who is so wonderful." Mrs. Mitchelson stormed out of the room, the front door slammed. Sandra rolled over and went back to sleep. That summer they sold the house.

In Bakersfield Mrs. Mitchelson worked at the Jolly Roger Fun and Games Lounge next door to the public library. Every day after school Sandra waited in the library and read magazines. She especially liked the large, slick magazines that contained numerous full-page advertisements. She enjoyed reading phrases such as "unmistakably the finest," "the affordability of excellence," "the passionate abandon of crushed velour." When the library closed at nine she sat outside on the bus bench and thought about the sharp, clear photographs. Fashions by Christian Dior, natural wood grain furniture, Chinese porcelain, a castle in Spain, a microwave oven with digital timer, an automobile with a leopard crouched and snarling on the hood. The doors of the Jolly Roger swung open and closed, releasing intermittent bursts of smoke, laughter and juke-box music. Buses roared past. Sometimes one of Mrs. Mitchelson's friends drove them home. Nervous, unshaven men, their cars were usually littered with plumbing or automotive tools; cigarettes with long gray ashes dangled from their mouths. They ate pretzels and laughed with Mrs. Mitchelson in the living room while Sandra went quietly to bed.

They lived in Pasadena, Glendale, Hawthorne, Encino. Sandra finished high school in Burbank, acquired a receptionist's job in Beverly Hills. In Compton they took a one bedroom apartment which included some cracked windowpanes and numerous discreet cockroaches. Weekdays, however, Sandra sat at an immaculate mahogany desk in the public relations firm of Zeitlin and Morgan. She answered telephone calls (often from television and film celebrities), organized the week's appointments in a large leather-bound black ledger, typed advertising copy, and allowed clients into the security building by activating a hidden white buzzer.

Sandra was usually alone in the office. Mr. Zeitlin had retired to compose Bermuda post-cards. Mr. Morgan—with his distinguished gray hair, taut polished cheek-bones and jogging outfit—arrived each day around elevenish, then quickly departed with Elaine, the leggy secretary, for the afternoon luncheon appointment. Occasionally Mr. Morgan's son Matthew dropped by and asked for Elaine. "Off with the old man again, huh? When am I supposed to get *my* chance?" Sandra admired Matthew—his capped white teeth, his knit ties, his shirts by Pierre Cardin. He resembled a man of "casual elegance," sipping Chivas Regal on a sailboat, displaying Jordache emblems at garden parties. Matthew was an executive with the Jiffy-Quick Messenger Corporation of Southern California. His solid-gold tie-clasp depicted the comical (but fleet-footed) Jiffy Man dashing unflappably to his appointed destination. "My Dad didn't just hand me the job, either," he assured Sandra. "I started off at the bottom, and absolutely refused any sort of preferential treatment. I even drove the delivery van one weekend, so nobody can say I didn't pay my dues. It literally took me months to get where I am today, and it was never any picnic, let me tell you. But I like to think that in the long run my employees will respect me for it."

At four o'clock Sandra pulled the plastic jacket over the IBM, replaced paper clips and memoranda in their appropriate drawers, and locked the office. On her way to the bus stop she window-shopped along Rodeo Drive, observed silk crepe de chine slacks at Mille Chemises, solid-gold Piaget quartz crystal watches at Van Cleef & Arpels. She admired the white, unblemished features and long cool necks of the mannequins; their postures were perfect, their expressions distant and unperturbed, as if they attended a fashionable cocktail party at the heart of some iceberg. Maseratis and Mercedes were parked along the curbs, and elderly women in low-cut blouses walked poodles on stainless-steel leashes. Everything and everybody appeared immaculate and eternal, like Pompeiian artifacts preserved in lava. Sandra avoided her own reflection in the sunny windowfronts—her pale white skin, her shiny polyester skirt—which made her feel like a trespasser in a museum. She caught the 6:15 bus and generally arrived home just after dark.

Mrs. Mitchelson started awake at the sound of Sandra's key in the lock, sat bolt upright on the living room couch. "Who's that? What do you want?"

Sandra opened the hall closet, removed a hanger. "It's only me. Go back to sleep."

Mrs. Mitchelson's dry tongue worked soundlessly in her mouth, she cleared her throat. "Well," she said experimentally. "Well, I wish I *could* go back to sleep. I wish I *could* get a minute's peace around this place." She gripped the frayed arm of the couch with both hands, pushed herself to her feet. "But don't worry about me. Just because I gave birth to you, just because I took care of you when *you* were sick and helpless." Mrs. Mitchelson took three short steps and landed in the faded rattan chair. The chair creaked sympathetically. "I'm not saying I was perfect. I'm not saying I didn't make my share of mistakes. But at least I *tried* to give you a good home—which is sure a hell of a lot more than your father ever did."

"Sit down, Mom. I'll get your dinner."

"Do you think it's easy for me? Do you? Getting older and weaker every day, so sick I can hardly breathe sometimes. Just sitting around this lousy apartment wondering how much longer I've got left in this miserable life."

"Please, Mom. Don't say things like that." Sandra folded

the comforter and slipped it under the couch. "Do you want Tater Tots or french fries with your dinner?"

Mrs. Mitchelson's attention was diverted by the teevee tray which stood beside her chair. The tray held a depleted gallon jug of Safeway brand bourbon, an uncapped litre bottle of Coca-Cola, and an unwashed Bullwinkle glass. "Why not? Why shouldn't I say it? I hope I *do* die. I hope I die tomorrow—how do you like that?" Mrs. Mitchelson absently cleaned the glass with the sleeve of her blue flannel bathrobe. "You wouldn't miss me. You'd finally be free of me, just like your father." She filled Bullwinkle waist-high with bourbon, added a few stale drops of Coke for texture. "When I needed your father, where was he? Traipsing all over the world, *that's* where he was. *You* might as well be a thousand miles away too, for all the good you ever do *me . . . Ah*." Mrs. Mitchelson put down the empty glass and snapped her dentures with satisfaction.

In the kitchenette Sandra turned on the stove, emptied a can of Spaghetti O's into a saucepan. She could hear the neck of the Safeway jug clink again against the rim of the glass.

"When I remember when I was younger, all the opportunities I had. I had a lot of boyfriends. They took me to nice restaurants, bought me expensive presents. Then I met your father. I was so stupid stupid stupid. I threw everything away for that louse. *Now* look at me."

Bullwinkle looked at her.

The following summer Mrs. Mitchelson was admitted to City Hospital. "This is just what you've been waiting for, isn't it? Now I'll be out of your hair for good." Mrs. Mitchelson's voice was uncharacteristically restrained. Sometimes she almost whispered, leaning toward the side of the bed where Sandra sat, clenching the ends of the stiff white sheet in her thin gray hands. "But just you wait. Now you'll learn what it's like to be alone. You'll know the hell I went through when your father left me for some cheap Filipino whore.'' Mrs. Mitchelson's eyes were wide and clear and moist, like the eyes of Bullwinkle on the drinking glass. Sandra sat quietly with her mother behind the cracked plastic partitions, listened faintly to the moans and cries of neighboring patients, read paperback romances in which elegant women were kidnapped and fiercely seduced by pirates, rebel cavalry officers, terrifically endowed plantation slaves. Mrs. Mitchelson's cirrhosis was complicated by undiagnosed leukemia, and she died unexpectedly just before dawn on a Monday morning. Sandra was fixing coffee in the kitchenette when the nurse called. Her mother had been wrong, she abruptly discovered. She did not feel alone, she did not feel betrayed. She did not, in fact, feel much of anything. She took the morning off from work, arranged disposition with the hospital crematorium, and smoked a pack of Mrs. Mitchelson's cigarettes.

The medical bills were formidable, and Sandra had less money than ever at the end of each month. Her window-shopping expeditions grew less frequent, and she took an earlier bus home. Without Mrs. Mitchelson to care for she rarely thought to fix dinner. She became pale and listless. Elaine said, "Why don't you lunch at *Ramone's* today? They've got an outdoor patio, and it's a beautiful day." Instead Sandra remained in the office alone, lunched on vended crackers, bagels and candy bars.

Then one night Sandra discovered Reverend Fanny Bright and the Worldwide Church of Prosperity. Reverend Fanny's sermons were broadcast live every Saturday evening from Macon, Georgia. Reverend Fanny told her followers, "You can't expect happiness to just come *knocking*. You must *pursue* riches, you must *pursue* happiness, you must *pursue* the power of Divine Creation. When you see something pretty you want to buy, how many times have you told yourself, 'I cannot afford this'? Is *that* what you think, children? Is *that* what you believe? Then you are *negating* the power of Divine Creation. You must convince yourself you can afford anything. You *can* afford it, you *will* purchase it, you *shall* possess it. You must impress your super-conscious with *affirmation*. The super-conscious is His workshop where, with the divine scissors of His power, He is constantly cutting out the events of your life. But first you must show Him the *patterns* of your desire, you must fill your *mind* with beautiful things." After each sermon Reverend Fanny pulled a chair up close to the audience and solicited tales of miraculous prosperity. Middle-aged men and women described flourishing investments, sudden cash gifts from strangers on the street, gratuitous office promotions. "All I want to tell you," one woman said, "is that I love you, Reverend Fanny. Prosperity has taught me how to love. Now I no longer feel so empty and alone."

Every month Sandra mailed the Church a check for ten dollars. In reply she received a mimeographed request for further donations. The stationery was inscribed with the Church motto: *If you do not wish to be denied riches, you must not deny riches to others.* Sandra closed out her savings, transferred the $2,386.00 to her previously minimal checking account, and prepared herself for imminent prosperity. She purchased navy cashmere sweaters, suede pants, a silk crepe blousson dress fringed with lace, a deep breasted brown satin coat, labels by Calvin Klein, Oscar De La Renta, Halston, Adolfo, Bill Blass, Ralph Lauren. She joined a health spa, subscribed to tanning treatments, visited prestigious beauty salons. Her checking balance dropped quickly to nineteen hundred, thirteen-fifty, one thousand. She did not question the beneficence of Divine Creation; instead she used her Visa card. Elaine said, "You're looking so much better, girl. Why don't we have a drink after work? I'm meeting a couple of Tokyo software executives, they told me to bring a friend.'' Mr. Morgan granted Sandra a fifty dollar raise and told her, ''You really bring a lot of class to the office,'' on his way to a toothpaste manufacturer and lobster bisque.

Church doctrine was unequivocally validated. Sandra increased her monthly contribution to thirty dollars.

Then one night Sandra discovered her super-conscious in a dream. She ascended a long winding staircase. She was wearing her white ankle-length ''Cameo lace'' nightgown from Vassarette, her Nazareno Gabrielli padded cashmere slippers. Her fingers ran lightly along a polished oak banister. The summit of stairs met a long off-white corridor lit by globed ceiling fixtures. The fixtures were white, opaque, and sprinkled with the silhouettes of mummified insects. At the end of the corridor a solitary door stood slightly ajar. Bright yellow light from behind the door cast long, angular shadows down the length of the corridor. Sandra stepped quietly, afraid of disturbing anyone. As she approached the door she grew light-headed, her ears popped, as if she were descending in an airplane. The tarnished aluminium doorknob rattled at her touch. She pushed open the door.

The room was small, windowless, lit by a naked overhead bulb. Cobwebs scribbled the pale walls and cornices. The plaster was pitted and crumbling, mapped by an extensive network of cracks and crevices. The hardwood floors were sagging, whorled and discolored. A full-feature model A-20 integrated amplifier sat in the middle of the floor beside a matching AM-FM stereo digital frequency synthesized tuner and cassette player. An identical system had been advertised in *Stereo Review*, and Sandra still recalled many of its vital statistics. A pair of three-way loudspeakers were stacked against the wall, with 12-inch woofers, 4-inch midrange drivers, and 1-inch dome tweeters housed in walnut veneer cabinetry. A mass of electric cords were joined by a plastic adaptor to a solitary wall outlet. A tiny green light activated on the amplifier's monochrome panel, an eight-track tape clacked faintly inside the tape player. The speakers suffused the room with white, cottony static.

Louis Armstrong began to sing, accompanied by bass, piano and drums.

> *Baby, take me down to Duke's Place,*
> *Wildest box in town is Duke's Place,*
> *Love that piano sound at Duke's Place . . .*

Sandra disliked jazz, pulled shut the door. The music diminished to a low persistent bass that fluttered in the off-white corridor like a staggered pulse. The door's surface was formica, with simulated wood grain. She tested the knob, the lock clicked soundly. Then she woke up.

It was still dark when the music awoke Sandra on the living room couch. She reached sleepily for the portable television. The green, baleful screen stared vacantly back at her, containing only her dim reflection—a shrunken body attached to one enormous, elongated hand. Louis Armstrong continued to sing.

> *Take your tootsies in to Duke's Place,*
> *Life is in the swim at Duke's Place . . .*

The bass thudded soundly in the floors, the walls, the cracked wooden frame of the couch.

Sandra turned on the lamp and saw the stereo components stacked against the far wall, partially hidden behind the teevee tray. The amplifier's monochrome panel glittered intricately. I am a miracle magnet, Sandra thought, recalling one of Reverend Fanny's prescribed affirmations. Beautiful things are drawn irresistibly to me. I give thanks that every day and in every way I grow richer and richer.

On her way to work Sandra mailed the Church a check for one hundred dollars.

That night she couldn't sleep. She lay on her back on the couch, her hands folded on her stomach. She closed her eyes and tried to visualize the off-white corridor, the half-open door. What did she want to find inside? A color teevee, jewelry, kitchen appliances, a new car? What kind of car, what color? Would it fit inside the room? How, exactly, had the room looked? She remembered the pitted walls, the stained floors, the quality of light—but she couldn't put all the elements together at once. A Maserati, she decided finally. Like the one Mr. Morgan drives. There, it's all decided. Now she was closing the door. Okay, the door is closed. Everything is very dark. Had she heard the living room floor creak just now? Yes, she was almost certain. Still, she kept her eyes closed a few more minutes.

She sat up and opened her eyes. The living room contained the portable teevee, the aluminium teevee tray, the new stereo, the broken wall clock, the dingy venetian blinds.

She closed her eyes and tried again. No matter how hard she concentrated she could not make the car appear. It was nearly dawn before she fell asleep, and only then did she stand again on the winding staircase. The wooden stairs were firm and cold against her feet; they even creaked occasionally. The car, she wondered. Will the car be there, or something else? It doesn't matter, she told herself. She would accept what was given. She wasn't choosy; she wasn't greedy. She only wanted her fair share. She walked to the end of the corridor, pushed open the door. Books were stacked haphazardly around the small, otherwise empty room. Dozens and dozens of books, as if waiting to be shelved by some divine librarian. Sandra stood at the doorway, but she did not go inside. The room's strange powers might harm her, she thought—jolt her like electricity, singe her like fire. She pulled the door shut.

When she awoke the next morning she examined her new books. They were accompanied by a bright orange and green brochure, which described them as "The Greatest Books Ever Written." *Madame Bovary, The Scarlet Letter, Fathers and Sons, The Red and the Black, Jude the Obscure.* Each volume was bound in genuine leather and filled with numerous illustrations by "the World's Greatest Modern Artists." She imagined the spines upright and glistening on a brand new bookshelf. A blond oak bookshelf, perhaps. With glass-panel doors, and gleaming gold fixtures . . . But any bookshelf will be fine, she reminded herself abruptly. Really, any kind at all. She wasn't in any sort of a hurry. She didn't want to test the power; she didn't want to challenge it unduly. She would accept what was given.

Every night the dream recurred and the room presented her with beautiful things. A Schumacher "Pride of Kashmir" Indian rug, a hand-carved Japanese console with iridescent moiré lacquer wash, a hand-cut glass chandelier by Waterford, a Miró original, a Roe Kasian dining set, a Giancarlo Ripa white shadow fox fur. The next time Matthew visited the office she was wearing Fernando Sanchez's latest, a sheer silk taffeta dress anchored to a black lace bra. Her ruby earrings were the color of pigeon's blood. Matthew sat on the edge of her desk.

"You like Japanese food?"

Sandra stopped typing, looked up. Her lashes were Borghese, her mascara Lancôme. "I guess I don't know. I've never had it before."

"Never?" Matthew's face was puzzled, as if confronted by an enigma. "Tempura, teriyaki, Misu soup? You're in for a real treat. I know the best place in town. They've got shrimp the size of my fist.'' He showed her his fist for emphasis. ''How does eight sound?''

''Eight?''

''All right. Eight-thirty—but try and be on time. I'll only honk twice. Here.'' He handed her the steno pad. ''I'll need your address. Draw me a little map or something.''

Matthew picked her up at nine and they drove directly to his apartment, a West Hollywood duplex. ''Is the restaurant nearby?'' Sandra asked. For the occasion she wore an obi—a broad black sash belt—with her cobalt blue, raw-silk dress. ''It just suddenly occurred to me,'' Matthew said. ''They probably aren't open Thursdays. I'm almost certain, in fact. If you're hungry, see what's in the fridge.'' In bed Matthew was fastidious. His hands and mouth made routine, scheduled stops at each of her erogenous zones, like miniature trains on a track. Sandra, meanwhile, observed herself in the mirrored ceiling. ''What's the matter with you?'' he asked finally. ''You didn't tell me you had problems with men.'' Matthew's body was sleek, firm, unblemished. His underwear was by Calvin Klein, his cologne by Ralph Lauren. Sandra said she just wanted him to hold her, and Matthew grew suddenly tense in her arms. He said he was short of cash at the moment—could she pay her own cab fare home? He *would* reimburse her.

Matthew stopped coming by the office. Whenever Sandra called his home she couldn't get past the girl at his answering service.

''Matthew Morgan residence—Mr. Morgan is out at the moment. Can I take a message?''

At this point Sandra usually heard the click of a second extension being lifted, and knew Matthew was listening when she asked, ''Has he picked up his messages today?''

"One second and I'll check. . . . This is Sandra again, right?"

"Yes."

"Well, I'm afraid he still hasn't called in. But you could leave another message, if you liked. . . ."

One day Sandra waited outside Matthew's office building until he emerged for lunch. "You know I really care about you," he said. "I just think it would be better if we didn't see each other for a while. It's nothing the matter with you, baby. It's *me*. I don't think I'm ready to make the kind of commitments you seem to expect from a man. You tend to be very possessive—which is *fine*, it's only *right*. . . ." He paused to wave at his secretary, who tapped one foot impatiently at the curb. "Look, baby. Let's talk about this later in the week, okay? We'll have lunch. And do you think I could borrow a twenty until then?" He palpated his vest pocket. "Seems I left my wallet in the office."

Matthew never called. Sandra waited at home, certain he would. She broke dates with Mr. Takata, the software executive, and Steve, her aerobics instructor. It was only a matter of time. Matthew would come around. She was a miracle magnet. She was one with the creative power. One night she received an Amana trash compactor, the next a Zenith Gemini 2000 color television. "You must not be afraid of total fulfillment," Reverend Fanny warned, her brows knit with sincerity. The glazed, speckless teevee screen crackled with static electricity as Sandra reached to increase the volume. "You mustn't fear, you mustn't doubt, you mustn't lose faith. *Total* fulfillment requires *total* commitment. Have you, for instance, hoarded away a little nest egg, some rainy-day money? Then you doubt the complete power of Divine Creation. Why put a time-lock on your security savings when your love can be bullish on the stock-exchange of heavenly devotion?"

That afternoon Sandra walked to the corner and mailed the Church a check for $327.43, the balance of her account. Later the same night Matthew called.

"Hello, Sandra?"

"Yes."

"Sandra, baby. It's me. Matthew. You remember me, don't you?"

"Of course I do."

"I know I should've called. But it's been really hectic in the messenger biz, you know?"

"I'm sure it has."

"You're not mad or anything, are you? I seem to sense a lot of hostility on your part. I know I owe you twenty and all—"

"No. I'm not mad. I'm glad you called. I was waiting for you to call."

"Good. Look, I was thinking. Let's have dinner tonight. All right with you? I'll pick you up a little after eight, we'll go find a nice quiet spot."

Matthew arrived at half past ten, and rang the doorbell.

"You think my car's safe parked around here? It's so late, I thought we could scrounge up a snack right here. You can show me around your apartment." Matthew entered the living room. "Hey, where'd all this great stuff come from?" He reached for the tape player—*Louis Armstrong's Greatest Hits*. Lengths of crumpled brown magnetic tape spilled onto the floor. "Seems you've got the tape caught on the heads. If you've got a screwdriver, I can probably fix it."

"I pushed a wrong button or something," Sandra explained quickly, took the tape from his hands and plugged it back into the player. "I'll have it fixed one of these days. I just like the way it looks. It really brightens up the room, don't you think?"

"What's down here? Is this the bedroom?"

Sandra followed Matthew through the door. He crouched in the corner of the bedroom, picked up and assessed one silver candelabrum. "This is worth a few bucks," he said.

"It's getting late. Aren't you tired?" Sandra asked, and began to straighten the Wamsutta silk sheets.

"Where'd you get all this loot? My old man doesn't pay you this well just to answer telephones."

"My father sends me things. My father has a very important job in Asia. Now, please—put those things down. Get into bed."

"What a sweet deal. I think I'd like to meet this old man of yours someday."

Sandra pushed Matthew's hands away from her belt. She just wanted him to hold her, she said again. This time, he obliged.

Sandra and Matthew were very happy together for a while. She enjoyed cooking his meals in the microwave, washing his clothes in the Maytag. Every morning she walked to Winchell's and brought him coffee and jelly donuts. Matthew took the next few weeks off from work. "I want to be with you more," he said, wiped a dollop of red jelly from his chin, and peered over Sandra's shoulder at the new Panasonic Omnivision VHS video recorder with wireless remote. "I never saw that before. Did it just arrive this morning or something?"

Every evening Sandra stopped by the market on her way home. Matthew requested steak, swordfish, veal, king crab, champagne, Jack Daniel's Tennessee Sour Mash. She began computing her checking balance in negative numbers. When she arrived home Matthew was usually on the phone in the bedroom. "—yeah, Bernie. It's me, Matt . . . I know I haven't been home—I don't see what it matters to you where I'm staying. I want you to put a grand on Blue Tone in the sixth . . . Bernie, don't insult me. You know my old man's good for it.''

Sandra collected soiled glasses and plates from the living room. On the burnished mahogany coffee table she noticed a tiny, soft white mound of powder centred on a small, rectangular mirror. A gold-plated razor blade, attached to a silver chain, lay beside it. She took the dishes into the kitchen, started hot water in the sink, wiped a bit of fried egg off the lid of the trash compactor. Her mail was stacked on the countertop. A lengthy, itemized Visa statement. The landlord's second eviction notice. Urgent utility bills with bold red borders. My mind is centred in infinite wealth, Sandra reminded herself, and opened the last envelope. Dear Friend, the letter began. Are you prepared to receive the wealth of Divine Creation? Then you must be prepared to dispense wealth to others. Wealth flows two ways, not one, thus maintaining universal harmony. The letters was concluded by Reverend Fanny's mimeographed scrawl. Sandra removed her checkbook from the kitchen drawer, computed her balance on the Texas Instruments Scientific Calculator. Zeitlin and Morgan would pay her Wednesday. Perhaps she could deposit the paycheck in time for her outstanding checks to clear. Her balance, then, would be $23.97. She thought for a moment, turned off the sink faucet, dried her hands on a towel. I am a money magnet. Every dollar I spend comes back to me multiplied. I have all the time, energy and money I require to accomplish all of my desires.

She wrote the Church a check for one thousand dollars. She licked and sealed the envelope, then heard the broiler door squeak open behind her. She turned.

''Porterhouse, huh? Great, baby. My favorite.'' Matthew slammed the broiler door shut. ''Listen, I need to ask you a little favor—*por favor?* Just a couple hundred for a day or two. My accountant's got all my assets tied up in some sort of bonds or something. I don't really understand all the technical details. It'll take me a few days to get hold of some cash. You know these accountants. They think it's their money, right?''

Matthew's smile was beautiful. His teeth actually sparkled, like the teeth in television commercials. Matthew and Sandra are very, very happy together, Sandra thought. Marriage, they both realize, is inevitable. They mean so much to each other. They will honeymoon in Brussels, where Matthew has important family. After a year they will return to the States where, with the aid of a personable nurse, Sandra will raise two beautiful, adopted children, a girl and a boy. Matthew will eventually be recruited into politics. "We need you," his influential friends will say. "You're the only man who can beat Patterson." Matthew will win by a narrow margin, but his re-election four years later will come in a landslide. They will rent a Manhattan penthouse, and Matthew will commute to Washington.

"I can write you a check," Sandra said.

One morning before she left for work Sandra made a long-distance call to Macon, Georgia. "Worldwide Church of Prosperity," the receptionist said. "How can we help each other?"

Sandra asked to speak with Reverend Fanny, and the receptionist said, "Oh, I'm afraid that simply isn't possible. Regretfully, the Reverend's numerous personal and public commitments make it virtually impossible for her to speak privately with each and every one of her brethren. But should you, perhaps, be contemplating sizeable donations—say, ten thousand or more, and all of it tax-deductible, of course— then I *might* be able to connect you with one of the Reverend's close advisers—"

"I *am* contemplating sizeable donations," Sandra assured

her. "I am eternally grateful to the power of Divine Creation. My life is abundant with beautiful things. But at the moment I'm experiencing some problems of *cash-flow*. . . ."

"Oh," the receptionist said.

"—I'm sure it's just a temporary problem—but I was wondering if there weren't any special prayers or affirmations for someone in my situation. You know, prayers which might *focus* my miracles a little more. And please, don't think I'm trying to be greedy or anything—"

"Cash is not wealth," the receptionist said. "Money only travels in one direction. True wealth flows both ways. If you would like to give me your address, I'll see to it you receive our free monthly newsletter."

On Friday Sandra received a series of overdraft charges from her bank, and a tense telephone call from the local Safeway manager. "I realize these things happen," the manager said. "Have to admit even I've bounced a few in my day. But how soon can I expect your check to clear?" Very soon, Sandra answered. She would deposit funds first thing tomorrow morning. She was so embarrassed. It wouldn't happen again.

"You'll get your damn money!" Mrs. Mitchelson used to shout, after the store's third call or so. "What's the matter with you people, anyway? Don't you realize I'm just a single woman trying to raise a child? No—*you* listen for a minute. You men always expect us to listen to you—well, *you* listen for a change. I'll pay you when I'm good and ready, and not a minute sooner. And *another* thing. You've got the worst stinking produce section in the city, do you know that? Your apples are wormy, your lettuce is wilted, your vegetables are rotten. Do you hear me? *Rotten*. Instead of me paying you, you should pay *me* for all the lousy produce I bought from your store and then had to throw away. That's what *I* think." After Mrs. Mitchelson hung up the phone she would fix herself a drink and then tell Sandra to go and pack her suitcase. "We're going to stay with your Aunt Lois again for a while," Mrs. Mitchelson would say. "Then maybe we can find a new home where the bastards will let us live in peace."

After Sandra hung up the phone, as a sort of grudging memorial to her mother, she climbed a stool, reached the Safeway jug down from a high, dusty shelf, and poured herself a drink. She carried her glass into the living room, which was crowded with mismatched and exorbitant furniture, video and stereo components, unopened crates of records, Abrams art books and glassware, like the award display on some television game show. Matthew was playing Galactic Midway, an arcade pinball machine by Bally. Bells chimed, lights flashed, hidden levers pumped the next gleaming silver ball into position. Gripping the machine's sides Matthew nudged it slightly from time to time. "Have a good day at work?" He pushed the reset button. On the scoreboard the digits clacked noisily around to zero.

"It was okay." Sandra cleared some stray pearls from the ottoman and sat down.

"Did I tell you the electric company called? Something about a last notice. I think I'd look into it if I were you."

On the coffee table the mound of soft white powder had nearly doubled in size, like a miniature avalanche. Sandra sipped her drink, glanced around the room.

After a while she asked, "Where's my new VHS? My video recorder. The one I got this week."

The flippers clacked noisily. Then Matthew hit the machine with his fist. "Damn!"

"The VHS. I asked what happened to it."

"How the hell do I know?" Matthew pushed the reset button. "Do I look like the maid or something? It's around some place. You probably haven't looked hard enough."

"I don't see it. It was in the living room this morning. It couldn't just get up and walk away."

"It'll turn up, you'll see. Everything turns up eventually," Matthew said, and pumped another ball into the game.

That night Sandra sat down and wrote a letter on her IBM Selectric.

Dear Reverend Fanny,

Please excuse the fact my check didn't clear. I had a very bad week last week. I tried to call and explain but the lady who answered the phone said you were very busy. I will try to make the check good at some date in the near future. I agree that if I expect to receive riches I must not deny riches to others, but I'm afraid my boyfriend Matthew whom I live with sold my Tiffany silverware set yesterday while I was at work in order to pay his gambling debts. Also he says he took my tape deck in to be repaired but I doubt that seriously. Also my electricity is being shut off tomorrow unless I pay them which I can't, and then what good will my new teevee or any of my new kitchen appliances be good for? I would appreciate any help or advice on these matters you might like to impart to me. I wish I could send you money like I usually do but I'll try to send you twice as much next time and hope you understand and forgive my present fiscal situation.

Yours faithfully,

Sandra Mitchelson

When Sandra fell asleep later that night she did not dream of the corridor. She dreamed instead of vast darkness, where silence filled everything like a heavy fluid. The fluid filled her mouth, throat, lungs. Breathing was impossible. I believe, she thought. I believe, I believe, I believe. She looked up and thought she detected, at the surface, a glimmer of white light. She tried to push herself up through the black weight but something gripped her ankle, something warm, pulsing, insistent. Like a tentacle, it moved up her leg. "Baby," the darkness said.

Sandra started upright in bed. The bedroom glowed with dim moonlight.

"Baby," Matthew said again. His arms wrapped themselves around her waist, his hands pulled her back into the weighted darkness.

On Monday when Sandra returned home from work she found Matthew in the bedroom, packing his Cricketeer wardrobe into the Samsonite. "I think I've done my part. I can honestly say I've done my share to make this relationship work." Underneath the packed clothes the tip of a silver candelabrum glinted dully. "But I'm the type of guy who demands a certain amount of honesty from a woman. Once she starts lying to me I know it's time to hit the road."

"I never lied," Sandra said. "I sent the electric company a check, just like I said. It must have gotten lost in the mail—"

"I'm not talking about that and you know it. I'm not talking about the fact there aren't any lights or any food in the house—or even that the television doesn't work. I'm not talking about what it's like living in the goddamn Stone Age. I'm talking about simple honesty—something you obviously know nothing about. I'm talking about the check you gave me for Bernie which wasn't worth the paper it was printed on. I'm talking about my reputation in this town, which is now just about shot because of you."

"I'll make it good," Sandra said. "It won't be any problem. We can sell the television, the washing machine—"

"It's just a little late for that. Bernie went to my old man for the dough. I'm free and clear. I've still got a job to go back to, or don't you remember. You didn't really expect me to live *here* all my life, did you? In *Compton?*" Matthew latched the suitcase and swung it off the bed.

"You have to stay. You can't leave," Sandra said, over and over again as she followed him down the hall and watched him walk out the front door.

The telephone was disconnected, the water, eventually the gas. Every night the vast, liquid darkness displaced Sandra's dream of the miraculous corridor. Elaine said. "You look like hell, girl. When was the last time you took a bath? There's a distinct odor creeping into this office, and don't think Mr. Morgan hasn't noticed it." At the end of the week Sandra returned home and found the front door sealed shut by the Sheriff's Department. The lock had been changed. She jimmied open the bedroom window, the one with the faulty latch.

Everything was gone. The brass bed, the pinball machine, the Maytag, the Lenox crystal. Rectangles of dust marked the former locations of impounded furniture. The room grew dark, and Sandra went to the window, turned open the venetian blinds. Outside it was dusk. She watched the phototropic streetlamps glow and gradually brighten, casting pale, watery red light through the blinds. Now she had nothing, and it didn't surprise her one bit. She was stupid, she never did anything right. Mrs. Mitchelson was right, Reverend Fanny was right, Matthew was right. Everybody was right, everybody except her. She was all alone; she was afraid of total commitment; she was dishonest—dishonest with herself. She was sick of being wrong all the time. Things must change; things were going to be different, now. *I* am going to be different, she thought. From now on *I'm* going to be right, *I'm* going to make the right decisions.

She just needed one more chance. Finally she knew what it was she wanted, and that was the important thing. It was all very simple, really, like psychoanalysis on television. She wanted someone who cared about her, someone who would stay with her. Staring out the window at the streetlamp Sandra leaned against the wall. Eventually she grew sleepy and closed her eyes.

She heard the door open behind her, the crack of the ruptured plastic seal.

Sandra opened her eyes. "Matthew?" She turned around. The door stood open, the living room remained empty. She walked to the door and looked out. The air was filled with blinding, devotional light. I am one with the creative power, Sandra reminded herself. I am not afraid. I believe, and I am not afraid. She stepped outside.

She stood again on the winding staircase. As she ascended she turned and caught a brief glimpse of the downstairs room. The light swirled and dust motes revolved slowly, like nebulas and constellations in some twilit planetarium. Large wooden packing crates were stacked everywhere, the lids nailed shut.

Sandra reached the summit of stairs. At the end of the corridor the door stood slightly ajar.

Quickly she crossed the length of the corridor, flung open the door and, without a second thought, stepped inside.

The overhead bulb flickered and extinguished with a sudden pop. She was not afraid, she told herself. The place was very cold and very dark. Slowly her eyes adjusted. Tall yellow weeds surrounded her, rippling as an icy breeze blew past. The foundation of the fish pond was broken and upthrust; all the water had drained away, leaving a few green puddles of algae. The skeletons of the monstruous goldfish, partially devoured by stray cats, lay strewn about the yard like weird leaves. She got down on her knees. Burrs and thorns scratched her legs. Her hands groped among the weeds, discovered fragments of the Japanese porcelain doll. The tattered rice-paper parasol was damp and stained with mildrew. She heard a noise and looked up.

A tall figure stood between her and the half open door.

"Daddy?" Sandra asked.

Another sudden breeze blew past. The door slammed shut.

"Isn't that just what I should have expected." The dark figure approached, briefly stumbled. "*Damn*—I could break my leg on these lousy gopher holes. Just look what a holy mess your father made of this place. But who's the first person you hope to see? Your father, your wonderful father. Your father who never called, who never wrote, who never came to visit, who certainly never provided one nickel of support. Your wonderful father who never really gave a good goddamn whether either of us lived or died."

Sandra sat down on the damp ground, weeds brushing against her face. The porcelain fragments crumbled apart in her hands.

"Aren't you a little old to be playing in the dirt? Here, get up." Mrs. Mitchelson offered her hand. Sandra took it, pulled herself to her feet. "Try and grow up a little, will you? I can't keep my eyes on you every minute. Just *look* at this mess." Mrs. Mitchelson slapped the dirt from Sandra's knees.

They took one another's hand. Mrs. Mitchelson's hand was cold and dry and soft. Sandra squeezed it tightly against her stomach, afraid of the dark.

"Try and remember that sometimes I need a little help and consideration too, you know. I can't do everything. I can only do the best I can, that's all. The best I can. Come on, now, and fix my dinner. It's been ages since I've had a decent meal in this dump."

Then, together in the deepening darkness, they made their way carefully across the ruined yard toward the shadows of the house.

Jane Yolen has written a number of tales about humans who develop relationships with beings who are anything but human. Her latest concerns an angry young student who becomes involved with someone who might in current parlance be called a "*real* foxy lady."

THE FOXWIFE

Jane Yolen

It was the spring of the year. Blossoms sat like painted butterflies on every tree. But the student Jiro did not enjoy the beauty. He was angry. It seemed he was always angry at something. And he was especially angry because he had just been told by his teachers that the other students feared him and his rages.

"You must go to a far island," said the master of his school.

"Why?" asked Jiro angrily.

"I will tell you if you listen," said his master with great patience.

Jiro shut his mouth and ground his teeth but was otherwise silent.

"You must go to the farthest island you can find. An island where no other person lives. There you must study by yourself. And in the silence of your own heart you may yet find the peace you need."

Raging, Jiro packed his tatami mat, his book and his brushes. He put them in a basket and tied the basket to his back. Though he was angry—with his master and with all the teachers and students in his school—he really *did* want to learn how to remain calm. And so he set out.

Sometimes he crossed bridges. Sometimes he waded rivers. Sometimes he took boats across the wild water. But at last he came to a small island where, the boatman assured him, no other person lived.

"Come once a week and bring me supplies," said Jiro, handing the boatman a coin. Then Jiro went inland and walked through the sparse woods until he came to a clearing in which he found a deserted temple.

"Odd," thought Jiro. "The boatman did not mention such a thing." He walked up the temple steps and was surprised to find the temple clean. He set his basket down in one corner, pulled out his mat, and spread it on the floor.

"This will be my home," he said. He said it out loud and there was an edge still to his voice.

For many days Jiro stayed on the island, working from first light till last. And though once in a while he became angry— because his brush would not write properly or because a dark cloud dared to hide the sun—for the most part he was content.

One day, when Jiro was in the middle of a particularly complicated text and having much trouble with it, he looked up and saw a girl walking across the clearing toward him.

Every few steps she paused and glanced around. She was not frightened but rather seemed alert, as if ready for flight.

Jiro stood up. "Go away," he called out, waving his arm.

The girl stopped. She put her head to one side as if considering him. Then she continued walking as before.

Jiro did not know what to do. He wondered if she was the boatman's daughter. Perhaps she had not heard him. Perhaps she was stupid. Perhaps she was deaf. She certainly did not belong on *his* island. He called out louder this time: "Go away. I am a student and must not be disturbed." He followed each statement with a movement of his arms.

But the girl did not go away and she did not stop. In fact, at his voice, she picked up her skirts and came toward him at a run.

Jiro was amazed. She ran faster than anyone he had ever seen, her dark russet hair streaming out behind her like a tail. In a moment she was at the steps of the temple.

"Go away!" cried Jiro for the third time.

The girl stopped, stared, and bowed.

Politeness demanded that Jiro return her bow. When he looked up again, she was gone.

Satisfied, Jiro smiled and turned back to his work. But there was the girl, standing stone-still by his scrolls and brushes, her hands folded before her.

"I am Kitsune," she said. "I care for the temple."

Jiro could contain his anger no longer. "Go away," he screamed. "I must work alone. I came to this island because I was assured no other person lived here."

She stood as still as a stone in a river and let the waves of his rage break against her. Then she spoke. "No other person lives here. I am Kitsune. I care for the temple."

After that, storm as he might, there was nothing Jiro could do. The girl simply would not go away.

She did care for the temple—and Jiro as well. Once a week she appeared and swept the floors. She kept a bowl filled with fresh camellias by his bed. And once, when he had gone to get his supplies and tripped and hurt his legs, Kitsune found him and carried him to the temple on her back. After that, she came every day as if aware Jiro needed constant attention. Yet she never spoke unless he spoke first, and even then her words were few.

Jiro wondered at her. She was little, lithe, and light. She moved with a peculiar grace. Every once in a while, he would see her stop and put her head to one side in that attitude of listening. He never heard what it was she heard, and he never dared ask.

At night she disappeared. One moment she would be there and the next moment gone. But in the morning Jiro would wake to find her curled in sleep at his feet. She would not say where she had been.

So spring passed, and summer, too. Jiro worked well in the quiet world Kitsune helped him maintain, and he found a kind of peace beginning to bud in his heart.

On the first day of fall, with leaves being shaken from the trees by the wind, Jiro looked up from his books. He saw that Kitsune sat on the steps trembling.

"What is it?" he asked.

"The leaves. Aieee, the leaves!" she cried. Then she jumped up and ran down to the trees. She leapt and played with the leaves as they fell about her. They caught in her hair. She blew them off her face. She rolled in them. She put her face to the ground and sniffed the dirt. Then, as if a fever had suddenly left her, she was still. She stood up, brushed off her clothing, smoothed her hair, and came back to sit quietly on the steps again.

Jiro was enchanted. He had never seen any woman like this before. He left his work and sat down on the steps beside her. Taking her hand in his, he stroked it thoughtfully, then brought it to his cheek. Her hand was warm and dry.

"We must be married," he said at last. "I would have you with me always."

"Always? What is always?" asked Kitsune. She tried to pull away.

Jiro held her hand tightly and would not let her go. And after awhile she agreed.

The boatman took them across to the mainland, where they found a priest who married them at once, though he smiled behind his hand at their haste. Jiro was supremely happy and he knew that Kitsune must be, too, though all the way in the boat going there and back again, she shuddered and would not look out across the waves.

That night Kitsune shared the tatami mat with Jiro. When the moon was full and the night whispered softly about the temple, Jiro awoke. He turned to look at Kitsune, his bride. She was not there.

"Kitsune," he called out fearfully. He sat up and looked around. He could not see her anywhere. He got up and searched around the temple, but she was not to be found. At last he fell asleep, sitting on the temple steps. When he awoke again at dawn, Kitsune was curled in sleep on the mat.

"Where were you last night?" he demanded.

"Where I should be," she said, and would say no more.

Jiro felt anger flowering inside, so he turned sharply from her and went to his books. But he did not try to calm himself. He fed his rage silently. All day he refused to speak. At night, exhausted by his own anger, he fell asleep before dark. He woke at midnight to find Kitsune gone.

Jiro knew he had to stay awake until she returned. A little before dawn he saw her running across the clearing. She ran up the temple steps and did not seem to be out of breath. She came right to the mat, surprised to see Jiro awake.

Jiro waited for her explanation, but instead of speaking she began her morning chores. She had fresh camellias in her hands, which she put in a bowl as if nothing were wrong.

Jiro sat up. "Where do you go at night?" he asked. "What do you do?"

Kitsune did not answer.

Jiro leaped up and came over to her. He took her by the

shoulders and began to shake her. "Where? Where do you go?" he cried.

Kitsune dropped the bowl of flowers and it shattered. The water spread out in little islands of puddles on the floor. She looked down and her hair fell around her shoulders, hiding her face.

Jiro could not look at the trembling figure so obviously terrified of him. Instead, he bent to pick up the pieces of the bowl. He saw his own face mirrored a hundred times in the spilled drops. Then he saw something else. Instead of Kitsune's face or her russet hair, he saw the sharp-featured head of a fox reflected there. The fox's little pointed ears were twitching. Out of its dark eyes tears began to fall.

Jiro looked up but there was no fox. Only Kitsune, beginning to weep, trembling at the sight of him, unable to move. And then he knew. She was a *nogitsone*, a were-fox, who could take the shape of a beautiful woman. But the *nogitsone's* reflection in the water was always that of a beast.

Suddenly Jiro's anger, fueled by his terror, knew no bounds. "You are not human," he cried. "Monster, wild thing, demon, beast. You will rip me or tear me if I let you stay. Some night you will gnaw upon my bones. Go away."

As he spoke, Kitsune fell to her hands and knees. She shook herself once, then twice. Her hair seemed to flow over her body, covering her completely. Then twitching her ears once, the vixen raced down the temple steps, across the meadow, and out of sight.

Jiro stood and watched for a long, long time. He thought he could see the red flag of her tail many hours after she had gone.

The snows came early that year, but the season was no colder than Jiro's heart. Every day he thought he heard the barking of a fox in the woods beyond the meadow, but he would not call it in. Instead he stood on the steps and cried out, "Away. Go away." At night he dreamed of a woman weeping close by his mat. In his sleep he called out, "Away. Go away."

Then when winter was full and the nights bitter cold, the sounds ceased. The island was deadly still. In his heart Jiro knew the fox was gone for good. Even his anger was gone, guttered in the cold like a candle. What had seemed so certain to him, in the heat of his rage, was certain no more. He wondered over and over which had been human and which had been beast. He even composed a haiku on it.

> *Pointed ears, red tail,*
> *Wife covered in fox's skin,*
> *The beast hides within.*

He said it over many times to himself, but he was never satisfied with it.

Spring came suddenly, a tiny green blade pushing through the snow. And with it came a strange new sound. Jiro woke to it, out of a dream of snow. He followed the sound to the temple steps and saw prints in the dust of white. Sometimes they were fox, sometimes girl, as if the creature who made them could not make up its mind.

"Kitsune," Jiro called out impulsively. Perhaps she had not died after all.

He looked out across the meadow and thought he saw again that flag of red. But the sound that had wakened him came once more, from behind. He turned, hoping to see Kitsune standing again by the mat with the bowl of camellias in her hand. Instead, by his books, he saw a tiny bundle of russet fur. He went over and knelt by it. Huddled together for warmth were two tiny kit foxes.

For a moment Jiro could feel the anger starting inside him. He did not want these two helpless, mewling things. He wanted Kitsune. Then he remembered that he had driven her away. Away. And the memory of that long, cold winter without her put out the budding flames of his new rage.

He reached out and put his hand on the foxlings. At his touch, they sprang apart on wobbly legs, staring up at him with dark, discerning eyes. They trembled so, he was afraid they might fall.

"There, there," he crooned to them. "This big, rough beast will not hurt you. Come. Come to me." He let them sniff both his hands and when their trembling ceased, he picked them up and cradled them against his body, letting them share his warmth. First one, then the other, licked his fingers. This so moved Jiro that, without meaning to, he began to cry.

The tears dropped onto the muzzles of the foxlings and they looked as if they, too, were weeping. Then, as Jiro watched, the kits began to change. The features of a human child slowly superimposed themselves on each fox face. Sighing, they snuggled closer to Jiro, closed their eyes, put their thumbs in their mouths, and slept.

Jiro smiled. Walking very carefully, as if afraid each step might jar the babies awake, he went down the temple steps. He walked across the clearing leaving man-prints in the umarked snow. Slowly, calmly, all anger gone from him, he moved toward the woods where he knew Kitsune waited. He would find her before evening came again.

A good salesman is supposed to be able to sell almost anything to anyone, or so it said—perhaps by salesmen themselves. Barry Levingston considered himself a first-class salesman, but he experienced some really trying moments after he had been granted an exclusive license by Queen Titania to sell computers in Faërie.

GOLDEN APPLES OF THE SUN

Gardner Dozois, Jack Dann, and Michael Swanwick

Few of the folk in Faërie would have anything to do with the computer salesman. He worked himself up and down one narrow, twisting street after another, until his feet throbbed and his arms ached from lugging the sample cases, and it seemed like days had passed rather than hours, and *still* he had not made a single sale. Barry Levingston considered himself a first-class salesman, one of the *best*, and he wasn't used to this kind of failure. It discouraged and frustrated him, and as the afternoon wore endlessly on—there was something funny about the way time passed here in Faerie; the hazy, bronze-colored Fairyland sun had hardly moved at all across the smoky amber sky since he'd arrived, although it should certainly be evening by *now*—he could feel himself beginning to lose that easy confidence and unshakable self-esteem that are the successful salesman's most essential stock-in-trade. He tried to tell himself that it wasn't really *his* fault. He was working under severe restrictions, after all. The product was new and unfamiliar to this particular market, and he was going "cold sell." There had been no telephone solicitation programs to develop leads, no ad campaigns, not so much as a demographic study of the market potential. Still, his total lack of success was depressing.

The village that he'd been trudging through all day was built on and around three steep, hive-like hills, with one street rising from the roofs of the street below. The houses were piled chockablock atop each other, like clusters of grapes, making it almost impossible to even find—much less *get* to—many of the upper-story doorways. Sometimes the eaves grew out over the street, turning them into long, dark tunnels. And sometimes the streets ran up sloping housesides and across rooftops, only to come to a sudden and frightening *stop* at a sheer drop of five or six stories, the street beginning again as abruptly on the far side of the gap. From the highest streets and stairs you could see a vista of the surrounding countryside: a hazy golden-brown expanse of orchards and forests and fields, and, on the far horizon, blue with distance, the jagged, snow-capped peaks of a mighty mountain range— except that the mountains didn't always seem to be in the same *direction* from one moment to the next; sometimes they were to the west, then to the north, or east, or south; sometimes they seemed much closer or farther away; sometimes they weren't there at *all*.

Barry found all this unsettling. In fact, he found the whole *place* unsettling. Why go *on* with this, then? he asked himself. He certainly wasn't making any headway. Maybe it was because he overtowered most of the fairyfolk—maybe they were sensitive about being so *short*, and so tall people annoyed them. Maybe they just didn't like humans; humans *smelled* bad to them, or something. Whatever it was, he hadn't gotten more than three words of his spiel out of his mouth all day. Some of them had even slammed doors in his face—something he had almost forgotten *could* happen to a salesman.

Throw in the towel, then, he thought. But . . . no, he *couldn't* give up. Not yet. Barry sighed, and massaged his stomach, feeling the acid twinges in his gut that he knew presaged a savage attack of indigestion later on. This was virgin territory, a literally untouched route. Gold waiting to be mined. And the Fairy Queen had given this territory to *him*. . . .

Doggedly, he plodded up to the next house, which looked something like a gigantic acorn, complete with a thatched cap and a crazily twisted chimney for the stem. He knocked on a round wooden door.

A plump, freckled fairy woman answered. She was about the size of an earthly two-year old, but a transparent gown seemingly woven of spidersilk made it plain that she was no child. She hovered a few inches above the doorsill on rapidly beating hummingbird wings.

"Aye?" she said sweetly, smiling at him, and Barry immediately felt his old confidence return. But he didn't permit himself to become excited. That was the quickest way to lose a sale.

"Hello," he said smoothly. "I'm from Newtech Computer Systems, and we've been authorized by Queen Titania, the Fairy Queen *herself*, to offer a *free* installation of our new home computer system—"

"That wot I not of," the fairy said.

"Don't you even know what a computer *is*?" Barry asked, dismayed, breaking off his spiel.

"Aye, I fear me, 'tis even so,' she replied, frowning

prettily. "In sooth, I know not. Belike you'll tell me of't, fair sir."

Barry began talking feverishly, meanwhile unsnapping his sample case and letting it fall open to display the computer within. "—balance your household accounts," he babbled. "Lets you organize your recipes, keep in touch with the stock market. You can generate full-color graphics, charts, graphs. . . ."

The fairy frowned again, less sympathetically. She reached her hand toward the computer, but didn't quite touch it. "Has the smell of metal on't," she murmured. "Most chill and adamant." She shook her head. "Nay, sirrah, 'twill not serve. 'Tis a thing mechanical, a clockwork, meet for carillons and orreries. Those of us born within the Ring need not your engines philosophic, nor need we toil and swink as mortals do at such petty tasks an you have named. Then wherefore should I buy, who neither strive nor moil?"

"But you can play *games* on it!" Barry said desperately, knowing that he was losing her. "You can play Donkey Kong! You can play *Pac-Man!* *Everybody* likes to play PacMan—"

She smiled slowly at him sidelong. "I'd liefer more delightsome games," she said.

Before he could think of anything to say, a long, long, *long* green-gray arm came slithering out across the floor from the hidden interior of the house. The arm ended in a knobby hand equipped with six grotesquely long, tapering fingers, now spreading wide as the hand reached out toward the fairy. . . .

Barry opened his mouth to shout a warning, but before he could, the long arm had wrapped bonelessly around her ankle, not once but *four* times around, and the hand with its scrabbling spider fingers had closed over her thigh. The arm yanked back, and she tumbled forward in the air, laughing.

"Ah, loveling, can you not wait?" she said with mock severity. The arm tugged at her. She giggled. "Certes, meseems you cannot!"

As the arm pulled her, still floating, back into the house, the fairy woman seized the door to slam it shut. Her face was flushed and preoccupied now, but she still found a moment to smile at Barry. "Farewell, sweet mortal!" she cried, and winked. "Next time, mayhap?"

The door shut. There was a muffled burst of giggling within. Then silence.

The salesman glumly shook his head. This was a goddam tank town, was what it was, he thought. Here there were no knickknacks and bric-à-brac lining the windows, no cast-iron flamingoes and eave-climbing plaster kitty cats, no mailboxes with fake Olde English calligraphy on them—but in spite of that it was still a tank town. Just another goddamn middleclass neighborhood with money a little tight and the people running scared. Place like this, you couldn't even *give* the stuff away, much less make a sale. He stepped back out into the street. A fairy knight was coming down the road toward him, dressed in green jade armor cunningly shaped like leaves, and riding an enormous frog. Well, why not? Barry thought. He wasn't having a lot of luck door-to-door.

"Excuse me, sir!" Barry cried, stepping into the knight's way. "May I have a moment of your—"

The knight glared at him, and pulled back suddenly on his reins. The enormous frog reared up, and leaped straight into the air. Gigantic, leathery, batlike wings spread, caught the thermals, carried mount and rider away.

Barry sighed and trudged doggedly up the cobblestone road toward the next house. No matter what happened, he wasn't going to quit until he'd finished the street. That was a compulsion of his . . . and the reason he was one of the top cold-sell agents in the company. He remembered a night when he'd spent five hours knocking on doors without a single sale, or even so much as a kind *word*, and then suddenly he'd sold $30,000 worth of merchandise in an hour . . . suddenly he'd been golden, and they couldn't say no to him. Maybe that would happen today, too. Maybe the next house would be the beginning of a run of good luck. . . .

The next house was shaped like a gigantic ogre's face, its dark wood forming a yawning mouth and heavy-lidded eyes. The face was made up of a host of smaller faces, and each of *those* contained other, even smaller faces. He looked away dizzily, then resolutely climbed to a glowering, thick-nosed door and knocked right between the eyes—eyes which, he noted uneasily, seemed to be studying him with interest.

A fairy woman opened the door—below where he was standing. Belatedly, he realized that he had been knocking on a dormer; the top of the door was a foot below him.

This fairy woman had stubby, ugly wings. She was lumpy and gnarled, and her skin was the texture of old bark. Her hair stood straight out on end all around her head, in a puffy nimbus, like the Bride of Frankenstein. She stared imperiously up at him, somehow managing to seem to be staring *down* her nose at him at the same time. It was quite a nose, too. It was longer than his hand, and sharply pointed.

"A great ugly lump of a mortal, an I mistake not!" she snapped. Her eyes were flinty and hard. "What's toward?"

"I'm from Newtech Computer Systems," Barry said, biting back his resentment at her initial slur, "and I'm selling home computers, by special commission of the Queen—"

"Go to!" she snarled. "Seek you to cozen me? I wot *not* what abnormal beast that be, but I have no need of mortal kine, nor aught else from your loathly world! Get you gone!" She slammed the door under his feet. Which somehow was every bit as bad as slamming it in his face.

"Sonofa*bitch*!" Barry raged, making an obscene gesture at

the door, losing his temper at last. "You goddamn flying fat pig!"

He didn't realize that the fairy woman could hear him until a round crystal window above his head flew open, and she poked her head out of it, nose first, buzzing like a jarful of hornets. "Wittold!" she shrieked. "Caitiff rogue!"

"Screw off, lady," Barry snarled. It had been a long, hard day, and he could feel the last shreds of self-control slipping away. "Get back in your goddamn hive, you goddamn pinocchio-nosed mosquito!"

The fairy woman spluttered incoherently with rage, then became dangerously silent. "So!" she said in cold passion. "*Noses*, is't? Would villify *my* nose, knave, whilst your *own* be uncommon squat and vile? A tweak or two will remedy *that*, I trow, and exchange the better for the worse!"

So saying, she came buzzing out of her house like an outraged wasp, streaking straight at the salesman.

Barry flinched back, but she seized hold of his nose with both hands and tweaked it savagely. Barry yelped in pain. She shrieked out a high-pitched syllable in some unknown language and began flying backward, her wings beating furiously, *tugging* at his nose.

He felt the pressure in his ears change with a sudden *pop*, and then, horrifyingly, he felt his face begin to *move* in a strangely fluid way, flowing like water, swelling out and out and *out* in front of him.

The fairy woman released his nose and darted away, cackling gleefully.

Dismayed, Barry clapped his hands to his face. He hadn't realized that these little buggers could *all* cast spells—he'd thought that kind of magic stuff was reserved for the Queen and her court. Like cavorting in hot tubs with naked starlets and handfuls of cocaine, out in Hollywood—a prerogative reserved only for the Elite. But when his hands reached his nose, they almost couldn't close around it. It was too large. His nose was now nearly two feet long, as big around as a Polish sausage, and covered with bumpy warts.

He screamed in rage. "Goddammit, lady, come back here and *fix* this!"

The fairy woman was perching half-in and half-out of the round window, lazily swinging one leg. She smiled mockingly at him. "There!" she said, with malicious satisfaction. "Art *much* improved, methinks! Nay, thank me not!" And, laughing joyously, she tumbled back into the house and slammed the crystal window closed behind her.

"Lady!" Barry shouted. Scrambling down the heavy wooden lips, he pounded wildly on the door. "Hey, look, a joke's a joke, but I've got *work* to do! *Lady!* Look, lady, I'm *sorry*," he whined. "I'm sorry I swore at you, honest! Just come out here and *fix* this and I won't bother you anymore. Lady, *please!*" He heaved his shoulder experimentally against the door, but it was as solid as rock.

An eyelid-shaped shutter snapped open above him. He looked up eagerly, but it wasn't the lady; it was a fat fairy man with snail's horns growing out of his forehead. The horns were quivering with rage, and the fairy man's face was mottled red. "Pox take you, boy, and your cursed brabble!" the fairy man shouted. "When I am foredone with weariness, must I be roused from honest slumber by your hurble-burble?" Barry winced; evidentally he had struck the Faërie equivalent of a night-shift worker. The fairy man shook a fist at him. "Out upon you, miscreant! By the Oak of Mughna, I demand SILENCE!" The window snapped shut again.

Barry looked nervously up at the eyelid-window, but somehow he *had* to get the lady to come out and fix this goddamn *nose*. "Lady?" he whispered. "*Please*, lady?" No answer. This wasn't working at all. He'd have to change tactics, and take his chances with Snailface in the next apartment.

"LADY!" he yelled. "OPEN UP! I'M GOING TO STAND HERE AND SHOUT AT THE TOP OF MY LUNGS UNTIL YOU COME OUT! YOU WANT THAT? DO YOU?"

The eyelid flew open. "This passes bearing!" Snailface ranged. "Now Cernunnos shrivel me, an I chasten not this boistrous doltard!"

"Listen, mister, I'm *sorry*," Barry said uneasily, "I don't mean to wake you up, honest, but I've *got* to get that lady to come out, or my ass'll really be grass!"

"Your *Arse*, say you?" the snail-horned man snarled. "Marry, since you would have it so, why, by Lugh, I'll do it, straight!" He made a curious gesture, roared out a word that seemed to be all consonants, and then slammed the shutter closed.

Again, there was a *popping* noise in Barry's ears, and a change of pressure that he could feel throughout his sinuses. *Another* spell had been cast on him.

Sure enough, there was a strange, prickly sensation at the base of his spine. "Oh, no!" he whispered. He didn't really want to look—but at last he forced himself to. He groaned. He had sprouted a long green tail. It looked and smelled suspiciously like grass.

"Ha! Ha!" Barry muttered savagely to himself. "Very funny! *Great* sense of humor these little winged people've got!"

In a sudden spasm of rage, he began to rip out handfuls of grass, trying to *tear* the loathsome thing from his body. The grass ripped out easily, and he felt no pain, but it grew back many times faster than he could tear it free—so that by the time he decided that he was getting nowhere, the tail trailed out six or seven feet behind him.

What was he going to do *now*?

He stared up at the glowering house for a long, silent moment, but he couldn't think of any plan of action that wouldn't just get him in *more* trouble with *someone*.

Gloomily, he gathered up his sample cases, and trudged off down the street, his nose banging into his upper lip at every step, his tail dragging forlornly behind him in the dust. Be damned if this wasn't even worse than cold-selling in *Newark*. He wouldn't have believed it. But *there* he had only been mugged and had his car's tires slashed. *Here* he had been hideously disfigured, maybe for life, and he wasn't even making any *sales*.

He came to an intricately carved stone fountain, and sat wearily down on its lip. Nixies and water nymphs laughed and cavorted within the leaping waters of the fountain, swimming just as easily up the spout as down. They cupped their pretty little green breasts and called invitingly to him, and then mischievously spouted water at his tail when he didn't answer, but Barry was in no mood for them, and resolutely ignored their blandishments. After a while they went back to their games and left him alone.

Barry sighed, and tried to put his head in his hands, but his enormous new nose kept getting in the way. His stomach was churning. He reached into his pocket and worried out a metal-foil packet of antacid tablets. He tore the packet open, and then found—to his disgust—that he had to lift his sagging nose out of the way with one hand in order to reach his mouth. While he chewed on the chalky-tasting pills, he stared glumly at the twin leatherette bags that held his demonstrator models. He was beaten. Finished. Destroyed. *Ruined*. Down and out in Faërie, at the ultimate rock bottom of his career. What a bummer! What a *fiasco!*

And he had had such high hopes for this expedition, too. . . .

Barry never really understood why Titania, the Fairy Queen, spent so much of her time hanging out in a sleazy little roadside bar on the outskirts of a jerkwater South Jersey town—perhaps *that* was the kind of place that seemed exotic to *her*. Perhaps she liked the rotgut hootch, or the greasy hamburgers—just as likely to be "venison-burgers," really, depending on whether somebody's uncle or backwoods cousin had been out jacking deer with a flashlight and a 30.30 lately—or the footstomping honky-tonk music on the juke box. Perhaps she just had an odd sense of humor. Who knew? *Not* Barry.

Nor did Barry ever really understand what *he* was doing there—it wasn't really his sort of place, but he'd been on the road with a long way to go to the next town, and a sudden whim had made him stop in for a drink. *Nor* did he understand why, having stopped in in the first place, he had then gone *along* with the gag when the beat-up old barfly on his left had leaned over to him, breathing out poisonous fumes, and confided, "*I'm* really the Queen of the Fairies, you know." Ordinarily, he would have laughed, or ignored her, or said something like, "And *I'm* the Queen of the May, sleazeball." But he had done none of these things. Instead, he had nodded gravely and courteously, and asked her if he could have the honor of lighting the cigarette that was wobbling about in loopy circles in her shaking hand.

Why did he do this? Certainly it hadn't been from even the *remotest* desire to get into the Queen's grease-stained pants—in her earthly incarnation, the Queen was a grimy, gray-haired, broken-down rummy, with a horse's face, a dragon's breath, cloudy agate eyes, and a bright-red rumblossom nose. No, there had been no ulterior motives. But he had been in an odd mood, restless, bored, and stale. So he had played up to her, on a spur-of-the-moment whim, going along with the gag, buying her drinks and lighting cigarettes for her, and listening to her endless stream of half-coherent talk, all the while solemnly calling her "Your Majesty" and "Highness," getting a kind of role-playing let's pretend kick out of it that he hadn't known since he was a kid and he and his sister used to play "grown-up dress-up" with the trunk of castoff clothes in the attic.

So that when midnight came, and all the other patrons of the bar froze into freeze-frame rigidity, paralyzed in the middle of drinking or shouting or scratching or shoving, and Titania manifested herself in the radiant glory of her *true* form, nobody could have been more surprised than *Barry*.

"My God!" he'd cried. "You really *are*—"

"The Queen of the Fairies," Titania said smugly. "You bet your buns, sweetie. I *told* you so, didn't I?" She smiled radiantly, and then gave a ladylike hiccup. The Queen in her new form was so dazzlingly beautiful as to almost hurt the eye, but there was still a trace of rotgut whiskey on her breath. "And because *you've* been a most true and courteous knight to one from whom you thought to see no earthly gain, I'm going to grant you a *wish*. How about *that*, kiddo?" She beamed at him, then hiccuped again; whatever catabolic effect her transformation had had on her blood-alcohol level, she was obviously still slightly tipsy.

Barry was flabbergasted. "I can't believe it," he muttered. "I come into a bar, on *im*pulse, just by *chance,* and the very first person I sit down next to turns out to be—"

Titania shrugged. "That's the way it goes, sweetheart. It's the Hidden Hand of Oberon, what you mortals call 'synchronicity.' Who knows what'll eventually come of this meeting— tragedy or comedy, events of little moment or of world-shaking weight and worth? Maybe even *Oberon* doesn't know, the silly old fart. Now, about that *wish*—"

Barry thought about it. What *did* he want? Well, he was a *salesman,* wasn't he? New worlds to conquer. . . .

Even Titania had been startled. She looked at him in surprise and then said, "Honey, I've been dealing with mortals for a lot of years now, but nobody ever asked for *that* before. . . ."

*   *   *

Now he sat on cold stone in the heart of the Faërie town, and groaned, and cursed himself bitterly. If only he hadn't been so ambitious! If only he'd asked for something *safe*, like a swimming pool or a Ferrari. . . .

Afterward, Barry was never sure how long he sat there on the lip of the fountain in a daze of despair—perhaps literally for weeks; it *felt* that long. Slowly, the smoky bronze disk of the Fairyland sun sank beneath the horizon, and it became night, a warm and velvety night whose very darkness seemed somehow luminous. The nixies had long since departed, leaving him alone in the little square with the night and the plashing waters of the fountain. The strange stars of Faërie swam into the sky, witchfire crystals so thick against the velvet blackness of the night that they looked like phosphorescent plankton sparkling in some midnight tropic sea. Barry watched the night sky for a long time, but he could find none of the familiar constellations he knew, and he shivered to think how far away from home he must be. The stars *moved* much more rapidly here than they did in the sky of Earth, crawling perceptibly across the black bowl of the night even as you watched, swinging in stately procession across the sky, wheeling and reforming with a kind of solemn awful grandeur, eddying and whirling, swirling into strange patterns and shapes and forms, spiral pinwheels of light. Pastel lanterns appeared among the houses on the hillsides as the night deepened, seeming to reflect the wheeling, blazing stars above.

At last, urged by some restless tropism, he got slowly to his feet, instinctively picked up his sample cases, and set off aimlessly through the mysterious night streets of the Faërie town. Where was he going? Who knew? Did it matter anymore? He kept walking. Once or twice he heard faint, far snatches of fairy music—wild, sad, yearning melodies that pierced him like a knife, leaving him shaken and melancholy and strangely elated all at once—and saw lines of pastel lights bobbing away down the hillsides, but he stayed away from those streets, and did his best not to listen; he had been warned about the bewitching nature of fairy music, and had no desire to spend the next hundred or so years dancing in helpless enchantment within a fairy ring. Away from the street and squares filled with dancing pastel lights and ghostly will-o'-the-'wisps—which he avoided—the town seemed dark and silent. Occasionally, winged shapes swooped and flittered overhead, silhouetted against the huge mellow silver moon of Faërie, sometimes seeming to fly behind it for several wingbeats before flashing into sight again. Once he met a fellow pedestrian, a monstrous one-legged creature with an underslung jaw full of snaggle teeth and one baleful eye in the middle of its forehead that blazed like a warning beacon, and stood unnoticed in the shadows, shivering, until the fearsome apparition had hopped by. Not paying any attention to where he was going, Barry wandered blindly downhill. He couldn't think at all—it was as if his brain had turned to ash. His feet stumbled over the cobblestones, and only by bone-deep instinct did he keep hold of the sample cases. The street ended in a long curving set of wooden stairs. Mechanically, dazedly, he followed them down. At the bottom of the stairs, a narrow path led under the footing of one of the gossamer bridges that looped like slender gray cobwebs between the fairy hills. It was cool and dark here, and almost peaceful. . . .

"AAAARRRRGGHHHHH!"

Something *enormous* leaped out from the gloom, and enveloped him in a single, scaly green hand. The fingers were a good three feet long each, and their grip was as cold and hard as iron. The hand lifted him easily into the air, while he squirmed and kicked futilely.

Barry stared up into the creature's face. "Yop!" he said. A double row of yellowing fangs lined a frog-mouth large enough to swallow him up in one gulp. The blazing eyes bulged ferociously, and the nose was a flat smear. The head was topped off by a fringe of hair like red worms, and a curving pair of ram's horns.

"Pay *up* for the use a my bridge," the creature roared, "or by Oberon's dirty socks, I'll crunch you whole!"

It never ends, Barry thought. Aloud, he demanded in frustration. "What bridge?"

"A wise guy!" the monster sneered. "*That* bridge, whadda ya *think*?" He gestured upward scornfully. "The bridge *over* us, dummy! The Bridge a Morrig the Fearsome! *My* bridge. I got a royal commission says I gotta right ta collect toll from *every* creature that sets foot on it, and you better believe that means *you*, buddy. I got you dead to rights. So cough up!" He shook Barry until the salesman's teeth rattled. "Or *else!*"

"But I *haven't* set foot on it!" Barry wailed. "I just walked *under* it!"

"Oh," the monster said. He looked blank for a moment, scratching his knobby head with his free hand, and then his face sagged. "Oh," he said again, disappointedly. "Yeah. I guess you're right. Crap." Morrig the Fearsome sighed, a vast noisome displacement of air. Then he released the salesman. "Jeez, buddy, I'm sorry," Morrig said, crestfallen. "I shouldn't'a'oughta have jerked ya around like that. I guess I got overanxious or sumpthin. Jeez, mac, you know how it is. Tryin' to make a buck. The old grind. It gets me down."

Morrig sat down, discouraged, and wrapped his immensely long and muscular arms around his knobby green knees. He brooded for a moment, then jerked his thumb up at the bridge. "That bridge's my only source a income, see?" He sighed gloomily. "When I come down from Utgard and set up this scam, I think I'm gonna get *rich*. Got the royal commission, all nice an' legal, everybody gotta *pay* me, right? Gonna clean *up*, right?" He shook his head glumly. "*Wrong.*

I ain't making a lousy *dime*. All the locals got *wings*. Don't
use the bridge at *all*." He spat noisily. "They're cheap little
snots, these fairyfolk are."

"*Amen*, brother," Barry said, with feeling. "I know *just*
what you mean."

"Hey!" Morrig said, brightening. "You care for a snort? I
got a jug a hootch right here."

"Well, actually . . ." Barry said reluctantly. But the troll
had already reached into the gloom with one long, triple-
jointed arm, and pulled out a stone crock. He pried off the
top and took a long swig. Several gallons of liquid gurgled
down his throat. "Ahhhh!" He wiped his thin lips. "That
hits the spot, all right." He thrust the crock into Barry's lap.
"Have a belt."

When Barry hesitated, the troll rumbled, "Ah, go ahead,
pal. Good for what ails ya. You got troubles too, aintcha, just
like me—I can tell. It's the lot a the workin' man, brother.
Drink up. Put hair on your *chest* even if you ain't got no
dough in your *pocket*." While Barry drank, Morrig studied
him cannily. "You're a mortal, aintcha, bud?"

Barry half-lowered the jug and nodded uneasily.

Morrig made an expansive gesture. "Don't worry, pal. *I*
don't care. I figure all a us workin' folks gotta stick *together*,
regardless a race or creed, or the bastards'll grind us *all*
down. Right?" He leered, showing his huge, snaggly, yellowing fangs in what Barry assumed was supposed to be a
reassuring grin. "But, say, buddy, if you're a mortal, how
come you got funny ears like that, and a tail?"

Voice shrill with outrage, Barry told his story, pausing
only to hit the stone jug.

"Yeah, buddy," Morrig said sympathetically. "They really worked you over, didn't they?" He sneered angrily.
"Them bums! Just *like* them little snots to gang up ona guy
who's just tryin' ta make an honest buck. Whadda *they* care

about the problems a the workin' man? Buncha booshwa snobs! Screw 'em all!''

They passed the seemingly bottomless stone jug back and forth again. "Too bad *I* can't do none a that magic stuff," Morrig said sadly, "or I'd fix ya right up. What a shame." Wordlessly, they passed the jug again. Barry sighed. Morrig sighed too. They sat in gloomy silence for a couple of minutes, and then Morrig roused himself and said, "*What* kinda scam is it you're tryin' ta run? I ain't never heard a it before. Lemme see the merchandise."

"What's the point—?"

"C'mon," Morrig said impatiently. "I wantcha ta show me the goods. Maybe *I* can figure out a way ta move the stuff."

Listlessly, Barry snapped open a case. Morrig leaned forward to study the console with interest. "Kinda pretty," the troll said; he sniffed at it. "Don't smell too bad, either. Maybe make a nice planter, or sumpthin."

"*Planter?*" Barry cried; he could hear his voice cracking in outrage. "I'll have you know this is a piece of high technology! Precision machinery!"

Morrig shrugged. "Okay, bub, make it march."

"Ah," Barry said. "I need someplace to plug it in. . . ."

Morrig picked up the plug and inserted it in his ear. The computer's CRT screen lit up. "Okay," Morrig said. "Gimme the pitch. What's it do?"

"Well," Barry said slowly, "let's suppose that you had a bond portfolio worth \$2,147 invested at 8¾ percent compounded daily, over eighteen months, and you wanted to calculate—"

"Two thousand four hundred forty three dollars and sixty-eight and seven-tenths cents," said the troll.

"Hah?"

"That's what it works out to, pal. Two hundred ninety-six dollars and change in compound interest."

With a sinking sensation, Barry punched through the figures and let the system work. Alphanumerics flickered on the CRT: $296.687.

"Can *everybody* in Faerie do that kind of mental calculation?" Barry asked.

"Yeah," the troll said. "But so what? No big deal. Who *cares* about crap like that anyway?" He stared incredulously at Barry. "Is that *all* that thing does?"

There was a heavy silence.

"Maybe you oughta reconsider that idea about the planters. . . ." Morrig said.

Barry stood up again, a trifle unsteady from all the hootch he'd taken aboard. "Well, that's *really* it, then," he said. "I might just as well chuck my samples in the river—I'll never sell in *this* territory. Nobody needs my product."

Morrig shrugged. "What do *you* care how they use 'em? You oughta *sell* 'em first, and then let the *customers* find a use for 'em afterward. That's logic."

Fairy logic, perhaps, Barry thought. "But how can you *sell* something without first convincing the customer that it's useful?"

"Here." Morrig tossed off a final drink, gave a bone-rattling belch, and then lurched ponderously to his feet, scooping up both sample cases in one hand. "Lemme show you. Ya just gotta be *forceful*."

The troll started off at a brisk pace, Barry practically having to run to keep up with his enormous strides. They climbed back up the curving wooden steps, and then Morrig somehow retraced Barry's wandering route through the streets of Faërie town, leading them unerringly back to the home of the short-tempered, pinocchio-nosed fairy who had cast the first spell on Barry—the Hag of Blackwater, according to Morrig.

Morrig pounded thunderously on the Hag's door, making the whole house shake. The Hag snatched the door open angrily, snarling, "What's to—GACK!" as Morrig suddenly grabbed her up in one enormous hand, yanked her out of the house, and lifted her up to face level.

"Good evenin', ma'am," Morrig said pleasantly.

"A murrain on you, lummox!" she shrieked. "Curst vile rogue! Release me at once! At *once*, you foul scoundrel! I'll—BLURK." Her voice was cut off abruptly as Morrig tightened his grip, squeezing the breath out of her. Her face turned blood-red, and her eyes bulged from her head until Barry was afraid that she was going to pop like an overripe grape.

"Now, *now*, lady," Morrig said in a gently chiding tone. "Let's keep the party polite, okay? You know your magic's too weak to use on *me*. And you shouldn't'a'oughta use no hard language. We're just two workin' stiffs tryin' ta make a honest buck, see? You give us the bad mouth, and, say, it just might make me *sore*." Morrig began shaking her, up and down, back and forth, his fist moving with blinding speed, shaking her in his enormous hand as if she were a pair of dice he was about to shoot in a crap game. "AND YOU WOULDN'T WANT TA MAKE ME SORE, NOW, WOULD YOU, LADY?" Morrig bellowed. "WOULD YOU?"

The Hag was being shaken so hard that all you could see of her was a blur of motion. "Givors!" she said in a faint little voice. "Givors, I pray you!"

Morrig stopped shaking her. She lay gasping and disheveled in his grasp, her eyes unfocused. "There!" Morrig said jovially, beaming down at her. "That's better, ain't it? Now I'm just gonna start all over again." He paused for a second, and then said brightly, " 'Evenin', ma'am! I'm sellin' . . .

uh. . . ." He scratched his head, looking baffled, then bright-
ened. ". . . . compukers!" He held up a sample case to show
her; she stared dazedly at it. "Now I could go on and on
about how swell these compukers are, but I can see you're
already anxious ta buy, so there ain't no need ta waste yer
valuable time like that. Ain't that right?" When she didn't
answer, he frowned and gave her a little shake. "Ain't that
right?"

"A-aye," she gibbered. "Aye!"

Morrig set her down, keeping only a light grip on her
shoulder, and Barry broke out the sales forms. While she was
scribbling frantically in the indicated blanks, Morrig rumbled,
"And, say, now that we're all gettin' along so good, how's
about takin' your spell offa my friend's nose, just as a gesture
a good will? You'll do that little thing for me, *won'tcha*?"

With ill-grace, the Hag obliged. There was a *pop*, and
Barry exulted as he felt his nose shrink down to its original
size. *Part* of the way home, anyway! He collected the sales
forms and returned the receipts. "You can let go of her
now," he told Morrig.

Sullenly, the Hag stalked back into her house, slamming
the door behind her. The door vanished, leaving only an
expanse of blank wood. With a freight-train rumble, the
whole house sank into the ground and disappeared from sight.
Grass sprang up on the spot where the house had been, and
started growing furiously.

Morrig chuckled. Before they could move on, another fairy
woman darted out from an adjacent door. "What bought the
Hag of Blackwater, so precious that straight she hastens to
hide herself away with it from prying eyes?" the other fairy
asked. "Must indeed be something wondrous rare, to make
her cloister herself with such dispatch, like a mouse to it's
hole, and then pull the very hole in after her! Aye, she knew
I'd be watching, I doubt not, the selfish old bitch! Ever has

she been jealous of my Art. Fain am I to know what the Hag would keep from my sight. Let *me* see your wares."

It was *then* that Barry had his master-stroke. "I'm sorry," he said in his snidest voice, "but I'm afraid that I can't show it to *you*. We're selling these computers by *exclusive* license of the *Queen*, and of course we can't sell them to just *anyone*. I'm afraid that we certainly couldn't sell *you* one, so—"

"What!" the fairy spluttered. "*No one* is better connected at Court than I! You *must* let me buy! And you do *not*, the Queen's majesty shall hear of this!"

"Well," said Barry doubtfully, "I don't know. . . ."

Barry and Morrig made a great team. They were soon surrounded by a swarm of customers. The demand became so great that they had no trouble talking Snailface into taking his spell off Barry as part of the price of purchase. In fact, Snailface became so enthusiastic about computers, that he bought *six* of them. Morrig had been right. Who cared what they used them for, so long as they *bought* them? That was *their* problem, wasn't it?

In the end, they only quit because they had run out of sales forms.

Morrig had a new profession, and Barry returned to Earth a happy man.

Soon Barry had (with a little help from Morrig, who was still hard at work, back in Faërie) broken all previous company sales records, many times over. Barry had convinced the company that the floodtide of new orders was really coming from heretofore untouched backwoods regions of West Virginia, North Carolina, and Tennessee, and everyone agreed that it was simply *amazing* how many hillbillies out there in the Ozarks had suddenly decided that they wanted home-computer systems. Business was booming. So, when, months later, the company opened a new branch office with great pomp and ceremony, Barry was there, in a place of honor.

The sales staff stood respectfully watching as the company president himself sat down to try out one of the gleaming new terminals. The president had started the company out of his basement when home computers were new, and he was only a college dropout from Silicon Valley, and he was still proud of his programming skills.

But as the president punched figures into the keyboard, long, curling, purple moose antlers began to sprout from the top of his head.

The sales staff stood frozen in silent horror. Barry gasped; then, recovering swiftly, he reached over the president's shoulder to hit the cancel key. The purple moose horns disappeared.

The Old Man looked up, puzzled. "Is anything wrong?"

"Only a glitch, sir," Barry said smoothly. But his hand was trembling.

He was afraid that there were going to be more such glitches.

The way sales were booming—a *lot* more.

Evidently, the fairyfolk had finally figured out what computers were *really* for. And Barry suddenly seemed to hear, far back in his head, the silvery peals of malicious elven laughter.

It was a *two*-way system, afterall. . . .

Many of us have on occasion had a strong desire to once again possess something we owned in our childhood—something we had lost or traded away. Fulfilling such a desire would appear to be almost impossible, unless that object had been traded to someone who never got rid of anything. Then all we'd have to do would be to locate our childhood acquaintance.

MY ROSE AND MY GLOVE

By Harvey Jacobs

James Huberman began collecting things in his earliest youth. He had an incredible sense of the future. When we were no more than nine or ten, he told me, "Someday my childhood will be worth a fortune. My father's toys already sell in antique shops for tremendous prices. My mother's old clothes are collector's items. I'm not going to make the mistake they made."

Of course, Huberman was a strange lad and the butt of many terrible jokes. When there was nothing else to do, it became the fashion to torture him in small ways. Once he was painted orange. Once an attempt was made to tattoo a picture of Hitler on his ass. Once his parakeet was held for a ransom of five hero sandwiches. Once he was locked in the school toilet over Washington's Birthday while the police searched for his body. Once a suicide note was "signed" by him and left, along with his underwear and raincoat, near a raging river. Huberman made the most of those woeful experiences. He not only pledged to remember his assassins, he actually preserved mementos. He saved what was left of the orange paint, he sat for hours on a warm cloth to transfer Hitler's picture and succeeded in creating a kind of Nazi Shroud of Turin, and when the parakeet died of exposure he stuffed it himself. While he was locked in the school toilet, he copied and filed the graffiti he found on the walls. The suicide note, the underwear, the raincoat, and a specimen from the river, along with an article from the local paper denying the incident, became an exhibit in Huberman's own Museum of Indignities.

I was Huberman's only friend—at least, his only active nonenemy. I had a premonition about him. I was afraid of his vengeance. Don't ask me why.

After high school, we all went our separate ways. Unlike Huberman, I was not a collector of either things or people. I dropped my roots into hostile soil . . . the communications business. After a few years in public relations, I realized that the essence of communications was noncommunication. I started out writing clear prose and making direct statements on behalf of my clients. Then I changed my style in favor of obfuscation and made it big. I grew moderately rich.

From time to time, I revisited my hometown. I always asked about Huberman, but nobody seemed to know his fate. He had opened an antique shop, predictably, then sold it and moved away. It must have been difficult for Huberman to sell anything, if ever he did sell anything. In the yearbook, under Huberman's picture, the caption read, "He has one saving grace . . ." with *saving* in italics. Clever. I wrote that.

Things went well for me. One afternoon—it was in winter, a silver snow was falling over New York—I remembered my

Rosebud, a toy motorcycle given to me by an uncle now dead. I had sold it to Huberman, or exchanged it for a Howdy Doody ring. He got the better of the bargain. He always did. The ring was rusty. Now, twenty years later, at the top of my profession, I wanted my motorcycle. I wanted it. And I assumed that Huberman must still have it. Huberman kept his dandruff. But I did not know where Huberman was to be found.

My desire for the motorcycle became an obsession. I began checking information listings in cities I thought might appeal to Huberman. He would enjoy old cities suffering population loss with growing slum problems. As buildings crumbled, Huberman would be there snapping up parapets and door frames for pennies. As populations emigrated, Huberman would wait by the road to buy up their leavings. I found Huberman in a suburb of Cleveland, a small city named Wyet that once manufactured carbon paper. They still had a small plant that turned out the stuff—maybe one box a year—and the Japs were threatening even that company. When I heard about Wyet, I couldn't wait to call information. Sure enough, Huberman, James, was listed.

I dialed the number slowly, enjoying the anticipation. Huberman looked so funny painted orange, so serious stuffing his bird. A voice grunted on the telephone—conserving energy, not wasting it on *hello*. That was promising.

"I want my motorcycle back."

"It'll cost you," said Huberman, and it was James Huberman beyond any doubt.

"Huberman, how are you?" I said. "How the hell have you been?"

"How should I be?"

"What are you up to?"

"The same. You?"

"The same. Nothing has changed. So, it's good to talk to you."

"Ah. The motorcycle?"

"I really do want it. Ask me not why."

"Who asked?"

"Well, I'm not surprised that you still have it. Nor that you knew me by my opening remark."

"So what?"

"Just conversing, Huberman. Listen, I'll tell you what. I have a client in Cleveland. Usually I don't make house calls, not anymore, but maybe I'll come on out there to visit his plant, and while I'm there I can run over to Wyet. We can lift a glass and talk about days gone by."

"I don't know. I'm busy," Huberman said.

"Listen, *friend*," I said, "I'm quite anxious to see you."

"You are?"

"I most certainly am. And I'm equally serious about my motorcycle."

"I'll be glad to give you a price," Huberman said. "But it will reflect the market."

"Did I call for a bargain? You know the trouble I went to to find you?"

"Trouble?"

"Trouble. Incredible anguish. I've talked with information operators in forty states."

"Mmm. Come then."

It was arranged. I flew to Cleveland and met with my client. When business was done, I called Huberman and we made plans for our reunion.

Once I called a girl I knew at college some fifteen years after the fact. She agreed to meet for a drink. On the way to our meeting place, I became very nervous. I suddenly felt the presence of time as weight. She must have felt the same. When we finally met, there was a split-second taking of inventory—we both looked thicker and older. She said, "Anything new?" and I said, "Not really, you?" And she said, "Not really." Meeting Huberman was different. I had always felt superior to him; everybody did. My career had blossomed into a fat and desirable flower. Huberman was stuck in Wyet, Ohio, still the man with the broom following a parade, Chaplinesque but unfunny. His pratfalls hurt. The very pleasure of comparing Huberman's track record with my own flooded me with guilt. I would offer him a large sum of money for the toy motorcycle. It would be a blatant handout, a bribe to lower his accusing eyes.

Reaching his street had a Dantesque quality. Wyet, the carbon-paper capital of America, had no lush houses left. On the main street, mannequins in new clothes looked like bag ladies. The town had the feeling of an abandoned spiderweb. And that was the classy neighborhood. The farther I got from the glittering center of Wyet, the worse it got. The web was torn. I found Huberman's "house." Not a house. A gigantic warehouse, certainly a relic of the days when every secretary carbon-copied to a long list. No more.

Of course Huberman, James, would have a warehouse. He had outgrown drawers and closets by the time he was fifteen. The warehouse would be bulging, and Huberman would know where every item could be found. That was Huberman.

Inches from the door, I nearly turned back. But I pressed the buzzer. After a wait, I heard boxes moving, pots clanging, and the slow progress of a presence moving through impossible obstacles. Then the knob turned.

"Yes? Ah. So you did come."

There he was, much different from before, yet the same. Huberman seemed taller and much fatter, yet he had a short, thin appearance. If that sounds confusing, it is because the man emitted conflicting signals. He had a huge belly but a thin face. He had long legs, but crotch to head he reminded me of a golf ball. He wore shoes made for bad feet, striped gray pants that must have come from some executive's annual-meeting suit, a sweatshirt with a faded picture of the Beatles, and an Army fatigue cap. His face hung in space, a planet without promise. But his eyes glittered. He was actually glad to see me. I held out my hand. Huberman looked at it; then he grabbed it and pumped.

"Come in. How are you? I'll make tea."

"Not necessary, Huberman. I can't stay too long. I thought it would be nice to touch base. A lot of years under the bridge."

"Years and years. You look well. Are you doing well?"

"I make a living. And you've got quite a place here."

"Six floors."

The floor was a garden of used TVs, bicycles, sleds, washing machines, sofas, chairs, tables, whatever. Bare bulbs hanging from twisted wires lit the place. I saw a pile of newspapers and magazines and another pile of song sheets and comic books. The piles were immense, as high as pyramids. I sang, "Give me my rose and my glove . . ."

"Why are you singing that?"

"It's from a song called 'People Will Say We're in Love.' About a man who saves souvenirs of a developing romance. The girl attempts to warn him—"

"I know the song," Huberman said. "Oklahoma. Rogers and Hammerstein. I bought the costumes from the original production. I have the *Playbill*. And one of Hammerstein's shoes."

"I always thought that song should be your theme, Huberman."

"I'm not sure I follow you."

"Forget it. A bit of whimsy."

We began walking upstairs. It was like navigating to the center of a hive. The walls were hung with posters of former presidents and film stars. We had to climb over a hill of manual typewriters and through a tunnel of radios in wooden cabinets.

"Be careful," Huberman said.

"Aren't you worried about fire?" I said.

Huberman stopped and turned. His face was almost purple. "I'm very worried about fire," he said.

I winced. Of course. It was the kind of question that didn't need asking. Are you worried about cancer? What else would Huberman be worried about, if not fire? With his luck he must know that someday a spark from something or a lightning bolt would start a tiny flame that would grow and devour his spectacular hoard. Some prankster might throw a firecracker or cigarette. He *should* worry. Especially him.

On the third floor, Huberman kept his living quarters. In the center of his mounds and piles was a clear area that held a bed, a table, two chairs, a TV, a sink connected to rubber tubes that led into the darkness to some source of water, and a hot plate wired to one of the ceiling fixtures.

"Home is where you hang your heart," Huberman said. That was very frivolous for him, and I chuckled. He laughed back at me. Huberman turned on his hot plate and filled a kettle made of chipped porcelain. He gathered up five or six used tea bags that had dried into knots and put them into a brown bag. He put the bag in a drawer. Then he took a new bag from a Lipton's package. One bag. He kept sugar in a tin that once held marshmallows, and powdered milk in a jar.

"This is cozy," I said.

"It serves the purpose," he said.

I sat and waited while he made tea. The tea was brewed from the single bag in large mugs with pictures of the young Queen Elizabeth. Huberman gave me the mug he dipped first. *One saving grace . . .*

"So, Huberman, here we are," I said.

"Long time, no see," Huberman said.

"And you seem content."

"I am. Are you?"

"Reasonably. So tell me: Any wife? Any kiddies?"

"I'm thinking seriously about marriage," Huberman said. "I have a girlfriend."

"Congratulations," I said. "I was married for a time. No children, though. Tell me about your girlfriend."

"She's smart, and she's got tits."

"Listen, nowadays that's plenty."

"I know. She's rich. Her father was a doctor. He left her well fixed. She loves me."

"I'm really glad."

"Why?"

"Why? Because. On general principles."

"Thank you. But I'm not sure yet."

"Risk. That's what life is about, Huberman. Don't hesitate because she's a doctor's daughter, smart, rich, and with tits. I mean, just because you're in the junk business. It's an honorable profession."

"Junk business?"

"Whatever. Antiques. Collectibles."

"I am a curator," Huberman said deliberately. "I am building a museum of art and artifacts. I live among priceless and beautiful things."

"Oh. Right."

"You think this is a temple of crap?"

"I never said that."

"The temple of crap is outside."

"I get your point, Huberman."

"You came for your cycle. We traded fairly. I gave you a Howdy Doody ring."

"The ring was rusty. It broke."

"Risk. That's what life is about, eh?"

"Score one for you, Huberman. I had my eyes open. It's curious. I was sitting in my office one day, and I began to think about that motorcycle. That's weird."

"It begins that way."

"I realized how much I wanted it. I also realize I shouldn't be telling you. That's not how I usually bargain."

"You can't have the motorcycle. You have nothing to trade. No wife. No children. Nothing."

"I have cash, Huberman."

"Cash? Are you serious? Cash? Now tell me you have stock certificates and municipal bonds." Huberman roared. He spilled his tea and coughed. He was really having himself a good time.

"I don't get the joke," I said.

"Finish your cup of tea. Come with me," Huberman said.

I finished my tea and followed Huberman up two more flights. We went though a fire door to another landscape of "art and artifacts." There, sorting through yellowing dentures in an Ivory Soap carton, was a hunched little man.

"He's cataloging," Huberman said. "Do you recognize him?"

"Should I?"

"He onced painted me orange," Huberman said.

"Bill Vanderweil? The football player?"

"The very same."

"What's he doing here?"

"He wanted his skates. We'd done a fair trade. I gave him lollipops. He liked lollipops. He gave me his skates. Then he wanted his skates."

"Bill Vanderweil. He must have really wanted his skates," I said.

"He did. Very much. He works here now. Very reasonably. He's been an enormous help. Look over there."

In the shadows, I saw a slender woman wiping thick dust

off a grandfather clock. It stood among a graveyard of grand-father clocks. There were hundreds.

"Jinny Sue Ellenbogel," Huberman said.

"The majorette?"

"Remember how she twirled her baton? Wasn't it elevating?"

"Jinny Sue. I had such a crush on her."

"She traded her baton for a rhinestone brooch, the silly bitch. Then she wanted her baton. It took time, but she understood that she needed her baton. Now she's employed here. Nonunion, I might add. Her boyfriend, Lobster Hallmark, killed my parakeet. He exposed it to the elements."

"Lobster Hallmark. The one with the convertible."

"The convertible is upstairs. He sits in it on his day off. He shifts the gears. I don't allow him to blow the horn except on Christmas."

"Listen, Huberman," I said, "I'm prepared to offer you twenty-five dollars for my motorcycle, but that's it."

"No deal. Come back when you're ready to do business."

"Thirty dollars. Not a penny more. I can live without the motorcycle. The driver's head is loose. The rear wheel is bent. Thirty is my final offer."

"Of course it is," Huberman said. "Would you like more tea? Some time to think?"

"No more tea," I said. "I drink Earl Grey. Not Lipton's."

"I'm sorry," Huberman said.

On the way down, we passed several children carrying boxes up the stairs Their faces looked familiar. But I didn't ask about their parents.

"Tell me something," Huberman said on the bottom landing. "What do you feel about the neutron bomb?"

"What do I feel? I hate it. How can you feel about a bomb that saves property and kills people?"

"Affectionate," said Huberman. "Let's lay it on the line.

You're in public relations. The neutron bomb is getting a lot of god-awful publicity. The other side of the story should be told.''

"What other side of the story?"

"The good side. The positive side. The life of objects. Objects are a life form, you know. A campaign could be mounted. People believe that plants have feelings, even consciousness. They need to be educated about things."

"You want me to mount a campaign that celebrates the neutron bomb?"

"We were friends, after a fashion. You never stomped on me. If you agree to the campaign, I'll give you your motorcycle. If not . . . well, what are friends for?"

"Never," I said. "Besides, my best client is a coal company with no involvement in nukes. How do you think they would feel if my organization—"

"The ball is in your court."

"Sixty dollars," I said. "The new tax laws exempt collectibles from Individual Retirement Accounts and Keogh Plans. Remember that, Huberman."

"Please consider," Huberman said, "the realities. There is every chance that life on earth will be destroyed or rendered senseless. Even if there is no war, a mechanized world with consequent leisure will destroy the population. Look what's happened to love. It's become sensation, hardly competitive with video games. And take video games. The most popular one features the perfect cannibal. It devours everything. Winning is consuming. But winning is losing. Because everything becomes nothing. So they come to me. And even when people cease to come for their batons, skates, convertibles— yes, motorcycles—*others* will come. What will *they* find? What I have collected and collated. This building is a time capsule. The only real history. Books lie. Film and tape can be edited. But my objects *are*. When *they* come here they will fondle real *things:* ratty mattresses, stained pillows, cups with rings at the bottom—glorious things. And *they* will play with my toys. *They* will ask themselves about the man who stocked this lode. His birthday will become a holiday."

"Like Washington. Huberman, you've never forgotten that incident in the toilet."

"If you want your motorcycle, it's going to cost you, my friend. But because you were my friend, I'm willing to let you share in this splendid adventure. A modest campaign, possibly some television, some print, a speech here and there. I'm not asking for billboards. Just explain that the shadow burned on a wall is as important as the shadow's father or mother. You know. Neutrons are your friends. Like that. All I want is equal time."

"Huberman, you're mad, but I want that motorcycle. One hundred dollars."

"Done."

"You'll take it?"

"Of course. I've got to eat. I've got to pay the electric bill. I'm considering marriage. CDs. I can't survive on ideals. Cash. No checks. No charge cards. No receipt. I'll get your motorcycle. I've already packed it. Gift wrapped."

Huberman got me the package. I gave him five tens and a fifty.

"Would you have taken thirty?" I said

"Who knows? Tell me, how's the old town? Is that little park still there, the one where they stripped me and tried to tattoo Hitler on my ass? Lord, those were gay times. But you can't go home again."

"The park is gone," I said. "It's a shopping center."

I drove to Cleveland and flew back to New York. I put the motorcycle on a shelf in my office. It looked marvelous there. I was glad to have it back. I think I would have done anything to get it.

The late Clark Ashton Smith was one of the prime fanta-
sists of his time. Together with Robert E. Howard and
H.P. Lovecraft he was one of the big three of the old
Weird Tales magazine. The following posthumous tale is
very different, however, from the exotic stories for which
he is best known. This story about an alcoholic and his
very unusual d.t.'s was apparently intended for Unknown
Worlds. Whether it was ever submitted to that magazine
is not known.

STRANGE SHADOWS

Clark Ashton Smith

Downing his thirteenth dry martini, Gaylord Jones drew a
complacent sigh and regarded the barroom floor with grave
attention. He was drunk. He knew that he was drunk. With
superb lucidity, he calculated the exact degree of his inebriation.

A great white light was pivoted in his brain. He could turn
this light, instantly, on the most obscure corners of the noth-
ingness called life. At last he was able to appreciate the
absurd logic of the cosmos. It was all very simple. Nothing
mattered in the least.

It was all very simple, and nothing mattered as long as one
could keep himself sufficiently pickled. Ah, that was the
problem. Reflecting long and deeply, Jones decided that just

one more martini would help to maintain his intoxication at the right stage.

He had, however, consumed three drinks in a row at this particular bar. The martinis were well mixed. The bartender's manners were unexceptionable. But Jones felt that he should not play any favorites when it came to barrooms. There were so many others that deserved his patronage. In fact, there was one just around the corner on his homeward route.

"I wonder often what the vintners buy one-half so precious as the stuff they sell," he quoted, muttering to himself, as he descended carefully from his seat.

Jones prided himself on knowing his capacity. So far, he had never had the misfortune to overestimate it. He could carry one, two, three, even four more drinks if necessary, without deviating from the proverbial chalk line. Every night, for at least a month past, he had collected a full cargo at various alcoholic ports between his office and hotel. The stuff never hurt him. He had never been known to stagger or even wobble at any point along the route. His morning headaches, if any, were light and fleeting.

He stood up and looked at himself in the mirror behind the bar. Yes, he could hold his liquor. No casual observer would be able to tell that he had had three martinis, let alone thirteen. His eyes were clear, his face no redder or paler than usual. He adjusted his tie neatly, bade the bartender a crisp goodnight, and started toward the door.

Of course, his locomotor faculties were under perfect control. He knew that they would not fail him as long as he observed due caution and didn't move too precipitately. His senses had never played him tricks either. But, as he crossed the long room, Jones received a curious impression. The room was empty except for a few patrons at the bar or remote tables. Yet once, twice, thrice, it seemed to him that he had trodden on someone's heels. It was a baffling and disconcerting sensation, since, visibly, no one was in front of him or even near at hand. With some effort, each time, he checked himself from stumbling.

Jones went on, feeling slightly disturbed and annoyed. Again, as he approached the door, the mysterious sensation was repeated. It was as if his toes had collided with the heel of some stranger who preceded him down the room. This time, Jones nearly fell on his face before he could recover himself.

"Who the hell—" he started to mumble. But, as before, there was no one, nothing, against whom or which he could have tripped. Looking down, he could see only his own shadow, now stretching doorward in the light cast by the electric chandeliers.

Jones stood peering at the shadow with a vague but growing puzzlement. It was a funny sort of shadow, he thought. There must be something queer about the lights in that barroom. It didn't look like his own shadow, or, in fact, the shadow of any human being. He wasn't squeamish. He had never been a stickler for aesthetic propriety or any kind of propriety. But he felt a sense of actual shock when he began to consider the various things that were wrong with the shadow's outline.

Though he himself was correctly attired, there was no suggestion that the caster of the shadow wore either clothing, hat, or shoes. Indeed, it hardly seemed to indicate any sort of creature that would wear clothing.

Jones thought of the gargoyles of Notre Dame. He thought of antique satyrs. He thought of goats and swine. The shadow was gargoylish, it was satyr-like. It was goatish and porcine—it was even worse. It was the adumbration of some shambling, obscene, pot-bellied monster, trying to stand upright like a man on its hind legs, and holding its forelegs a little away from the body on each hand.

Its edges were hairy like the silhouette of an ape. Appendages that were huge ears or horns rose above its swollen head. The rear shanks were bent at a bestial angle. Something like a tail depended between them. The four feet gave the appearance of hooves. The two lifted feet were visibly cloven.

Apart from these deformities of outline, the shadow possessed an unnatural thick blackness. It was like a pool of tar. Sometimes it seemed to swell upward from the floor, to take on a third dimension.

Sobriety had almost returned to Jones. But now the thirteen cumulative martinis resumed their work. By one of those sudden shifts of a drunkard's mood, he began to forget his feelings of shock and perplexity. The shadow's very grotesquery began to amuse him.

"Must be another guy's shadow," he chuckled. "But what a guy!"

He stepped forward cautiously, holding out his right arm at a dead level and parting all the fingers of his right hand. The shadow moved with him. Its right fore-member rose and protruded at the angle of his arm. But still there was only the shadow of a cloven hoof where the shadows of five outspread fingers should have registered.

Jones shook his head bewilderedly. Maybe it was the lights, after all. There must be some explanation.

He stepped backward, maintaining a balance that had become slightly precarious. This time, the shadow did not follow his change of position. It lay as before, its hind hooves separated from his own nattily shod feet by an interval of light.

Jones felt a confused outrage. Here was a problem that defied the blazing white logic of alcohol. What could one make of a shadow that not only failed to reproduce its owner's periphery, but refused to follow all his movements?

To make matters worse, he saw that the shadow had now

begun to display an activity of its own. Lurching and weaving while he stood stock still, it danced abominably from side to side on the floor, like the shadow of a drunken satyr. It capered and cavorted. It made vile gestures with its forelegs.

At this moment a patrolman, parched, no doubt, from his long evening vigil, entered the barroom. He was formidably tall and broad. Giving Jones the tail of a truculent eye, he passed on toward the bar without seeming to notice the outrageous behavior of Jones' errant shadow.

Behind the patrolman's bulk there trailed a shadow like that of some diminutive monkey. It appeared to cower at his heels. It seemed to scamper and scuttle behind the arrogant pomp of his advance. It was incredibly thin, wizened, puny-looking.

Jones rubbed his eyes. Here, perhaps, was something to reassure him. If his own shadow had gone screwy, the policeman's was equally haywire.

This conclusion was instantly confirmed. The shadow that, by courtesy, Jones called his own, had ceased its indecorous caperings. It wheeled about suddenly and ran past him as if following the officer. At the same time the policeman's monkeylike shadow detached itself from its owner's heels and fled swiftly toward a remote corner of the room. Jones' shadow pursued it in great, goatish leaps, with gesticulations of obscene anger and menace. The officer, quite oblivious of his loss, continued barward. Jones heard him order a beer.

Jones decided that he had lingered all too long in that particular drinking-place. Matters had grown slightly embarrassing, not to say compromising. Shadow or no shadow, he would speed his progress to the next bar. After two or three additional martinis, he could manage well enough without a shadow. Good riddance, anyway. Let the policeman keep the damned thing in order if he could.

The street outside was well lighted but almost empty of

pedestrians. With a sense of urgency and compulsion, Jones hurried to the saloon around the corner. He avoided looking down at the pavement as he went.

Ordering three martinis, he drank them down as fast as the bartender could mix and pour them. The result was all that he had hoped for. His feeling of cosmic detachment and independence returned to him. What was a shadow, anyway? The one cast by the bartender's hand and arm, moving over the bar, was not that of a normal human limb; but Jones refused to consider it. He could take his shadows or leave them.

He took three more drinks. His sense of alcoholic caution told him that it was now curfew time. Promptly, though a little unsteadily, he began the last lap of his homeward journey.

Somewhere on the way, he perceived rather vaguely that his shadow had rejoined him. It was more monstrous than ever under the streetlamps—more obscene and unnatural. Then, suddenly, there were *two* shadows. This, however, was not surprising, since he had begun to see telephone posts, lights, cars, hydrants, people, and other objects along his route all in duplicate.

He awoke the next morning with a dull headache and a confused impression that the scheme of things had somehow gone wrong. Just how or why it had gone wrong he could not remember at first. But he had had one or two drinks too many and had fallen asleep in his clothes on top of the bedding.

Groaning, he pulled himself from the bed and stood up groggily with his back to the bright sunlight that streamed in through his apartment windows. It seemed that something sprang with him as he rose—a black, solid silhouette that stood erect for an instant in the air. Horribly startled, he saw the thing resolve itself into a shadow stretching across the floor. It was the gargoylish, goatish, satyrish, porcine shadow of the previous night. It was something that neither sunlight nor lamplight, by any trick or distortion, could conceivably have wrought from Jones' head, limbs and body. In the bright glare, it was blacker, grosser, more hirsute than before. Curiously, it was less elongated than a shadow should have been in the full early light.

It was like some foul incubus of legend—a separate entity that companioned him in place of his rightful shadow.

Jones felt thoroughly frightened. Sober, with the profound, excessive sobriety of the morning after, he remembered all the strange phenomena of the past evening. He did not believe in the supernatural. Plainly, he had become the victim of a set of bizarre hallucinations, confined to one subject. Otherwise, his sensory perceptions were quite normal. Perhaps, without realizing it, he had been drinking too much and had developed a new kind of delirium tremens. He knew that alcoholism didn't always result in the seeing of mauve elephants and cerise reptiles.

Or maybe it was something else. There were all sorts of obscure mental diseases, symptomized by aberrant or deluded sense-perceptions. He knew that the possibilities were infinitely terrifying.

Averting his eyes from the shadow, he fled to his bathroom, where there was no direct sunlight. Even here he had the sensation of being accompanied. Again, as in the barroom, he seemed to stumble over the heels of some unseen person who had preceded him.

With nightmare difficulty he concentrated on the tasks of washing and shaving himself. A dreadful gulf had opened at his feet amid the solid reality of things.

A clock struck somewhere in the apartment house, and Jones realized that he had overslept and must hurry to his office. There was no time for breakfast, even if he had not lacked the appetite.

Dogged by his weirdly altered shadow, he went out on the

crowded street in the clear April morning. Embarrassment mingled with his sense of horror. It seemed that everyone must notice that black changeling that followed him like a wizard's familiar.

However, the early throng, hurrying intently to the day's work or pleasure, paid no more attention to Jones and his shadow than on any other morning. It was more and more obvious that he suffered from some sort of visual hallucination: for the people about him were apparently quite untroubled by the oddities which he perceived in their shadows as well as in his own.

Studying these shadows with a morbid fascination as they passed by on the walls and pavements, Jones well-nigh forgot the dark miscreation at his own heels. It was like looking at the shadows of some hellish menagerie. Among them all, there was none that corresponded to the visible physique of its owner. And now and then some person went by, like the legendary vampire, without appearing to cast a shadow at all.

Demure young girls were attended by adumbrations that might have been those of lascivious she-apes or coquetting sphinxes. A benign priest was followed by the shadow of some murderous devil. A rich and popular society matron was paired with the four-legged shadow of a humpbacked cow. Shadows like those of hogs and hyenas trotted behind respectable bankers and aldermen.

Jones noted that the shadows cast by inorganic objects, such as trees and buildings, had not shared in the change. But the shadows of animals bore as little likeness to their casters as those of men. Oddly, those of dogs and horses were often quasi-human, seeming to indicate a rise rather than a degradation in the scale of being.

Sometimes, as on the evening before, Jones witnessed the incredible behavior of shadows that moved and acted with complete detachment from their owners. He saw pantomimes that were grotesque, ludicrous, often indecent.

It was in the mental state of a man bewitched that he reached the office of his young but thriving insurance business. Miss Owens, the rather mature typist, was already settled at her machine. She raised her well-plucked eyebrows at his lateness.

Jones noted mechanically that his business partner, Caleb Johnson, was even later than himself. A moment afterwards, Johnson entered. He was heavy-set, darkly florid, older than Jones. As usual, he looked like the aftermath of a season of misspent nights. The rings under his eyes were strongly marked as those of a raccoon's tail. Miss Owens did not appear to notice his entrance, but bent closer above her machine.

Johnson grunted by way of greeting. It was a one-syllable, Anglo-Saxon grunt. He went to his desk, which was opposite Miss Owens'. The office settled to its daily routine.

Jones, trying to control his whirling wits and fix them on his work, was thankful for the diffused light at that hour. Somehow, he succeeded in applying himself to a pile of letters, and even dictated a few replies. Several clients came in. There were some new applicants for fire and accident insurance. It reassured Jones a little, to find that he could talk and answer questions without betraying the incoherence of his thoughts.

Part of the morning went by. At times the mad mystery that troubled him receded to the margin of consciousness. It was too unreal, too much like the phantasms of dreams. But he would go easy on drinking in the future. No doubt the hallucinations would wear off when he had freed his system from any residue of alcohol. Perhaps his nerves were already righting themselves and he wouldn't see any more crazy shadows.

At that moment he happened to look over toward Johnson and Miss Owens. The rays of the sun in its transit had now entered the broad plate-glass window, spreading obliquely across them both and casting their shadows on the floor.

Jones, who was no prude, almost blushed at the outlines formed by Miss Owens' shadow. It showed a figure that was not only outrageously unclothed but betrayed proclivities more suitable to a witches' Sabbat than a modern business office. It moved forward in an unseemly fashion while Miss Owens remained seated. It met the shadow cast by Johnson . . . which, without going into detail, was hardly that of a respectable business man. . . .

Miss Owens, looking up from her Remington, intercepted Jones' eye. His expression seemed to startle her. A natural flush deepened her brunette rouge.

"Is anything wrong, Mr. Jones?" she queried.

Johnson also looked up from the account book in which he was marking entries. He too appeared startled. His heavy-lidded eyes became speculative.

"Nothing is wrong, as far as I know," said Jones, shame-facedly, averting his eyes from the shadows. He had begun to wonder about something. Johnson was a married man with two half-grown children. But there had been hints. . . . More than once, Jones had met him with Miss Owens after business hours. Neither of them had seemed particularly pleased by such meetings. Of course, it wasn't Jones' affair what they did. He was not interested. What did interest him now was the behavior of the shadows. After all, was there at times some hidden relevance, some bearing upon reality, in the phenomena that he had regarded as baseless hallucinations? The thought was far from pleasant in one sense. But he decided to keep his eyes and his mind open.

*   *   *

Jones had lunched with more semblance of appetite than he had believed possible. The day drew on toward five o'clock. The lowering sun filled a westward window with its yellow blaze. Johnson stood up to trim and light a cigar. His strong black shadow was flung on the gold-lit door of the company's big iron safe in the corner beyond.

The shadow, Jones noted, was not engaged in the same action as its owner. There was nothing like the shadow of a cigar in its outthrust hand. The black fingers seemed trying to manipulate the dial on the safe's door. They moved deftly, spelling out the combination that opened the safe. Then they made the movement of fingers that draw back a heavy hinged object. The shadow moved forward, stooping and partly disappearing. It returned and stood errect. Its fingers carried something. The shadow of the other hand became visible. Jones realized, with a sort of startlement, that Johnson's shadow was counting a roll of bills. The roll was apparently thrust into its pocket, and the shadow went through the pantomime of closing the safe.

All this had set Jones to thinking again. He had heard, vaguely, that Johnson gambled—either on stocks or horses, he couldn't remember which. And Johnson was the firm's bookkeeper. Jones had never paid attention to the bookkeeping, apart from noting cursorily that the accounts always seemed to balance.

Was it possible that Johnson had been using, or meant to use, the firm's money for irregular purposes? Large sums were often kept in the safe. Offhand, Jones thought that there must be more than a thousand dollars on hand at present.

Oh, well, maybe it was preferable to think that excess cocktails had endowed him with a new brand of heeby-jeebies. Maybe a doctor could tell him something. He had never cared especially for doctors: their imaginations, if any, seemed to run toward the sadistic and macabre. But perhaps one of them could persuade him that the shadow pantomime he had just witnessed was merely a manifestation of deranged nerves. It would be better than believing that Johnson was a possible embezzler.

That evening he visited a doctor instead of making the usual round of barrooms.

The doctor frowned very learnedly as Jones described his strange affliction. He took Jones' pulse and temperature, tested his knee-jerk and other reflexes, flashed a light into his eyes, looked at his tongue.

"You haven't any fever, and there's no sign of d.t.," he reassured finally. "I don't think you're likely to go insane—at least not for some time. Probably it's your eyes. You'd better see a good oculist tomorrow. In the meantime I'll prescribe a sedative for your nervousness. Of course you ought to ease up on liquor—maybe the alcohol is affecting your eyesight."

Jones hardly heard the doctor's advice. He had been studying the doctor's shadow, flung across an expensive rug by a tall and powerful floor-lamp. It was the least human and most unpleasant of all the shadows he had yet seen. It had the contours and the posture of a ghoul stooping over ripe carrion.

After leaving the doctor's office, Jones remembered that he had a fiancee. He had not seen her for a week. She did not approve of martinis—at least not in such quantities as Jones had been collecting nightly for the past month. Luckily—unless he collected them in her company—she was unable to tell whether he had two drinks or a dozen. He was very fond of Marcia. Her quaint ideas about temperance weren't too much of a drawback. And anyway he was going to be temperate himself till he got rid of the shadows. It would be something to tell Marcia.

On second thought he decided to leave out the shadow part. She *would* think he had the heeby-jeebies.

Marcia Dorer was a tall blonde, slender almost to thinness. She gave Jones a brief kiss. Sometimes her kisses made him feel slightly refrigerated. This was one of the times.

"Well, where have you been keeping yourself?" she asked. There was a sub-acid undertone in her soprano. "In front of all the bars in town, I suppose?"

"Not today," said Jones gravely. "I haven't had a drink since last night. In fact, I have decided to quit drinking."

"Oh, I'm glad," she cooed, "if you really mean it. I know liquor can't be good for you—at least, not so much of it. They say it does things to your insides."

She pecked him again, lightly, between cheek and lips. Just at that moment Jones thought to look at their shadows on the parlor wall. What would Marcia's shadow be like?

In spite of the queer phenomena he had already seen, Jones was unpleasantly surprised, even shocked. He hardly knew what he had expected; but certainly it wasn't anything like this.

To begin with, there were *three* shadows on the wall. One was Jones', porcine, satyrlike as usual. In spite of his physical proximity to Marcia, it stood far apart from hers.

Marcia's shadow he could not clearly distinguish from the third one, since, with its back turned to Jones', it was united with the other in a close embrace. It resembled Marcia only in being the shadow of a female. The other shadow was plainly male. It lifted a grossly swollen, bearded profile above the head of its companion. It was not a refined-looking shadow. Neither was Marcia's.

Marcia had never embraced him like that, thought Jones. He felt disgusted; but after all he couldn't be jealous of an unidentified shadow.

Somehow, it was not a very successful evening. Jones

turned his eyes away from the wall and refrained from looking at it again. But he could not forget the shadows. Marcia
chattered without seeming to notice his preoccupation; but
there was something perfunctory in her chatter, as if she too
were preoccupied.

"I guess you'd better go, darling," she said at last. "Do
you mind? I didn't sleep well, and I'm tired tonight."

Jones looked at his wristwatch. It was only twenty minutes
past nine.

"Oh, all right," he assented, feeling a vague relief. He
kissed her and went out, seeing with the tail of his eye that
the third shadow was still in the room. It was still on the
parlor wall, with Marcia's shadow in its arms.

Halfway down the block, beside a lamp post, Jones passed
Bertie Filmore. The two nodded. They knew and liked each
other very slightly. Jones peered down at Filmore's shadow
as he went by. Filmore was a floorwalker in a department
store—a slim, sleek youth who neither drank, smoked nor
indulged in any known vice. He attended the Methodist church
every Sunday morning and Wednesday evening. Jones felt a
profane and cynical curiosity as to what his shadow would
look like.

The adumbration that he saw was shortened by the nearby
lamp. But its profile was unmistakably the gross, bearded
profile of the third shadow on Marcia's wall! It bore no
resemblance to Filmore.

"What the hell!" thought Jones, very disagreeably startled. "Is there something in this?"

He slackened his pace and glanced back at Filmore's reced-
ing figure. Filmore sauntered on as if out for an airing,
without special objective, and did not turn to look back at
Jones. He went in at the entrance of Marcia's home.

"So that's why she wanted me to leave early," Jones
mused. It was plain to him now . . . plain as the clinching

shadows. Marcia had expected Filmore. The shadows weren't all Katzenjammer, not by a jugful.

His pride was hurt. He had known that Marcia was acquainted with the fellow. But it was a shock to think that Filmore had displaced him in her affections. In Jones' estimation, the fellow was a cross between a Sunday School teacher and a tailor's dummy. No color or character to him.

Chewing the cud of his bitterness, Jones hesitated at several barroom doors. Perhaps he would see worse shadows if he killed another row of martinis. Or . . . maybe he wouldn't. What the hell. . . .

He went into the next bar without hesitating.

The morning brought him a headache worthy of the bender to which twenty—or was it twenty-one—more or less expert mixologists had contributed.

He reached his office an hour behind time. Surprisingly, Miss Owens, who had always been punctual, was not in evidence. Less surprisingly, Johnson was not there either. He often came late.

Jones was in no mood for work. He felt as if all the town clocks were striking twelve in his head. Moreover, he had a heart which, if not broken, was deeply cracked. And there was still the nerve-wracking problem of those strangely distorted and often misplaced shadows.

He kept seeing in his mind the shadows on Marcia's wall. They nauseated him . . . or perhaps his stomach was slightly upset from more than the due quota of martinis. Then, as many minutes went by and neither Miss Owens nor Johnson appeared, he recalled the queer shadow-play in his office on the previous afternoon. Why in hell hadn't he thought of that before? Perhaps—

His unsteady fingers spun the combination of the safe, drew back the door. Cash, negotiable bonds, a few checks that had come in too late for banking—all were gone. Johnson must have returned to the office that night. Or perhaps he had cleaned out the safe before leaving in the late afternoon. Both he and Miss Owens had stayed after Jones' departure. They often did that, and Jones hadn't thought much about it since both were busy with unfinished work.

Jones felt paralyzed. One thing was clear, however: Johnson's shadow had forewarned him with its pantomime of opening the safe, removing and counting money. It had betrayed its owner's intention before-hand. If he had watched and waited, Jones could no doubt have caught his partner in the act. But he had felt so doubtful about the meaning of the shadows, and his main thought when he left the office had been to see a doctor. Later, the discovery of Marcia's deceit had upset him, made him forget all else.

The telephone broke into his reflections with its jangling. A shrill female voice questioned him hysterically. It was Mrs. Johnson. "Is Caleb there? Have you seen Caleb?"

"No I haven't seen him since yesterday."

"Oh, I'm so worried, Mr. Jones. Caleb didn't come home last night but phoned that he was working very late at the office. Said he might not get in till after midnight. He hadn't come in when I fell asleep; and he wasn't here this morning. I've been trying to get the office for the past hour."

"I was late myself," said Jones. "I'll tell Johnson to call you when he comes. Maybe he had to go out of town suddenly." He did not like the task of telling Mrs. Johnson that her husband had embezzled the firm's cash and had probably eloped with the typist.

"I'm going to call the police," shrilled Mrs. Johnson. "Something dreadful must have happened to Caleb."

Jones kept remembering that other shadow-scene in his office which had made him almost blush. More as a matter of form than anything else, he rang up the apartment house at which Miss Owens roomed. She had returned there as usual the previous evening but had left immediately with a valise, saying that she was called away by the sudden death of an aunt and would not be back for several days.

Well, that was that. Jones had lost a good typist, together with more cash than he could afford to lose. As to Johnson— well, the fellow had been no great asset as a partner. Jones, who had no head for figures, had been glad to delegate the book keeping to him. But he could have hired a good accountant at far less expense.

There was nothing to do but put the matter in the hands of the police. Jones had reached again for the receiver, when the mailman entered, bringing several letters and a tiny registered package.

The package was addressed to Jones in Marcia's neat and somewhat prim handwriting. One of the letters bore the same hand. Jones signed for the package and broke the letter open as soon as the mailman had gone. It read:

Dear Gaylord:

I am returning your ring. I have felt for some time past that I am not the right girl to make you happy. Another man, of whom I am very fond, wishes to marry me. I hope you will find someone better suited to you than I should be.

Always yours,
Marcia

Jones put the little package aside without opening it. His thoughts were bitter. Marcia must have written to him and mailed the package early that morning. Filmore, of course, was the other man. Probably he had proposed to her the night before, after Jones had passed him on the street.

Jones could definitely add a sweetheart to his other losses. And he had gained, it seemed, a peculiar gift for seeing shadows that did not correspond to their owners' physical outlines . . . which did not always duplicate their movements . . . shadows that were sometimes revelatory of hidden intentions, prophetic of future actions.

It seemed, then, that he possessed a sort of clairvoyance. But he had never believed in such things. What good was it doing him anyway?

After he had phoned the police about Johnson, he would call it a day and gather enough drinks to dissolve the very substance of reality into a shadow.

In this day of hair styling salons et al, finding a good old-fashioned barber shop, especially one that does more than just cut hair, isn't too easy. Losing it once found would be more than just a little disconcerting.

A LITTLE TWO-CHAIR BARBER SHOP ON PHILLIPS STREET

Donald R. Burleson

It doesn't take any new barber of mine long to figure out that while I'm getting a haircut I would rather just sit in the chair and drowse than talk about sports or politics or the weather. I don't even read a magazine. It's the only time I feel completely released from responsibility, completely pampered and taken care of. I close my eyes and let the buzzing of the clippers and the snipping of the scissors lull me away to the private caverns of sleep.

Thus it was that I sat dreaming away on a recent Saturday afternoon, barely aware of the squawking of the inevitable talcum-powder-dusted radio on the shelf below the mirror, or of the hearty conversation going on at the other chair about some football game, or of the occasional rumble of traffic going by just outside the open door. It was a little two-chair shop on Phillips Street, and I had never noticed it before—mainly, I guess, because I almost never chanced to come down Phillips Street at all. The street was an obscure little lane just one block long that began and ended with nondescript smoke-blackened brick frontage punctuated erratically with graffiti, outdated posters, and hopeless-looking "For Lease" signs. Wedged between more lively thoroughfares, it was the sort of street that you could walk down with a mind full of thoughts and scarcely even notice.

That afternoon I had come there to look into a little second-hand bookshop, listed in the phone book, that I somehow hadn't gotten around to visiting. I had found it readily enough—one of those little hole-in-the-wall places with battered bins of cheap, ragged, volumes lining the sidewalk in front, and the promise of dusty labyrinths of shelves within. But I had also spotted the barber shop next door and had decided to give that a try first.

The barber nearest the door was an old man, a pot-bellied chap with a dark complexion and great shock of white hair that apparently hadn't known the attentions of a member of his own profession for quite some time. When I entered, he snicked his scissors smartly in the air over his customer's head and nodded, eyeing me, I thought, a little oddly as I sat down to wait. In any case, the man seemed well disposed, once I was finally in the chair, to let me drowse the way I like to do. Soon I was warmly ensconced in the cozy privacy and carefree flow of my thoughts.

I think crazy things sometimes while I'm getting a haircut; I mean *really* crazy. You could be put away someplace for thinking the sorts of things that run through my head on the inside while the barber's instruments are humming and nibbling away at the outside. Sometimes I'm worlds apart from the everyday talk and activity going on around me. And on that particular Saturday afternoon, while the other customer, a high school kid, talked loudly about some spectacular touchdown, with the usual assortment of waiting customers chiming in from the chairs along the wall, where they browsed their well-thumbed girlie magazines, I was mentally far away, in vastly different fields, and smugly glad that nobody could know what I was thinking.

I was indulging, in fact, in my favorite barber-chair fantasy: imagining that the barber was a witch doctor or medicine man who danced about me, ministering to my needs. I know how strange that must sound, but barbers in olden times did often double as surgeons; they even used to bleed patients. (It's said that the traditional red and white stripes on the barber pole may derive from the rolls of white towels streaked red in this process.) And besides, I happened to be feeling rather poorly that day and was in the mood to be pampered. I had recently been diagnosed as suffering from high blood pressure; my doctor had declared salt to be a no-no and regular exercise a must, though this regimen hadn't yet seemed to help. So maybe it wasn't so insane a fantasy after all.

As the barber hummed a formless tune between remarks about the football game, I imagined him intoning some ancestral ritual chant that ululated eerily on the night wind, beneath a black jungle sky wreathed with gnarled trees and fragmented by dark curls of smoke that rose from a crackling native fire. As the barber's electric clippers hummed beside my head, I thought of great green buzzing insects that were part of the healing ceremony. Somewhere in the clearing, within the circle of firelight, an ancient and wizened woman, her face wrinkled like the over-folded visage of a lizard, would be chewing these pungent-smelling insects in a nearly toothless mouth that, at other times, spoke a timeless, weirdly inflected, and unimaginable language.

The buzzing clippers gave way to the snipping of scissors

at the top of my head, and my beguiled fancy transmuted them into great gourd-rattlers which the venerated witch doctor shook and brandished vigorously as he pranced, hideously painted and masked, around my receptive form, he himself entranced by the ageless and incomprehensible chant that he was mouthing. Every muscle in my body relaxed utterly as I gave myself over to the care of this undulating shaman and his incantatory power over the nature-spirits. My eyes remained closed in reverie; I was a docile and willing patient.

The nearby conversation about football gradually grew muffled and oddly distorted, and soon I imagined that the speaking voices were in another language. Well, I thought, that couldn't be all that strange, in a neighborhood full of Poles and Italians and Greeks and Canadian French, though why they had suddenly abandoned English I couldn't understand—maybe through some clannish desire to exchange remarks that they didn't want me, an outsider, to be privy to. But it was no language that I could even identify.

I felt awkward and out of place, and kept my eyes closed. To my surprise, one of the speakers in this unaccountable exchange was my barber, who increasingly seemed to dominate the scene, his voice rising little by little to a kind of chant.

The barber chair now felt peculiarly scratchy and hard, and all of a sudden I realized that I seemed to be sitting in it crosslegged. Good God—had I unconsciously drawn my legs up into the chair? What would people think if they noticed it? Maybe they already had. With a start of embarrassment, I flicked open my eyes.

I was indeed sitting crosslegged—but on a thatched mat on the ground near a roaring fire that sent black billows of smoke spiraling up over the great overhanging trees and into the night sky. I was nude; I could feel the warmth from the fire on my body and face, and my head seemed to be smeared

with some oily substance that smelled like mint. Around me
in great prancing circles gyrated a grotesque figure, painted
all over in zigzagging red patterns and naked except for a
repellently grimacing yellow and blue mask that covered the
head and came halfway down the chest, tufts of white hair
floating at the edges. This figure was bellowing some rhyth-
mic, hypnotic chant that I could understand nothing of at all,
and was vigorously shaking two enormous and intricately
colored gourds, producing a rattling cadence that seemed to
blend unobtrusively with the song that he intoned. Unable to
move, I merely watched, fascinated. In the light cast by the
licking flames, I saw other dancing figures and a shriveled
old woman sitting off to my left, her eyes glazed over
catatonically as she chewed something I no longer cared to
try very hard to imagine.

Without warning all sound and movement ceased. The
cavorting figures froze in their tracks; the masked dancer
dropped dustily in an inert heap on the ground before me. I
wondered if he was still breathing, but in the next moment he
straightened up and motioned to someone at his side. A
muscular young celebrant squatted beside me and began daub-
ing a vile-smelling orange paste on my throat, which immediately went quite numb. The man produced some object that I
could not quite see clearly and, with the masked doctor
watching solemnly, made a painless incision, whereupon the
one in the medicine mask came forward to me on his knees
with what appeared to be a long transparent reed in his hand,
placing one end of it at my throat and sucking on the other. A
deep, concerted moan went up all around, and the other
dancers began moving again, encircling me and periodically
lunging in my direction with terrifying, wide-eyed shrieks.

All of this so distracted me that I didn't at first notice the
second incision.

The man in the mask was still sucking steadily on the tube,

but now the tube ran to my chest, and my whole frame was suddenly shaken by an access of hideous, searing pain. The tube itself—the long slender reed now puffed so full of dark, coursing blood—was writhing spasmodically, like some sly serpent insinuating itself into my body. God in heaven—the thing was inserted directly into my heart!

Gouts of smoke swirled into the sky, black against black, and as the dancers continued to lunge and shriek in nightmare profusion and the masked shaman nodded over his work, my senses blurred, the scene growing dim and diffuse. The firelight seemed to expand, turning pallid and grainy-looking, and I felt myself slipping into a faint. My eyes closed wearily.

With a sudden jerk I opened my eyes again, to see the barber calmly putting down his familiar implements. He levered the chair back down for me to dismount. "Done," he said, and immediately rejoined the sports talk that filled the air of the shop, pausing only to interject, "Next!"

I paid him and left, vaguely aware of a little discomfort and wondering if perhaps I'd caught a cold. I postponed my book-browsing and went home, but I didn't come down with anything after all.

I returned to the bookstore on Phillips Street two days later, but right away had the distressing feeling that I was awfully mixed up about something. The window next door was that of a rather dingy-looking little bakery from which aromas of fresh-baked bread and steaming apple pies wafted out to the sidewalk, making odd alchemy with the auto exhaust. I stepped into the bookshop—my God, could there be two? could I be on the wrong street?—and nodded to the woman behind the cash register, an owlish creature who looked rather like the stereotype of an elderly town librarian.

"Say, what happened to the barber shop next door?"

She looked at me as if I had asked her for a railway ticket to Saturn. "Next door? That's the Keating Bake Shoppe."

I stared at her helplessly. "But wasn't there a—I thought this was Phillips Street."

"It is," she said with some impatience. "The bakery's been there ever since I was a little girl. I get my doughnuts there every morning. Always have." As if to prove her point, she reached into a paper bag and pulled forth a doughnut, which she was munching on as I left the store.

It's really too bad, because I have a hard time finding a barber that will leave me to my thoughts while cutting my hair the way I like it. The odd thing is, my doctor told me just this morning that my blood pressure is down to normal.

Clea the Fox was both an accomplished sorceress and a proficient swordswoman. She possessed at least one other talent. She was also a skilled artificer, which Raalt the Thief learned to his chagrin.

TAKING HEART

Stephen L. Burns

The past-midnight quiet in Yuelianq Thief-Keep came to a sudden end when a knife came flashing out of the dark.

The knife buried itself point-first in the wooden crescent of stool showing between the night-jailer's legs. Jailer, stool, and his upraised wineskin went toppling over backward. He had barely hit the floor when a soft, hoarse voice came out of the same dark nowhere as the knife.

"Silence, on your life! How much are you paid, Guard?"

The jailer dared to peek fearfully over his overturned stool, past the knife. "Little," he whispered.

"Enough to be worth your life this night?"

The jailer shook his head so violently that his earrings rattled.

A piece of darkness detached itself from the unlit corridor, and became a small figure robed and hooded in black. "Up," came the voice. Within the dark hood, no face could be seen, but the blade of a knife protruded from one long sleeve, bright, sharp and ready. The jailer scrambled to his feet, eyes on the knife.

"Your keys, guard. We pay a visit to the thief Raalt." The knife showing from one sleeve winked out of sight. The sleeve moved, and before the jailer's amazed eyes the black-handled knife embedded in the stool pulled itself free and flew past him like a darting bird. It vanished inside the sleeve hilt-first.

"Take your lamp and lead the way."

The jailer halted before one particular cell door in the dank stone corridor, and gestured toward the iron-bound door.

One black sleeve swept outward. "Open it." The nightshade visitor's voice showed no overt edge, yet it was there, as a leather sheath contains the ready steel edge of a sword. The jailer heard that silent edge and unlocked the door with a nervous rattle of keys. He picked up his greaselamp and, with an unhappy sigh, went into the cell.

The thief Raalt was a large, hard-muscled man, handsome and blond-maned. He lay sleeping on the rank straw piled at the far end of the cell. Stout chains rimed with rust ran from the shackles on his thick wrists to a massive iron ring set in the rough stone of the cell's back wall. His ankles were shackled as well, the chains just as sturdy.

He roused at the light in his eyes. "A *visitor*," the jailer husked.

Raalt looked past the jailer and saw the mysterious, part-of-the-dark form of the black-robed visitor. It stepped closer, ominously silent.

Raalt drew into a crouch, paled, but did not look away. "Are you Arrmik, come for your Heart?"

It had been the Heart of Arrmik that he had stolen, and after a long chase and fierce struggle, he had been captured. He had brought down fourteen guards and soldiers before he had been overmastered by a pike blow to the back of the head. He was still alive only because he had managed to hide the Heart before his capture. Its return was greatly desired.

The robed figure drew closer yet. Rallt's muscles began to twitch as he readied himself to battle the thing.

Then the cell suddenly filled with the sound of light chiming laughter. The sleeve-shrouded hands threw back the hood and pulled down a black veil, revealing a woman with short midnight hair and wide-set black eyes. Her elfin face was alight with mischievous delight.

"*Clea!*" Raalt groaned. His mouth twisted angrily and he slumped back to the straw with a jangle of chains.

"How would you like to be free of this awful place, dear Raalt?" She grinned at him and winked. "Can the reputation of the Great Thief Raalt bear the shame of being rescued by a woman?"

Raalt wondered what god bore him such a grudge.

"There is a price, of course! I get half of what the Heart of Arrmik brings or I leave you here." She shook her head sadly. "The torture is to begin at dawn. I hear that they can keep a man in living agony for days—*weeks* if he is really strong . . ."

Raalt groaned again. Being captured was bad enough; having to be rescued was worse yet. That it was Clea who would rescue him, and the price she demanded, was almost too bitter a turn to bear. He stared bleakly at his shackles and rattled his chains dejectedly. He thought about hooks, hammers, pincers and red-hot irons probing tender places. He shuddered. What other choice did he have?

"I agree," he said sullenly, promising himself dire retribution.

Clea's smile was like the twist of a knife. "Swear an Oath on the souls of your father and mother that you will obey me and not try to betray me until after we have gained the Heart and sold it.''

"No!" Raalt shouted. "You ask too much!"

"Probably." Clea turned to go.

"Wait!" Raalt looked as if he were swallowing something that went down hard and tasted bad. He was; it was his pride. "I so swear," he grated, his teeth clenched. "—And I further swear that you will pay for this!"

Clea shrugged, her smile unchanged by his threat. "Set him free." The jailer scurried to comply. "Now I will leave a little puzzle in your name."

As Raalt stepped free from his chains, Clea went to the wall where the iron ring was fastened. Using a bit of chalk taken from her pocket she drew a large square around the ring. It started from the floor and looked like a low door with the ring at its center. She scribed a symbol at each corner of the square, then above the square she scrawled the word BEWARE. A pinch of powder taken from a black leather pouch was then rubbed onto the stone just over the ring. Raalt's spine tingled as he sensed magic being gathered.

"Now." She moved her hand and instantly one of the black-handled knives was in it. Whispering some oddly cadenced chant under her breath, she tapped the powdered spot with the knife's hilt.

There was a long sighing sound and the whole square went black, as if that section of wall had suddenly opened on a chasm of night. The iron ring dropped to the floor with a dull *chang*, its anchoring part having disappeared along with the section of wall that held it. Raalt stared at the hole as if he expected some fell creature to come climbing out of it at any moment.

Clea grinned, obviously pleased with her work. "That should give them something to ponder." She nudged the iron ring over the dark threshold with her toe. It fell,

dragging chains and shackles behind it. There was no sound
of a bottom being struck.

"Now they will believe that you escaped by some power
that they know not, and it will occupy them for a while." She
winked at Raalt. "It will not hurt your reputation, either.
They will think you a wizard now, and fear you more!"

"You thought of everything," Raalt muttered in grudging
admiration. He had to admit that it was a pleasure to watch
Clea's devious mind at work—when it was not working
against him.

"Don't I always?"

Clea led Raalt to a place just outside the Thief-Keep's
walls and halted him by a thick clump of bushes. Under the
bushes three bound and gagged soldiers writhed like armored
worms. She retrieved a tunic, hooded cloak, sword, sheath
and belt, handing them to him silently.

Once Raalt was dressed, they put some distance between
themselves and the Keep's somber stone walls. Clea set the
pace, moving quietly as a hawk's shadow on the ground.
Raalt stalked along beside her, already chafing under the
unhappy bargain he had been forced to strike. Only his oath
and the memory of experiences of other days kept him in
check.

He had last clashed with Clea some two years before. She
had turned up just in time to turn the tide in a pitched battle
with a horde of Nariman Tribesmen who wanted to relieve
Raalt and his two confederates of the spoils from the robbery
of a gem merchant. Clea had joined the fighting like a demon
incarnate, those inexplicable black-handled knives of hers
leaving and returning to her hands like edged lightning and
never missing their marks.

The skirmish was nearing an end when Raalt had broken
away on horseback with the chest of gems. He had never

planned to share the booty and cared little how the end of the battle went.

Clea had seen him and waded through a knot of six tribesmen, scattering them like leaves. She had run him down on foot and unhorsed him. He had tried to defend his prize with his sword, but she had evaded his every stroke and thrust. She led him away from the chest, disarmed him, then doubled back to take his sword, horse, and his share of the gems, leaving him unarmed and smarting to face his disgruntled associates. He had just barely been able to talk his way out of that with his skin intact. That had not been the first time they had clashed.

Now here she was again, and she had forced him to swear that damned oath—which made it that much harder for him to find a way to master her.

Clea interrupted his thoughts. "We should be far enough away now. Tell me where you hid the Heart."

Raalt squared his broad shoulders. First things first. Get the Heart, then figure out how to keep it from her . . . There *had* to be a way. "I did not have much time to hide it. The guards were hard on my heels—"

"Because you were too stupidly certain of your strength to plan your theft carefully." Clea said scornfully. "You just grabbed it and ran, didn't you?"

Raalt bristled, his hand falling to his sword-hilt. "Why do it otherwise?" he snarled. "I am not some weak woman, bent on avoiding a fight! I brought down fourteen guards, alone, and got the Heart to a safe place!"

He caught himself and took a deep breath to master his anger. Allowing her to provoke him would not bring the Heart closer. He spoke stiffly. "I flung the Heart into the fountain in the old Eastern Square." He looked grim, as if he had just told her that it was in a cave guarded by a thousand hungry Bloodwraiths.

Clea frowned, puzzled. "That is not too shabby a place."

"Thank you. But we still have to get it out somehow. . . ."

Clea shrugged. "You just wade in and dive for it—the fountain cannot be all that deep."

Raalt paled. "Into all that *water?* Never!" He shuddered, just thinking about it. He would rather face Bloodwraiths or Sandmaws. Once, on a small bet, he had climbed laughing into a cage to wrestle a gûr-rhakhar, and feared nothing with blade, teeth or claws. But he could not abide the water. He was a child of dry, barren lands and unable to change.

Clea hung her head and rubbed her forehead as if she had a headache. "Then how were you going to regain the Heart if you are afraid of the water?"

"I am *not* afraid!" Raalt snapped. "I just do not *like* the damned water! As for the Heart, I would probably threaten someone into getting it for me—I guess I had not thought about it. Not yet."

"No, it is not likely that you would have." Clea shook her head sadly. "Come on, let us get it now. You will not get wet, I promise."

They approached the old Eastern Square through an unlit, trash-strewn alley. When they reached the alley's end they peered out from behind some piled bales, taking care that they were not seen.

"There are a few people about," Clea whispered. "Let us think this through and plan it out."

"Why bother?" Raalt pulled his sword partway out of its sheath. "We—*you*—get the Heart out of the cursed water. I cover you, and anyone daring to interfere gets a belly full of steel! How would *you*," he stressed the word scornfully, "do it?"

Clea regarded him bleakly. "Raalt, truly you are as strong and fast as the best of them, and you know your blade better than most. You are a good thief, but your artlessness will one day be the death of you.'' She turned away, leaving Raalt to decide if he had been given a compliment. She scanned torch and moonlit square carefully, her sharp black eyes missing nothing. ''I do not see any guards or soldiers about, but you never can tell. . . . Exactly where did the Heart land?''

''Right in the center of the fountain. It sank quickly.''

Clea nodded and pointed to an amply fleshed, kohl-eyed prostitute lounging in a doorway about a third of the way around the square from their hiding-place. ''We will use her, I think.'' She pointed to a still-open wine stall. ''—and that place. Wait here.''

Before Raalt could argue or question, Clea was gone. ''Damn her,'' he muttered, resigning himself to waiting and thinking of various ways he might wrest the spoils from the Heart out of her hands. The oath she had bound him to reduced his other options.

Clea reappeared quickly. ''Everything is set up,'' she said, sounding very pleased. ''Here is the plan. You and I pretend that we are drunk.''

Raalt said nothing, wishing he was drunk—and alone.

''We wander over to that winestall and buy a skin of wine—here is some coin. Just a man and his woman out at the evening's dregs, buying some wine before we go someplace private. Got that?''

Raalt frowned, but nodded.

''We laugh often and look harmless and happy. After we buy the wine, we move toward the fountain. But before we get there, I will break away from you, laughing and teasing. When I reach the fountain I will dive in—just acting silly, it would seem. You follow behind, pick up my clothing, and go to the fountain's rim still playing your role. Got that?''

Raalt thought that Clea's plan was getting more ridiculous by the moment. But he would let her have her way—his time would come. He nodded curtly.

"The whore's cue is my leaving your side. She goes to the winestall and starts an argument over the price of a flask. I told her to be loud and crude, so that anyone watching will have to divide their attention between her and us.

"I find the Heart and you have my robe ready at the side of the fountain so that I can step right into it. I will pass the Heart so that nobody can see that I have taken something from the fountain. Then we leave, still keeping up our act— just two drunken lovers and no one the wiser!"

Raalt's impatience flared. "But why go through all that nonsense, Clea?" He gestured toward the square. "Nobody watches, and even if someone does and tries to interfere, he will die regretting it!"

Raalt had learned his craft from the Great Thief Wegan, and he had always told Raalt that fancy plans were for those without the might or confidence to simply take what they wanted. Anyone uncomfortable with that forthright approach would be better off as a pickpocket or priest if they still wanted to steal but lacked the balls for a man's methods.

"Was anyone watching when you stole the Heart?" Clea glared up at him.

"I didn't think so," he snarled, clenching his fists. "I got away!"

"But only for a while! Use your head *and* your arm! That will make you more than twice as strong! Never leave anything to chance—*never!*" Clea checked her scorn and continued more gently. "Theft is a game and an art; always be at least ten steps ahead and make every move beautiful."

Raalt had suffered enough of Clea's impudence. He quivered with repressed violence, and was on the verge of breaking his oath when Clea touched his arm and said, "I'm sorry." He felt a strange tingling sensation that spread from her touch and caught a vague whiff of some sweet spice. The anger seemed to sigh out of him all at once and on its own.

Clea linked her arm in his, her smile winsome and apologetic. "Ready partner?"

He shrugged uneasily, wondering where his anger had gone. The tingle was gone and the scent faded before he could place it.

Clea's smile turned into a comradely grin. "Let us be at it, then!"

Arm in arm they weaved out of the alley and onto the moonlit square. Clea's laugh rang out high and sweetly girlish, sounding silly from too much wine. She clung to Raalt's arm as if afraid that he would get away from her, and her hip bumped against him at every step. She seemed every inch a giddy young girl.

Though stiff and uncomfortable at first, Raalt soon began to swagger as he relaxed into his assigned role. The change that Clea had undergone helped. She scarcely resembled the ever-contrary, sharp-tongued creature come to plague his life again. Now that she was not seemingly going out of her way to rub him wrong, she seemed more attractive, more like the kind of woman he knew and could bend to his will. The way she hung on his arm made him realize how small and waif-like she really was, made him realize that she must have her own weak spots.

Then he remembered something else Wegan had taught him, a thing he himself knew to be true; that a woman's heart was her weakest part.

It was like a light dawning inside. All the signs had been there. She had sought and saved him, brought him fine clothes and a weapon. Even her constant arguing could be seen as a kind of wry courtship, as with children. As part of her plan she got to hold him and play at romance. Had she not desired that, she would have made another plan.

Raalt looked down at Clea, smiling in his new knowledge.

His face took on the devilish grin that had led a hundred maids to his bed. *A woman's heart is her weakest part;* that would be a part of the way he would out-fox Clea the Fox. He tightened his arm around her and winked conspiratorily. The smile she returned was open, lovely. *Vulnerable.* Raalt laughed aloud.

They arrived at the winestall. Raalt dickered hard for the wine, falling into the spirit of the exchange. Partway through his haggling, Clea tugged at his sleeve, indicating that she wanted to whisper something to him. He bent to listen, but instead of words, he received a wet tongue in his ear, provoking a laugh from the beaky, bearded merchant. Her wet probing continued longer than he might have expected—though not as long as he would have liked—and there seemed to be nothing of play-acting in it. Again he caught that soft scent—cinnamon perhaps.

The bargaining done and wine in hand, they wandered toward the center of the square. Clea laughed often and kept rubbing against him as they walked. An occasional eye turned their way, sometimes set in a frowning face, but more often followed by an approving nod.

They were partway across the square when Clea broke away, giggling and teasing. She threw her robe off her shoulders, laughing as she let it drop to the ground. She danced back a step, her black eyes bright and merry. Her small fingers flew at the buttons of her cotton undergarment as she pranced backwards.

Just before she reached the fountain the last button came free and the cotton chemise pooled around her feet, leaving her pale and naked in the moon's lambent light. Raalt stumbled to a halt, his eyes seeing nothing but the dancing white flame of her small body.

Part of his mind had been worrying at different ways to deal Clea out of the Heart's spoils once he had captured her heart, but the dry bones of his plans turned to dust as she captured his full attention with the simple fact of her beauty. Behind him he half-heard a woman begin to curse stridently.

Clea leapt to the rim of the fountain, calling him. She blew him a kiss, then turned and dived into the fountain.

Raalt bent and picked up her robe, fear and desire grappling inside him. He had a terrible urge to run and dive in after her. Before he could steel himself for such an act of bravery, the sound of the argument reached a more fevered pitch. He heard and remembered what he was supposed to do.

He hurried to pick up her other garment, then almost ran to the side of the fountain. He stood shifting his weight from one foot to the other, staring at the water and thinking that he never could have really followed her into it. The square remained quiet. Fingering his sword, he turned back toward the water, beginning to fear that Clea had drowned—or worse. She had been under a very long time, and who knew what horrors all that water might hide?

Suddenly her head broke the moon-rimed surface before him. Her hand came out of the water and she thrust the leather pouch that the Heart had been in when he had stolen it into his hand. He closed his fingers around it in relief—he had wondered if the water would willingly give it up.

"Quick, my robe," Clea gasped, her breath short from the time she had spent submerged. Raalt held it up, still clutching the pouch, licking his lips at the sight of her as he draped the robe over her shoulders. It broke his heart to see her covered again.

When the pouch had touched his hand he had felt a powerful impulse to take the Heart and her robe and run, turning the tables. But the earlier sight of her burned in his mind like a beacon too bright to turn away from. He stayed.

Now wearing her robe, Clea stepped closer and embraced him, running her wet hands down along his spine and making him shiver. "I have some rooms for us already," she whispered. "Let us go celebrate!"

Raalt lifted her from the fountain rim and set her on the ground. Clea took his arm and held on tight. Together they left the fountain and headed across the square.

"See what we can do together, partner?" Clea breathed softly, smiling up at him.

"And the night is still young," he replied, stopping her for a kiss. She responded with considerable passion. He was certain of it—that tantalizing, elusive scent was cinnamon.

They passed the edge of the square, Raalt glowed like a lamp; the Heart was once again in hand and Clea was as good as his. He swore to himself that by morning she would be begging him to keep her half of what the Heart brought. His oath would hold; she would betray herself. The thought of seeing Clea brought low made his grin grow even wider.

Raalt could scarcely believe the luxury of the rooms Clea had arranged. They had two large rooms interconnected by an arched door hung with glittering beadwork. The main room was larger, and had a door to the street. The smaller room, containing kitchen and bath, opened onto a small garden.

The whitewashed stone walls of the main room were hung with spills of silk and dyed cotton hangings. One side of the room, on the street-door end, held a mountain of cushions and pillows, all soft and richly embroidered. On the other side there was a huge silk-curtained bed. The furniture was all of rich dark woods or carved stone. Nightingales sang from wicker cages, filling the incense-sweet air with soft music. The room was lit by fragrant beeswax tapers, and there was bread, fruit, cheese and wine already on hand.

Raalt toured the main room in wonder, the still-wet pouch

momentarily forgotten in his hand. The room confirmed his estimation of Clea's motives; this was a love nest if ever there was one.

Clea was just turning from pouring them wine when she saw that he was about to open the pouch. She paled and nearly dropped their cups. *"Don't open that!"* she shouted, real fear in her voice.

Raalt halted uncertainly. "Why not?"

"Gods! That is the Heart of Arrmik!" She came only a step closer, and stood as if ready to flinch away instantly.

"So?" he said uneasily, his fingers on the thong binding the pouch shut.

"The Heart is *cursed!* Only the Priest of Arrmik can look upon it and live—that is why it is kept covered! Did you not know? Do you not bother to learn something of what you steal?"

"Well," Raalt began unhappily, feeling his control over her beginning to slip away. He did not want to admit that he did not, and had not; knowing that it was valuable was enough. He was tempted to open the pouch anyway, just to prove that her fears were unfounded, but decided against it on the off-chance that she was right. You could never be certain about curses; sometimes they were just words to frighten away the gullible, but now and again they had a power better left unprovoked.

Clea went to Raalt's side. "I am sorry, but I did not want to lose you." The smile she gave him would have made the face of a stone statue crack as it tried to smile back. "Put it in your belt for safe-keeping tonight."

She handed him his cup. "I will have to find something else for you to unwrap and enjoy."

Raalt grinned hungrily at her thinly veiled invitation and put the pouch away. Then he helped himself to his wine.

Clea watched him over the rim of her cup and spoke

offhandedly. "It is a good thing that you did not try to open that pouch while you were stealing it—they would have found you dead with it still in your hand. You would have drowned on dry land!"

Raalt choked on his wine. Clea had to thump him on the back several times before he was able to get his breath back.

"I—I would have dr—dr—" He could not say it out loud.

Clea giggled and ran her fingertip down along the hinge of his jaw, down the side of his neck and to the center of his chest. "Arrmik is a God of Desert Water," she breathed. "It is told that once he drowned an entire city that turned from his worship." Her fingers played over Raalt's chest knowingly, making his breath catch, making the tide of visions of drowning recede a bit. He threw back another gulp of wine.

Clea's maddening fingers continued their work. Her tongue wet her lips and she looked at Raalt expectantly.

Raalt forced the last of the water-thoughts from his mind and put his cup aside. He gathered Clea into his arms, crushing her small body against his, enveloped in the just-reappeared cinnamon scent, reveling in the helpless way she clung to him. Their mouths met and she held on even more desperately.

Raalt broke the kiss, and when he saw the heavy-lidded look in her dark eyes he wanted to crow in triumph. The Fox was almost skinned.

As his hands were slipping down her back to cup her buttocks, she slipped out of his embrace unexpectedly. "Now wait," she said, her face elfin and mischievous. "Let us not hurry! I am going to bathe before we go any farther—the water in that fountain was *filthy!*" She wrinkled her nose to show what she meant.

"You think so, do you?" Raalt chuckled, moving toward her with his arms poised to catch her. She danced back out of his grasp, shaking her finger at him and laughing.

"You do not want to bed a woman smelling of stale water and camel lips, do you? Work on the wine and I will be done before you even miss me."

Raalt opened his mouth to protest. Clea darted forward and put her finger to his lips. "No complaining or I make *you* take one!"

Raalt gave her his most wolfish grin. "I drink. *You* hurry."

"I will," she said huskily, meeting his eyes.

Raalt let her lead him to the big drift of pillows and waited while she removed his cloak, sword, and belt for him as if she were a slave girl. He dropped to the pillows and took the mug and flask she handed him, pleased with this new Clea. She was his, and by daybreak the Heart would be his as well.

He watched her move to the other end of the room, her slim hips swaying provocatively. She flashed him a smile full of tender promise, then stepped through the beaded curtain.

Listening to her splashing, Raalt patted the pouch and drank his wine, well pleased. He had good wine, a rich room, the Heart, his freedom, and best of all the sweet knowledge that he had finally found Clea's weakness—and she was falling without a struggle. He could already see himself count-ing her share of the spoils from the Heart—not that she should have had one in the first place.

What delicious justice; she had tried to take his Heart, but he had captured hers instead. Clea the Fox had met her match in Raalt the Thief, and high time too.

He was working on his fifth mug of wine when he decided that she had been splashing long enough, by damn. He stood up just a bit unsteadily and stretched, every muscle standing out in sharp relief. He grinned wickedly as he shed his tunic and then dropped his clout. After a last sip of wine he headed for the beaded curtain wearing a big smile and nothing else.

Raalt passed through the clicking beads, grinning and scratching his crotch. One good look and she would be out of that tub quick enough.

When his eyes fell on the tub his grin crumbled to dust and his knees nearly buckled under him. There in the big wooden tub sat the ample-fleshed, kohl-eyed whore from the fountain square. Clea was nowhere to be seen.

The whore leered and winked. "There y'are buck! The young Missy says how you be ready for sport, an' I guess y'truly be! Ah, y'lookin' so—"

"*Where is she?*" Raalt roared, his handsome face going black with rage, his hands groping for the sword left behind in the other room. He balled his fists and advanced on the woman in the tub.

The whore cringed back, splashing. "She *gone*, Master," she cried. "She leave me as present, she did! One gold Finger to fight with wineman, two more to hide in garden till she come f'me, then wait in tub f'you, Master!"

Raalt moaned and spun around, then ran back to his discarded clothing, searching for the pouch. When he found it he snatched it up and worried at the thong, cursing steadily, his face fearful.

At last the thong gave way. He upended the pouch and out dropped a large wet rock. He squeezed his eyes shut in denial and clenched the rock in his fist as he slumped to the pillows in defeat. Clea had beaten him yet again; led him down the garden path only to step in fresh wet dung.

He felt someone touch his shoulder, and looked up to see the wet and dripping corpulent courtesan. She spoke fearfully.

"Missy tol' me—an I near forget—to tella y'best 'member what she say 'bout bein' ten steps 'head." The poor woman looked like she expected him to strike her.

Raalt did clench his fist again, but after a moment his hand dropped limply. The rock fell from his fingers, dropped to the pillows, then rolled to the floor. He clamped his jaw to keep in another moan, and hung his head to hide his face.

The kohl-eyed whore knew what to do. She stepped closer and drew Raalt's head against her ample belly.

She cradled his head tenderly and ran her fingers through his hair. "There now," she crooned, "there, there, my baby."

Just as that tender moment was occurring, Clea was already on a fast horse and riding out of Yuelianq. She had already disposed of the Heart of Arrmik and her saddlebags were heavy with gold.

It had been easy—too easy really. But the game had been great sport, and it had been profitable. She regretted that she had not been able to stay to see the look on Raalt's face—that might have been worth half of the gold after all.

Almost as precious as the gold was the bit of rumor she had heard while in Yuelianq. It seemed that Timoor of Morn was a poor loser and had put a good price on her head. That sounded like an interesting challenge; trying to sell her own head, collecting the price herself, and keeping it on her shoulders in the bargain.

But with a bit of careful planning. . . .

Clea threw back her hood and dug her heels into the horse's side, spurring him to a run. She laughed aloud and left Yuelianq behind, riding toward the setting moon.

Although the science of meteorology has made great advances in the past few years, some storms still come as complete surprises to even the best weather forecasters. Certainly "The Storm" was not predicted by anyone, but whether it was really unexpected is a question of belief.

THE STORM

David Morrell

Gail saw it first. She came from the Howard Johnson's toward the heat haze in the parking lot where our son Jeff and I were hefting luggage into our station wagon. Actually, Jeff supervised. He gave me his excited ten-year-old advice about the best place for this suitcase and that knapsack. Grinning at his sun-bleached hair and nut-brown freckled face, I told him I could never have done the job without him.

It was 8 A.M., Tuesday, August 2, but even that early, the thermometer outside our motel unit had risen to eighty-five. The humidity was thick and smothering. Just from my slight exertion with the luggage, I'd sweated through my shirt and jeans, wishing I'd thought to put on shorts. To the east, the sun blazed, white and swollen, the sky an oppressive, chalky blue. This'd be one day when the station wagon's costly air conditioning wouldn't be a luxury but a necessity.

My hands were sweat-slick as I shut the hatch. Jeff nodded, satisfied with my work, then grinned beyond me. Turning, I saw Gail coming toward us. When she left the brown parched grass, her brow creased as her sandals touched the heat-softened asphalt parking lot.

"All set?" she asked.

Her smooth white shorts and cool blue top emphasized her tan. She looked trim and lithe and wonderful. I'm not sure how she did it, but she seemed completely unaffected by the heat. Her hair was soft and golden. Her subtle trace of makeup made the day seem somehow cooler.

"Ready. Thanks to Jeff," I answered.

He grinned up proudly.

"Well, I paid the bill. I gave them back the key," Gail said. "Let's go." She paused. "Except—"

"What's wrong?"

"Those clouds." She pointed past my shoulder.

I turned—and frowned. In contrast with the blinding, chalky, eastern sky, I stared at numbing, pitch-black western clouds. They seethed on the far horizon, roiling, churning. Lightning flickered like a string of flashbulbs in the distance, the thunder so muted it rumbled hollowly.

"Now where the hell did *that* come from?" I said. "It wasn't there before I packed the car."

Gail squinted toward the thunderheads. "You think we should wait till it passes?"

"It isn't close." I shrugged.

"But it's coming fast." She bit her lip. "And it looks bad."

Jeff grabbed my hand. I glanced at his worried face.

"It's just a storm, son."

He surprised me, though. I'd misjudged what worried him.

"I want to go back home," he said. "I don't want to wait. I miss my friends. Please, can't we leave?"

I nodded. "I'm on your side. Two votes out of three, Gail. If you're really scared, though . . ."

"No. I . . ." Gail drew a breath and shook her head. "I'm being silly. It's just the thunder. You know how storms bother me." She ruffled Jeff's hair. "But I won't make us wait. I'm homesick, too."

We'd spent the past two weeks in Colorado, fishing, camping, touring ghost towns. The vacation had been perfect. But as eagerly as we'd gone, we were just as eager to be heading back. Last night, we'd stopped here in North Platte, a small, quiet town off Interstate 80, halfway through Nebraska. Now, today, we hoped we could reach home in Iowa by nightfall. .

"Let's get moving then," I said. "It's probably a local storm. We'll drive ahead of it. We'll never see a drop of rain."

Gail tried to smile. "I hope."

Jeff hummed as we got in the station wagon. I steered toward the interstate, went up the eastbound ramp, and set the cruise control at fifty-five. Ahead, the morning sun glared through the windshield. After I tugged down the visors, I turned on the air conditioner, then the radio. The local weatherman said hot and hazy.

"Hear that?" I said. "He didn't mention a storm. No need to worry. Those are only heat clouds."

I was wrong. From time to time, I checked the rear-view mirror, and the clouds loomed thicker, blacker, closer, seething toward us down the interstate. Ahead, the sun kept blazing fiercely though. Jeff wiped his sweaty face. I set the air conditioner for DESERT, but it didn't seem to help.

"Jeff, reach in the ice chest. Grab us each a Coke."

He grinned. But I suddenly felt uneasy, realizing too late he'd have to turn to open the chest in the rear compartment.

"Gosh," he murmured, staring back, awestruck.

"What's the matter?" Gail swung around before I could stop her. "Oh, my God," she said. "The clouds."

They were angry midnight chasing us. Lightning flashed. Thunder jolted.

"They still haven't reached us," I said. "If you want, I'll try outrunning them."

"Do *something*."

I switched off the cruise control and sped to sixty, then sixty-five. The strain of squinting toward the white-hot sky ahead of us gave me a piercing headache. I put on Polaroids.

But all at once, I didn't need them. Abruptly, the clouds caught up to us. The sky went totally black. We drove in roiling darkness.

"Seventy. I'm doing seventy," I said. "But the clouds are moving faster."

"Like a hurricane," Gail said. "That isn't possible. Not in Nebraska."

"I'm scared," Jeff said.

He wasn't the only one. Lightning blinded me, stabbing to the right and left of us. Thunder actualy shook the car. Then the air became an eerie, dirty shade of green, and I started thinking about tornadoes.

"Find a place to stop!" Gail said.

But there wasn't one. The next town was Kearney, but we'd already passed the exit. I searched for a roadside park, but a sign said Rest Stop, Thirty Miles. I couldn't just pull off the highway. On the shoulder, if the rain obscured another driver's vision, we could all be hit and killed. No choice. I had to keep on driving.

"At least it isn't raining," I said.

As I did, the clouds unloaded. No preliminary sprinkle. Massive raindrops burst around us, gusting, roaring, pelting.

"I can't see!" I flicked the windshield wipers to their highest setting. They flapped in sharp, staccato, triple time. I peered through murky, undulating, windswept waves of water, struggling for a clear view of the highway.

I was going too fast. When I braked, the station wagon fishtailed. We skidded on the slippery pavement. I couldn't breathe. The tires gripped. I felt the jolt. Then the car was in control.

I slowed to forty, but the rain heaved with such force against the windshield, I still couldn't see.

"Pull your seatbelts tight," I told Gail and Jeff.

Though I never found that rest stop, I got lucky when a flash of lightning showed a sign, the exit for the next town, called Grand Island. Shaking from tension, I eased down the off-ramp. At the bottom, across from me, a Best Western motel was shrouded with rain. We left a wake through the flooded parking lot and stopped under the motel's canopy. My hands were stiff from clenching the steering wheel. My shoulders ached. My eyes felt swollen, raw.

Gail and Jeff got out, rain gusting under the canopy as they ran inside. I had to move the car to park it in the lot. I locked the doors, but though I sprinted, I was drenched and chilled when I reached the motel's entrance.

Inside, a small group stared past me toward the storm—two clerks, two waitresses, a cleaning lady. I shook.

"Mister, use this towel," the cleaning lady said. She took one from a pile on her cart.

I thanked her, wiping my dripping face and soggy hair.

"See any accidents?" a waitress asked.

With the towel around my neck I shook my head.

"A storm this sudden, there ought to be accidents," the waitress said as if doubting me.

I frowned when she said *sudden*. You mean it's just starting here?"

A skinny clerk stepped past me to the window. "Not too

long before you came. A minute maybe. I looked out this window, and the sky was bright. I knelt to tie my shoe. When I stood up, the clouds were here—as black as night. I don't know where they came from all of a sudden, but I never saw it rain so hard so fast.''

"But—" I shivered, puzzled. "It hit us back near Kearney. We've been driving in it for an hour."

"You were on the edge of it, I guess," the clerk said, spellbound by the storm. "It followed you."

The second waitress laughed. "That's right. You brought it with you."

My wet clothes clung cold to me, but I felt a deeper chill.

"Looks like we've got other customers," the second clerk said, pointing out the window.

Other cars splashed through the torrent in the parking lot.

"Yeah, we'll be busy, that's for sure," the clerk said. He switched on the lobby's lights, but they didn't dispel the outside gloom.

The wind howled.

I glanced through the lobby. Gail and Jeff weren't around. "My wife and son." I said, concerned.

"They're in the restaurant," the second waitress said, smiling to reassure me. "Through that arch. They ordered coffee for you. Hot and strong."

"I need it. Thanks."

Dripping travelers stumbled in.

We waited an hour. Though the coffee was as hot as promised, it didn't warm me. In the air-conditioning, my soggy clothes stuck to the chilly chrome-and-plastic seat. A bone-deep, freezing numbness made me sneeze.

"You need dry clothes," Gail said. "You'll catch pneumonia."

I'd hoped the storm would stop before I went out for the

clothes. But even in the restaurant, I felt the thunder rumble. I couldn't wait. My muscles cramped from shivering. "I'll get a suitcase," I said and stood.

"Dad, be careful." Jeff looked worried.

Smiling, I leaned down and kissed him. "Son, I promise."

Near the restaurant's exit, one waitress I'd talked to came over. "You want to hear a joke?"

I didn't, but I nodded politely.

"On the radio," she said. "The local weatherman. He claims it's hot and clear."

I shook my head, confused.

"The storm." She laughed. "He doesn't know it's raining. All his instruments, his radar and his charts, he hasn't brains enough to look outside and see what kind of day it is. If anything, the rain got worse." She laughed again. "The biggest joke—that dummy's my husband."

I remembered she'd been the waitress who joked that I'd brought the storm with me. Her sense of humor troubled me, but I laughed to be agreeable and went to the lobby.

It was crowded. More rain-drenched travelers pushed in, cursing the weather. They tugged at sour, dripping clothes and bunched before the motel's counter, wanting rooms.

I squeezed among them at the big glass door, squinting out at the wildest storm I'd ever seen. Above the exclamations of the crowd, I heard the shriek of the wind.

My hand reached for the door.

It hesitated. I really didn't want to go out.

The skinny desk clerk suddenly stood next to me. "It could be you're not interested," he said.

I frowned, surprised.

"We're renting rooms so fast we'll soon be all full up," he said. "But fair is fair. You got here first. I saved a room. In case you plan on staying."

"I appreciate it. But we're leaving soon."

"You'd better take another look."

I did. Lightning split a tree. The window shook from thunder.

A scalding bath, I thought. A sizzling steak. Warm blankets while my clothes get dry.

"I changed my mind. We'll take that room."

All night, thunder shook the building. Even with the drapes shut, I saw brilliant streaks of lightning. I slept fitfully, waking with a headache. Six A.M.; it still was raining.

On the radio the weatherman sounded puzzled. As the lightning's static garbled what he said, I learned that Grand Island was suffering the worst storm in its history. Streets were flooded, sewers blocked, basements overflowing. An emergency had been declared, the damage in the millions. But the cause of the storm seemed inexplicable. The weather pattern made no sense. The front was tiny, localized, and stationary. Half a mile outside Grand Island—north and south, east and west—the sky was cloudless.

That last statement was all I needed to know. We quickly dressed and went downstairs to eat. We checked out shortly after seven.

"Driving in this rain?" the desk clerk said. He had the tact to stop before he said, "You're crazy."

"Listen to the radio," I answered. "Half a mile away, the sky is clear."

I'd have stayed if it hadn't been for Gail. Her fear of storms—the constant lightning and thunder—made her frantic.

"Get me out of here," she said.

And so we went.

And almost didn't reach the interstate. The car was hubcap-deep in water. The distributor was damp. I nearly killed the battery before I got the engine started. The brakes were soaked. They failed as I reached the local road. Skidding, blinded, I swerved around the blur of an abandoned truck, missing the entrance to the interstate. Backing up, I barely saw the ditch in time. But finally, we headed up the ramp, rising above the flood, doing twenty down the highway.

Jeff was white-faced. I'd bought some comics for him, but he was too scared to read them.

"The odometer," I told him. "Watch the numbers. Half a mile, and we'll be out of this."

I counted tenths of a mile with him. "One, two, three. . ."

The storm grew darker, stronger.

"Four, five, six . . ."

The numbers felt like broken glass wedged in my throat.

"But Dad, we're half a mile away. The rain's not stopping."

"Just a little farther."

But instead of ending, it got worse. We had to stop in Lincoln. The next day, the storm persisted. We pressed on to Omaha. We could normally drive from Colorado to our home in Iowa City in two leisured days.

But *this* trip took us seven long, slow, agonizing days. We had to stop in Omaha and then Des Moines and towns whose names I'd never heard of. When we at last reached home, we felt so exhausted, so frightened we left our bags in the car and stumbled from the garage to bed.

The rain slashed against the windows. It drummed on the roof. I couldn't sleep. When I peered out, I saw a waterfall from the overflowing eaves trough. Lightning struck a hydro pole. I settled to my knees and recollected every prayer I'd ever learned and then invented stronger ones.

The hydro was fixed by morning. The phone still worked. Gail called a friend and asked the question. As she listened to the answer, I was startled by the way her face shrank and her eyes receded. Mumbling "Thanks," she set the phone down.

"It's been dry here," she said. "Then last night at eight the storm began."

"But that's when we arrived. My God, what's happening?"

"Coincidence." She frowned. "The storm front moved in our direction. We kept trying to escape. Instead, we only followed it."

The fridge was bare. I told Gail I'd get some food and warned Jeff not to go outside.

"But Dad, I want to see my friends."

"Watch television. Don't go out till the rain stops."

"It won't end."

I froze. "What makes you say that?"

"Not today it won't. The sky's too dark. The rain's too hard."

I nodded, relaxing. "Then call your friends. But don't go out."

When I opened the garage door, I watched the torrent. Eight days since I'd seen the sun. Damp clung on me. Gusts angled toward me.

I drove from the garage and was swallowed.

Gail looked overjoyed when I came back. "It stopped for forty minutes." She grinned with relief.

"But not where I was."

The nearest supermarket was half a mile away. Despite my umbrella and raincoat, I'd been drenched when I lurched through the hissing automatic door of the supermarket. Fighting to catch my breath, I'd fumbled with the inside-out umbrella and muttered to a clerk about the goddamn endless rain.

The clerk hadn't known what I meant. "But it started just a minute ago."

I shuddered, but not from the water dripping off me.

Gail heard me out and gaped. Her joy turned into frightened disbelief. "As soon as you came back, the storm began again."

The bottom fell out of my soggy grocery bag. I found a weather station on the radio. But the announcer's static-garbled voice sounded as bewildered as his counterparts through Nebraska.

His report was the same. The weather pattern made no sense. The front was tiny, localized, and stationary. Half a mile away, the sky was cloudless. In a small circumference, however, Iowa City was enduring its most savage storm on record. Downtown streets were . . .

I shut off the radio.

Thinking frantically, I told Gail I was going to my office at the university to see if I had mail. But my motive was quite different, and I hoped she wouldn't think of it.

She started to speak as Jeff came into the kitchen, interrupting us, his eyes bleak with cabin fever. "Drive me down to Freddie's, Dad?"

I didn't have the heart to tell him no.

At the school the parking lot was flecked with rain. There weren't any puddles, though. I live a mile away. I went into the English building and asked a secretary, though I knew what she'd tell me.

"No, Mr. Price. All morning it's been clear. The rain's just beginning."

In my office I phoned home.

"The rain stopped," Gail said. "You won't believe how beautiful the sky is, bright and sunny."

I stared from my office window toward a storm so black and ugly I barely saw the whitecaps on the angry churning river.

Fear coiled in my guts, then hissed and struck.

*   *   *

The pattern was always the same. No matter where I went, the storm went with me. When I left, the storm left as well. It got worse. Nine days of it. Then ten. Eleven. Twelve. Our basement flooded, as did all the other basements in the district. Streets eroded. There were mudslides. Shingles blew away. Attics leaked. Retaining walls fell over. Lightning struck the hydro poles so often the food spoiled in our freezer. We lit candles. If our stove hadn't used gas, we couldn't have cooked. As in Grand Island, an emergency was declared, the damage so great it couldn't be calculated.

What hurt most was seeing the effect on Gail and Jeff. The constant chilly damp gave them colds. I sneezed and sniffled too but didn't care about myself because Gail's spirits sank the more it rained. Her eyes became dismal gray. She had no energy. She put on sweaters and rubbed her listless, aching arms.

Jeff went to bed much earlier than usual. He slept later. He looked thin and pale.

And he had nightmares. As lightning cracked, his screams woke us. Again the hydro wasn't working. We used flash-lights as we hurried to his room.

"Wake up, Jeff! You're only dreaming!"

"The Indian!" He moaned and rubbed his frightened eyes.

Thunder rumbled, making Gail jerk.

"What Indian?" I said.

"He warned you."

"Son, I don't know what—"

"In Colorado." Gail turned sharply, startling me with the hollows the darkness cast on her cheeks. "The weather dancer."

"You mean that witch doctor?"

On our trip we'd stopped in a dingy desert town for gas and seen a meager group of tourists studying a roadside Indian display. A shack, trestles, beads and drums and belts. Skeptical, I'd walked across. A scruffy Indian, at least a hundred, dressed in threadbare faded vestments, had chanted gibberish while he danced around a circle of rocks in the dust.

"What's going on?" I asked a woman aiming a camera.

"He's a medicine man. He's dancing to make it rain and end the drought."

I scuffed the dust and glanced at the burning sky. My head ached from the heat and the long oppressive drive. I'd seen too many sleazy roadside stands, too many Indians ripping off tourists, selling overpriced inauthentic artifacts. Imperfect turquoise, shoddy silver. They'd turned their back on their heritage and prostituted their traditions.

I didn't care how much they hated us for what we'd done to them. What bothered me was behind their stoic faces they laughed as they duped us.

Whiskey fumes wafted from the ancient Indian as he clumsily danced around the circle, chanting.

"Can he do it?" Jeff asked. "Can he make it rain?"

"It's a gimmick. Watch these tourists put money in that so-called native bowl he bought at Sears."

They heard me, rapt faces suddenly suspicious.

The old man stopped performing. "Gimmick?" He glared.

"I didn't mean to speak so loud. I'm sorry if I ruined your routine."

"I made that bowl myself."

"Of course you did."

He lurched across, the whiskey fumes stronger. "You don't think my dance can make it rain?"

"I couldn't care less if you fool these tourists, but my son should know the truth."

"You want convincing?"

"I said I was sorry."

"White man always say they're sorry."

Gail came over, glancing furtively around. Embarrassed, she tugged at my sleeve. "The gas tank's full. Let's go."

I backed away.

"You'll see it rain! You'll pray it stops!" the old man shouted.

Jeff looked terrified, and that made me angry. "Shut your mouth! You scared my son!"

"He wonders if I can make it rain? Watch the sky! I dance for you now! When the lightning strikes, remember me!"

We got in the car. "That crazy coot. Don't let him bother you. The sun cooked his brain."

"All right, he threatened me. So what?" I said. "Gail, you surely can't believe he sent this storm. By dancing? Think. It isn't possible."

"Then tell me why it's happening."

"A hundred weather experts tried but can't explain it. How can I?"

"The storm's linked to you. It never leaves you."

"It's . . ."

I meant to say "coincidence" again, but the word had lost its meaning and smothered in my lungs. I studied Gail and Jeff, and in the glare of the flashlights I realized they blamed me. We were adversaries, both of them against me.

"The rain, Dad. Can't you make it stop?"

I cried when he whispered "Please."

Department of Meteorology. A full professor, one associate, and one assistant. But I'd met the full professor at a cocktail party several years ago. We sometimes met for tennis. On occasion, we had lunch together. I knew his office hours and braved the storm to go to see him.

Again the parking lot was speckled with increasing raindrops when I got there. I ran through raging wind and shook

my raincoat in the lobby of his building. I'd phoned ahead.
He was waiting.

Forty-five, freckled, almost bald. In damn fine shape though,
as I knew from many tennis games I'd lost.

"The rain's back." He shook his head disgustedly.

"No explanation yet?"

"I'm supposed to be the expert. Your guess would be as
good as mine. If this keeps up, I'll take to reading tea
leaves."

"Maybe superstition's . . ." I wanted to say "the answer," but I couldn't force myself.

"What?" He leaned forward.

I rubbed my aching forehead. "What causes thunderstorms?"

He shrugged. "Two different fronts collide. One's hot and
moist. The other's cold and dry. They bang together so hard
they explode. The lightning and thunder are the blast. The
rain's the fallout."

"But in *this* case?"

"That's the problem. We don't have two different fronts.
Even if we did, the storm would move because of vacuums
the winds create. But this storm stays right here. It only shifts
a half a mile or so and then comes back. It's forcing us to
reassess the rules."

"I don't know how to . . ." But I told him. Everything.

He frowned. "And you believe this?"

"I'm not sure. My wife and son do. Is it possible?"

He put some papers away. He poured two cups of coffee.
He did everything but rearrange his bookshelves.

"Is it possible?" I said.

"If you repeat this, I'll deny it."

"How much crazier can—?"

"In the sixties, when I was in grad school, I went on a
field trip to Mexico. The mountain valleys have such complicated weather patterns they're perfect for a dissertation. One

place gets so much rain the villages are flooded. Ten miles away another valley gets no rain whatsoever. In one valley I studied, something had gone wrong. It normally had lots of rain. For seven years, though, it had been completely dry. The valley next to it, normally dry, was getting all the rain. No explanation. God knows, I worked hard to find one. People were forced to leave their homes and go where the rain was. In this seventh summer they stopped hoping the weather would behave the way it used to. They wanted to return to their valley, so they sent for special help. A weather dancer. He claimed to be a descendent of the Mayans. He arrived one day and paced the valley, praying to all the compass points. Where they intersected in the valley's middle, he arranged a wheel of stones. He put on vestments. He danced around the wheel. One day later it was raining, and the weather pattern went back to the way it used to be. I told myself he'd been lucky, that he'd somehow read the signs of nature and danced when he was positive it would rain, no matter if he danced or not. But I saw those clouds rush in, and they were strange. They didn't move till the streams were flowing and the wells were full. Coincidence? Special knowledge? Who can say? But it scares me when I think about what happened in that valley."

"Then the Indian I met could cause this storm?"

"Who knows? Look, I'm a scientist. I trust in facts. But sometimes 'superstition' is a word we use for science we don't understand."

"What happens if the storm continues, if it doesn't stop?"

"Whoever lives beneath it will have to move, or else they'll die."

"But what if it follows someone?"

"You really believe it would?"

"It does!"

He studied me. "You ever hear of a superstorm?"

Dismayed, I shook my head.

"On rare occasions, several storms will climb on top of each other. They can tower as high as seven miles."

I gaped.

"But this storm's already climbed that high. It's heading up to ten now. It'll soon tear houses from foundations. It'll level everything. A stationary half-mile-wide tornado."

"If I'm right, though, if the old man wants to punish me, I can't escape. Unless my wife and son are separate from me, they'll die, too."

"Assuming you're right. But I have to emphasize—there's no scientific reason to believe you are."

"I think I'm crazy."

Eliminate the probable, then the possible. What's left must be the explanation. Either Gail and Jeff would die, or they'd have to leave me. But I couldn't bear losing them.

I knew what I had to do. I struggled through the storm to get back home. Jeff was feverish. Gail kept coughing, glaring at me in accusation.

They argued when I told them, but in desperation they agreed.

"If what we think is true," I said, "once I'm gone, the storm'll stop. You'll see the sun again."

"But what about you? What'll happen?"

"I wish I knew. Pray for me."

We kissed and wept.

I packed the car. I left.

The interstate again, heading west. The storm, of course, went with me.

Iowa. Nebraska. I spent three insane, disastrous weeks getting to Colorado. Driving through rain-swept mountains was a nightmare. But I finally reached that dingy desert town. I found that sleazy roadside stand.

No trinkets, no beads. As the storm raged, turning dust to mud, I searched the town, begging for information. "That old Indian. The weather dancer."

"He took sick."

"Where is he?"

"How should I know? Try the reservation."

It was fifteen miles away. The road wound narrow, mucky. I passed rocks so hot they steamed from rain. The car slid, crashing in a ditch, resting on its drive shaft. I ran through lightning and thunder, drenched and moaning when I stumbled to the largest building on the reservation. It was low and wide, made from stone. I pounded on the door. A man in uniform opened it, the agent for the government.

I told him.

He stared suspiciously. Turning, he spoke a different language to some Indians in the office. They answered.

He nodded. "You must want him bad," he said, "if you came out here in this storm. You're almost out of time. The old man's dying."

In the reservation's hospital, the old man lay motionless under sheets, an I.V. in his arm. Shriveled, he looked like a dry, empty cornhusk. He slowly opened his eyes. They gleamed with recognition.

"I believe you now," I said. "Please, make the rain stop."

He breathed in pain.

"My wife and son believe. It isn't fair to make them suffer. Please." My voice rose. "I shouldn't have said what I did. I'm sorry. Make it stop."

The old man squirmed.

I sank to my knees, kissed his hand, and sobbed. "I know

I don't deserve it. But I'm begging. I've learned my lesson. Stop the rain.''

The old man studied me and slowly nodded. The doctor tried to restrain him, but the old man's strength was more than human. He crawled from bed. He chanted and danced.

The lightning and thunder worsened. Rain slashed the windows. The old man danced harder. The frenzy of the storm increased. Its strident fury soared. It reached a crescendo, hung there—and stopped.

The old man fell. Gasping, I ran to him and helped the doctor lift him in bed.

The doctor glared. ''You almost killed him.''

''He isn't dead?''

''No thanks to you.''

But I said, ''Thanks''—to the old man and the powers in the sky.

I left the hospital. The sun, a common sight I used to take for granted, overwhelmed me.

Four days later, back in Iowa, I got the call. The agent from the government. He thought I'd want to know. That morning, the old man had died.

I turned to Gail and Jeff. Their colds were gone. From warm sunny weeks while I was away, their skin was brown again. They seemed to have forgotten how the nightmare had nearly destoryed us, more than just our lives, our love. Indeed, they now were skeptical about the Indian and told me the rain would have stopped, no matter what I did.

But they hadn't been in the hospital to see him dance. They didn't understand.

I set the phone down and swallowed, sad. Stepping from our house—it rests on a hill—I peered in admiration toward the sky.

I turned and faltered.

To the west, a massive cloud bank approached, dark and thick and roiling. Wind began, bringing a chill.

September 12. The temperature was seventy-eight. It dropped to fifty, then thirty-two.

The rain had stopped. The old man did what I asked. But I hadn't counted on his sense of humor.

He stopped the rain, all right.

But I knew the snow would never end.

Here, from a multiple-award-winning author, is an outstanding fantasy. It is also a love story—dealing as it does with a young man's sacrifice on behalf of his beloved.

A CABIN ON THE COAST

Gene Wolfe

It might have been a child's drawing of a ship. He blinked, and blinked again. There were masts and sails, surely. One stack, perhaps another. If the ship was really there at all. He went back to his father's beach cottage, climbed the five wooden steps, wiped his feet on the coco mat.

Lissy was still in bed, but awake, sitting up now. It must have been the squeaking of the steps, he thought. Aloud he said, "Sleep good?"

He crossed the room and kissed her. She caressed him and said, "You shouldn't go swimming without a suit, dear wonderful swimmer. How was the Pacific?"

"Peaceful. Cold. It's too early for people to be up, and there's nobody within a mile of here anyway."

"Get into bed, then. How about the fish?"

"Salt water makes the sheets sticky. The fish have seen them before." He went to the corner, where a showerhead poked from the wall. The beach cottage—Lissy called it a cabin—had running water of the sometimes and rusty variety.

224

"They might bite 'em off. Sharks, you know. Little ones."

"Castrating woman." The shower coughed, doused him with icy spray, coughed again.

"You look worried."

"No."

"Is it your dad?"

He shook his head, then thrust it under the spray, finger-combing his dark curly hair.

"You think he'll come out here? Today?"

He withdrew, considering. "If he's back from Washington, and he knows we're here."

"But he couldn't know, could he?"

He turned off the shower and grabbed a towel, already damp and a trifle sandy. "I don't see how."

"Only he might guess." Lissy was no longer smiling. "Where else could we go? Hey, what did we do with my underwear?"

"Your place. Your folks'. Any motel."

She swung long golden legs out of bed, still holding the sheet across her lap. Her breasts were nearly perfect hemispheres, except for the tender protrusions of their pink nipples. He decided he had never seen breasts like that. He sat down on the bed beside her. "I love you very much," he said. "You know that?"

It made her smile again. "Does that mean you're coming back to bed?"

"If you want me to."

"I want a swimming lesson. What will people say if I tell them I came here and didn't go swimming?"

He grinned at her. "That it's that time of the month."

"You know what you are? You're filthy!" She pushed him. "Absolutely filthy! I'm going to bite your ears off." Tangled in the sheet, they fell off the bed together. "There they are!"

"There what are?"

"My bra and stuff. We must have kicked them under the bed. Where are our bags?"

"Still in the trunk. I never carried them in."

"Would you get mine? My swimsuit's in it."

"Sure," he said.

"And put on some pants!"

"My suit's in my bag, too." He found his trousers and got the keys to the Triumph. Outside the sun was higher, the chill of the fall morning nearly gone. He looked for the ship and saw it. Then it winked out like a star.

That evening they made a fire of driftwood and roasted the big greasy Italian sausages he had brought from town, making giant hot dogs by clamping them in French bread. He had brought red supermarket wine, too; they chilled it in the Pacific. "I never ate this much in my life," Lissy said.

"You haven't eaten anything yet."

"I know, but just looking at this sandwich would make me full if I weren't so hungry." She bit off the end. "Cuff tough woof."

"What?"

"Castrating woman. That's what you called me this morning, Tim. Now *this* is a castrating woman."

"Don't talk with your mouth full."

"You sound like my mother. Give me some wine. You're hogging it."

He handed the bottle over. "It isn't bad, if you don't object to a complete lack of character."

"I sleep with you, don't I?"

"I have character, it's just all rotten."

"You said you wanted to get married."

"Let's go. You can finish that thing in the car."

"You drank half the bottle. You're too high to drive."

"Bullshoot."

Lissy giggled. "You just said bullshoot. Now *that's* character!"

He stood up. "Come on, let's go. It's only five hundred miles to Reno. We can get married there in the morning."

"You're serious, aren't you?"

"If you are."

"Sit down."

"You were testing me," he said. "That's not fair, now is it?"

"You've been so worried all day. I wanted to see if it was about me—if you thought you'd made a terrible mistake."

"We've made a mistake," he said. "I was trying to fix it just now."

"You think your dad is going to make it rough for you—"

"Us."

"—for us because it might hurt him in the next election."

He shook his head. "Not that. All right, maybe partly that. But he means it, too. You don't understand him."

"I've got a father myself."

"Not like mine. Ryan was almost grown up before he left Ireland. Taught by nuns and all that. Besides, I've got six older brothers and two sisters. You're the oldest kid. Ryan's probably at least fifteen years older than your folks."

"Is that really his name. Ryan Neal?"

"His full name is Timothy Ryan Neal, the same as mine. I'm Timothy Jr. He used Ryan when he went into politics because there was another Tim Neal around then, and we've always called me Tim to get away from the Junior."

"I'm going to call him Tim again, like the nuns must have when he was young. Big Tim. You're Little Tim."

"O.K. with me. I don't know if Big Tim is going to like it."

Something was moving, it seemed, out where the sun had set. Something darker against the dark horizon.

"What made you Junior anyway? Usually it's the oldest boy."

"He didn't want it, and would never let Mother do it. But she wanted to, and I was born during the Democratic convention that year."

"He had to go, of course."

"Yeah, he had to go, Lissy. If you don't understand that, you don't understand politics at all. They hoped I'd hold off for a few days, and what the hell, Mother'd had eight with no problems. Anyway, he was used to it—he was the youngest of seven boys himself. So she got to call me what she wanted."

"But then she died." The words sounded thin and lonely against the pounding of the surf.

"Not because of that."

Lissy upended the wine bottle; he saw her throat pulse three times. "Will I die because of that, Little Tim?"

"I don't think so." He tried to think of something gracious and comforting. "If we decide we want children, that's the risk I have to take."

"*You* have to take? Bullshoot."

"That both of us have to take. Do you think it was easy for Ryan, raising nine kids by himself?"

"You love him, don't you?"

"Sure I love him. He's my father."

"And now you think you might be ruining things for him. For my sake."

"That's not why I want us to be married, Lissy."

She was staring into the flames; he was not certain she had even heard him. "Well, now I know why his pictures look so grim. So gaunt."

He stood up again. "If you're through eating . . ."

"You want to go back to the cabin? You can screw me right here on the beach—there's nobody here but us."

"I didn't mean that."

"Then why go in there and look at the walls? Out here we've got the fire and the ocean. The moon ought to be up pretty soon."

"It would be warmer."

"With just that dinky little kerosene stove? I'd rather sit here by the fire. In a minute I'm going to send you off to get me some more wood. You can run up to the cabin and get a shirt, too, if you want to."

"I'm O.K."

"Traditional roles. Big Tim must have told you all about them. The woman has the babies and keeps the home fires burning. You're not going to end up looking like him, though, are you, Little Tim?"

"I suppose so. He used to look just like me."

"Really?"

He nodded. "He had his picture taken just after he got into politics. He was running for ward committeeman, and he had a poster made. We've still got the picture, and it looks like me with a high collar and a funny hat."

"She knew, didn't she?" Lissy said. For a moment he did not understand what she meant. "Now go and get some more wood. Only don't wear yourself out, because when you come back we're going to take care of that little thing that's bothering you, and we're going to spend the night on the beach."

When he came back she was asleep, but he woke her carrying her up to the beach cottage.

Next morning he woke up alone. He got up and showered and shaved, supposing that she had taken the car into town to get something for breakfast. He had filled the coffeepot and put it on before he looked out the shoreside window and saw the Triumph still waiting near the road.

There was nothing to be alarmed about, of course. She had awakened before he had and gone out for an early dip. He had done the same thing himself the morning before. The little patches of green cloth that were her bathing suit were hanging over the back of a rickety chair, but then they were still damp from last night. Who would want to put on a damp, clammy suit? She had gone in naked, just as he had.

He looked out the other window, wanting to see her splashing in the surf, waiting for him. The ship was there, closer now, rolling like a derelict. No smoke came from its clumsy funnel and no sails were set, but dark banners hung from its rigging. Then there was no ship, only wheeling gulls and the empty ocean. He called her name, but no one answered.

He put on his trunks and a jacket and went outside. A wind had smoothed the sand. The tide had come, obliterating their fire, reclaiming the driftwood he had gathered.

For two hours he walked up and down the beach, calling, telling himself there was nothing wrong. When he forced himself not to think of Lissy dead, he could only think of the headlines, the ninety seconds of ten o'clock news, how Ryan would look, how Pat—all his brothers—would look at him. And when he turned his mind from that, Lissy was dead again, her pale hair snarled with kelp as she rolled in the surf, green crabs feeding from her arms.

He got into the Triumph and drove to town. In the little brick station he sat beside the desk of a fat cop and told his story.

The fat cop said, "Kid, I can see why you want us to keep it quiet."

Tim said nothing. There was a paperweight on the desk—a baseball of white glass.

"You probably think we're out to get you, but we're not.

Tomorrow we'll put out a missing persons report, but we don't have to say anything about you or the senator in it, and we won't.''

"Tomorrow?"

"We got to wait twenty-four hours, in case she should show up. That's the law. But kid—'' The fat cop glanced at his notes.

"Tim."

"Right. Tim. She ain't going to show up. You got to get yourself used to that.''

"She could be . . .'' Without wanting to, he let it trail away.

"Where? You think she snuck off and went home? She could walk out to the road and hitch, but you say her stuff's still there. Kidnapped? Nobody could have pulled her out of bed without waking you up. Did you kill her?''

"No!'' Tears he could not hold back were streaming down his cheeks.

"Right. I've talked to you and I don't think you did. But you're the only one that could have. If her body washes up, we'll have to look into that.''

Tim's hands tightened on the wooden arms of the chair. The fat cop pushed a box of tissues across the desk.

"Unless it washes up, though, it's just a missing person, O.K.? But she's dead, kid, and you're going to have to get used to it. Let me tell you what happened.'' He cleared his throat.

"She got up while you were still asleep, probably about when it started to get light. She did just what you thought she did—went out for a nice refreshing swim before you woke up. She went out too far, and probably she got a cramp. The ocean's cold as hell now. Maybe she yelled, but if she did she was too far out, and the waves covered it up. People think drowners holler like fire sirens, but they don't—they don't have that much air. Sometimes they don't make any noise at all.''

Tim stared at the gleaming paperweight.

''The current here runs along the coast—you probably know that. Nobody ought to go swimming without somebody around, but sometimes it seems like everybody does it. We lose a dozen or so a year. In maybe four or five cases we find them. That's all.''

The beach cottage looked abandoned when he returned. He parked the Triumph and went inside and found the stove still burning, his coffee perked to tar. He took the pot outside, dumped the coffee, scrubbed the pot with beach sand and rinsed it with salt water. The ship, which had been invisible through the window of the cottage, was almost plain when he stood waist-deep. He heaved the coffeepot back to the shore and swam out some distance, but when he straightened up in the water, the ship was gone.

Back inside he made fresh coffee and packed Lissy's things in her suitcase. When that was done, he drove into town again. Ryan was still in Washington, but Tim told his secretary where he was. ''Just in case anybody reports me missing,'' he said.

She laughed. ''It must be pretty cold for swimming.''

''I like it,'' he told her. ''I want to have at least one more long swim.''

''All right, Tim. When he calls, I'll let him know. Have a good time.''

''Wish me luck,'' he said, and hung up. He got a hamburger and more coffee at a Jack-in-the-Box and went back to the cottage and walked a long way along the beach.

He had intended to sleep that night, but he did not. From time to time he got up and looked out the window at the ship, sometimes visible by moonlight, sometimes only a dark presence in the lower night sky. When the first light of dawn came, he put on his trunks and went into the water.

For a mile or more, as well as he could estimate the distance, he could not see it. Then it was abruptly close, the long oars like the legs of a water spider, the funnel belching sparks against the still-dim sky, sparks that seemed to become new stars.

He swam faster then, knowing that if the ship vanished he would turn back and save himself, knowing, too, that if it only retreated before him, retreated forever, he would drown. It disappeared behind a cobalt wave, reappeared. He sprinted and grasped at the sea-slick shaft of an oar, and it was like touching a living being. Quite suddenly he stood on the deck, with no memory of how he came there.

Bare feet pattered on the planks, but he saw no crew. A dark flag lettered with strange script flapped aft, and some vague recollection of a tour of a naval ship with his father years before made him touch his forehead. There was a sound that might have been laughter or many other things. The captain's chair would be aft, too, he thought. He went there, bracing himself against the wild roll, and found a door.

Inside, something black crouched upon a dais. "I've come for Lissy," Tim said.

There was no reply, but a question hung in the air. He answered it almost without intending to. "I'm Timothy Ryan Neal, and I've come for Lissy. Give her back to me."

A light, it seemed, dissolved the blackness. Cross-legged on the dais, a slender man in tweeds sucked at a long clay pipe. "It's Irish, are ye?" he asked.

"American," Tim said.

"With such a name? I don't believe ye. Where's yer feathers?"

"I want her back," Tim said again.

"An' if ye don't get her?"

"Then I'll tear this ship apart. You'll have to kill me or take me, too."

"Spoken like a true son of the ould sod," said the man in tweeds. He scratched a kitchen match on the sole of his boot and lit his pipe. "Sit down, will ye? I don't fancy lookin' up like that. It hurts me neck. Sit down, and 'tis possible we can strike an agreement."

"This is crazy," Tim said. "The whole thing is crazy."

"It is that," the man in tweeds replied. "An' there's much, much more comin'. Ye'd best brace for it, Tim me lad. Now sit down."

There was a stout wooden chair behind Tim where the door had been. He sat. "Are you about to tell me you're a leprechaun? I warn you, I won't believe it."

"Me? One o' them scamperin', thievin', cobblin' little misers? I'd shoot meself. Me name's Daniel O'Donoghue, King o' Connaught. Do ye believe that, now?"

"No," Tim said.

"What would ye believe, then?"

"That this is—some way, somehow—what people call a saucer. That you and your crew are from a planet of another sun."

Daniel laughed. " 'Tis a close encounter you're havin', is it? Would ye like to see me as a tiny green man wi' horns like a snail's? I can do that, too."

"Don't bother."

"All right, I won't, though 'tis a good shape. A man can take it and be whatever he wants, one o' the People o' Peace or a bit o' a man from Mars. I've used it for both, and there's nothin' better."

"You took Lissy," Tim said.

"And how would ye be knowin' that?"

"I thought she'd drowned."

"Did ye now?"

"And that this ship—or whatever it is—was just a sign, an omen. I talked to a policeman and he as good as told me, but I didn't really think about what he said until last night, when I was trying to sleep."

"Is it a dream yer havin'? Did ye ever think on that?"

"If it's a dream, it's still real." Tim said doggedly. "And anyway, I saw your ship when I was awake, yesterday and the day before."

"Or yer dreamin' now ye did. But go on wi' it."

"He said Lissy couldn't have been abducted because I was in the same bed, and that she'd gone out for a swim in the morning and drowned. But she could have been abducted, if she had gone out for the swim first. If someone had come for her with a boat. And she wouldn't have drowned, because she didn't swim good enough to drown. She was afraid of the water. We went in yesterday, and even with me there, she would hardly go in over her knees. So it was you."

"Yer right, ye know," Daniel said. He formed a little steeple of his fingers. " 'Twas us."

Tim was recalling stories that had been read to him when he was a child. "Fairies steal babies, don't they? And brides. Is that why you do it? So we'll think that's who you are?"

"Bless ye, 'tis true," Daniel told him. " 'Tis the Fair Folk we are. The jinn o' the desert, too, and the saucer riders ye say ye credit, and forty score more. Would ye be likin' to see me wi' me goatskin breeches and me panpipe?" He chuckled. "Have ye never wondered why we're so much alike the world over? Or thought that we don't always know just which shape's the best for a place, so the naiads and the dryads might as well be the ladies o' the Deeny Shee? Do ye know what the folk o' the Barb'ry Coast call the hell that's under their sea?"

Tim shook his head.

"Why, 'tis Domdaniel. I wonder why that is, now. Tim, ye say ye want this girl."

"That's right."

"An' ye say there'll be trouble and plenty for us if ye don't have her. But let me tell ye now that if ye don't get her, wi' our blessin' to boot, ye'll drown—hold your tongue, can't ye, for 'tis worse than that—if ye don't get her wi' our blessin', 'twill be seen that ye were drownin' now. Do ye take me meaning?"

"I think so. Close enough."

"Ah, that's good, that is. Now here's me offer. Do ye remember how things stood before we took her?"

"Of course."

"They'll stand so again, if ye but do what I tell ye. 'Tis yerself that will remember, Tim Neal, but she'll remember nothin'. An' the truth of it is, there'll be nothin' to remember, for it'll all be gone, every stick of it. This policeman ye spoke wi', for instance. Ye've me word that ye will not have done it."

"What do I have to do?" Tim asked.

"Service. Serve us. Do whatever we ask of ye. We'd sooner have a broth of a girl like yer Lissy than a great hulk of a lad like yerself, but then, too, we'd sooner be havin' one that's willin', for the unwillin' girls are everywhere—I don't doubt but ye've seen it yerself. A hundred years, that's all we ask of ye. 'Tis short enough, like Doyle's wife. Will ye do it?"

"And everything will be the same, at the end, as it was before you took Lissy?"

"Not everythin', I didn't say that. Ye'll remember, don't ye remember me sayin' so? But for her and all the country round, why 'twill be the same."

"All right," Tim said. "I'll do it."

" 'Tis a brave lad ye are. Now I'll tell ye what I'll do. I said a hundred years, to which ye agreed—"

Tim nodded.

"—but I'll have no unwillin' hands about me boat, nor no ungrateful ones neither. I'll make it twenty. How's that? Sure and I couldn't say fairer, could I?"

Daniel's figure was beginning to waver and fade; the image of the dark mass Tim had seen first hung about it like a cloud.

"Lay yerself on yer belly, for I must put me foot upon yer head. Then the deal's done."

The salt ocean was in his mouth and his eyes. His lungs burst for breath. He revolved in the blue chasm of water, tried to swim, at last exploded gasping into the air.

The King had said he would remember, but the years were fading already. Drudging, dancing, buying, spying, prying, waylaying, and betraying when he walked in the world of men. Serving something that he had never wholly understood. Sailing foggy seas that were sometimes of this earth. Floating among the constellations. The years and the slaps and the kicks were all fading, and with them (and he rejoiced in it) the days when he had begged.

He lifted an arm, trying to regain his old stroke, and found that he was very tired. Perhaps he had never really rested in all those years. Certainly, he could not recall resting. Where was he? He paddled listlessly, not knowing if he were swimming away from land, if he were in the center of an ocean. A wave elevated him, a long, slow swell of blue under the gray sky. A glory—the rising or perhaps the setting sun—shone to his right. He swam toward it, caught sight of a low coast.

He crawled onto the sand and lay there for a time, his back struck by drops of spray like rain. Near his eyes, the beach seemed nearly black. There were bits of charcoal, fragments of half-burned wood. He raised his head, pushing away the earth, and saw an empty bottle of greenish glass nearly buried in the wet sand.

When he was able at last to rise, his limbs were stiff and cold. The dawnlight had become daylight, but there was no warmth in it. The beach cottage stood only about a hundred yards away, one window golden with sunshine that had entered from the other side, the walls in shadow. The red Triumph gleamed beside the road.

At the top of a small dune he turned and looked back out to sea. A black freighter with a red and white stack was visible a mile or two out, but it was only a freighter. For a moment he felt a kind of regret, a longing for a part of his life that he had hated but that was now gone forever. I will never be able to tell her what happened, he thought. And then: Yes, I will, if only I let her think I'm just making it up. And then: No wonder so many people tell so many stories. Good-bye to all that.

The step creaked under his weight, and he wiped the sand from his feet on the coco mat. Lissy was in bed. When she heard the door open she sat up, then drew up the sheet to cover her breasts.

"Big Tim," she said. "You did come. Tim and I were hoping you would."

When he did not answer, she added, "He's out having a swim, I think. He should be around in a minute."

And when he still said nothing: "We're—Tim and I—we're going to be married."

DAW

TANITH LEE

"Princess Royal of Heroic Fantasy"—*The Village Voice*

The Birthgrave Trilogy
- [ ] THE BIRTHGRAVE — (UE1776—$3.50)
- [ ] VAZKOR, SON OF VAZKOR — (UE1972—$2.95)
- [ ] QUEST FOR THE WHITE WITCH — (UE1996—$2.95)

THE FLAT EARTH SERIES
- [ ] NIGHT'S MASTER — (UE1657—$2.25)
- [ ] DEATH'S MASTER — (UE1741—$2.95)
- [ ] DELUSION'S MASTER — (UE1932—$2.50)
- [ ] DELIRIUM'S MISTRESS — (to come)

OTHER TITLES
- [ ] THE STORM LORD — (UE1867—$2.95)
- [ ] DAYS OF GRASS — (UE2094—$3.50)

ANTHOLOGIES
- [ ] RED AS BLOOD — (UE1790—$2.50)
- [ ] THE GORGON — (UE2003—$2.95)

DAW

DAW Books now in select format